The Stones Of Power
Book 3
Crimson Tides

BY AARON MCGOWAN

The Stones Of Power
Book 3
Crimson Tides

Published 2021
Elpis Project ©2011-2021 by Aaron McGowan

The characters and events in this book are fictitious. Any similarity to real persons, living or dead, is coincidental and not intended by the author.

McGowan, Aaron.
Elpis / Aaron McGowan

Summary: To avenge the death of his parents and the destruction of his village, Terico seeks to obtain the four fragments of the Elpis—a source of power that will allow his enemy Delkol to conquer the world.

ISBN: 000-0-0000000-0-0

1st Edition

Published by Hellfun Publishing Pty. Limited

•Part IX•
SILENT REGRETS AND DREAMS

Lanek watched as Rilv stood her ground, while the stranger continued to walk toward her. He was just a few meters away now, and either didn't care for the hostage child's life or truly believed Rilv wouldn't actually kill the girl. To be completely honest, Lanek wasn't sure if Rilv was serious in her threat or not.

"Who are you?" Rilv asked.

"I am Kechi, servant of Mareba Shire," the man said, stopping a couple meters in front of Rilv. "And you will be handing your Hader to me immediately." He raised the Hader in his right hand, its swirls of light shifting between green and black.

So this man worked for Shire royalty? Lanek found it curious that Kechi didn't claim allegiance to Augurc Shire, but rather another man entirely—a noble in his fifties and wheelchair-bound, Lanek recalled reading. Mareba Shire was supposedly greatly opposed to the Brotherhood following the fall of Delkol, as all the Shire governing body claimed. The question was, was Kechi obtaining Haders just for himself, for the good of the Shire Kingdom in general, for the intent of giving Mareba Shire power over Augurc, or even for the Brotherhood specifically?

Rilv glanced at the Hader pointed directly toward her. Her own Hader was still pointed at the child she kept levitated above the battered shrine. "You can't threaten me. Any attack you send my way, I can easily push away with my own Hader."

Lanek knew she could move multiple things at the same time, but it seemed Rilv was straining herself just to keep the hostage suspended in the air. Would she actually be able to move aside Kechi's attack and still keep the child from falling to her death? And if not, would she lose control of the child the moment she was attacked? Lanek wished he was closer to where the girl was positioned, and wished the stranger was enough of a distraction to give Lanek time to reach the girl before Rilv would notice. Yet Rilv was keeping as much control over the situation as she possibly could, even when facing a confident enemy with two Haders.

"I don't need to threaten you," Kechi said, grinning wildly. "You *will* be handing your Hader to me immediately."

It was as if his words were meant to force her to just walk over and give him her Hader. Was Kechi's Hader the power to control someone's mind? Lanek watched Rilv, worried she was going to do just as Kechi ordered.

Instead she simply stood in place, frowning. If Kechi was using his Hader, it was clearly having no effect on Rilv.

A sword rose from the ground a couple meters to Rilv's right, a weapon likely forced aside earlier by Rilv's telekinesis or Kitoh's shield of water. The sword's blade turned and pointed at Kechi, who gritted his teeth. Rilv seemed to be managing just fine holding the child in the air and maneuvering the sword at the same time, and Lanek had to wonder if Kechi was going to pose a threat at all. Did he not have good control over his Haders? Or was Rilv too strong, and capable of resisting Kechi's power?

Was this Lanek's chance to try rescuing the girl above the shrine? Rilv had her mind intently focused on two things at once—this was the best chance Lanek was going to get. He spotted a green Nexi left on the ground by the villagers, and decided he could use it to save the child. He'd only get one chance at it, and he'd have to be quick. Finding a path behind some villagers just in front of what was left of the shrine wall, Lanek bolted toward the green Nexi stone, as quiet and fast as he could.

"Stop, Lanek!" Rilv yelled, jolting Lanek to a halt as he was reaching for the vine Nexi. "Despite what this man claims, I will kill this child if you or anyone else makes a move to rescue her!"

The crying child wobbled in the air a bit more, and Lanek wasn't sure if this was Rilv shaking the girl to make a point, or if Rilv was losing control with her concentration waning.

Lanek backed away from the green Nexi, trying to think of some other way to reach the child. But there was nothing...

Rilv still kept her floating sword aimed at Kechi, who continued to hold his Hader tight, still pointed at Rilv. Was he still trying to force Rilv to hand over her Hader? He almost looked like he was breaking a sweat, trying to wield his Hader's power against her.

The sword flew toward Kechi, even faster than Lanek anticipated. Kechi only had time to step back, unable to dodge quickly enough.

And yet the sword missed him entirely. By a good meter, the sword lunged to his left, flying into a hillside a ways past Kechi.

Rilv's eyes widened slightly—was this how she looked when surprised?

"I see," Kechi said. "We can't use our Haders against each other."

"I suggest you back away then," Rilv said. "If you don't, the child will die. You have five seconds."

Kechi laughed. "You're still bluffing! But that's fine. I'll rescue the child, and just let the angry mob take you down... You're too weak to resist much longer."

A stream of red liquid rushed toward the girl in the air, far too quick for Rilv to react to in time. The child screamed, villagers screamed, people pointed and gasped, others stumbled back in surprise. Nullen knelt down, gasping for breath, and Rilv tried using her Hader to maneuver the hostage away from the strange substance. The red liquid held a tight grip on the child, as if the water had solidified to some degree.

Was this the power of Kechi's second Hader? Lanek looked and saw him with his left fist raised, a Hader glowing silver and red between his fingers.

The red liquid held the screaming girl tight, pushing against the tugs of Rilv's Hader. Rilv trembled and began to take deep breaths. She was being pushed past her limit. In one swift movement, the red liquid brought the child away from the shrine and down on the ground, a little ways in front of Fenley and her relatives. The crimson substance dropped to the ground, splattering across the dirt path like bloodstains.

Perhaps it *was* blood. And when Lanek looked over the area near the side of the shrine, where several elves had died, Lanek couldn't find any bloodstains among them.

Did Kechi gather all the blood together and maneuver it with his Hader, just as a tan Nexi could mold earth and a dark blue Nexi could mold water? Kechi's control of blood was much quicker than base Nexi abilities, however, and he seemed capable of controlling how solid or liquid the blood was. This wasn't an ability to be treated lightly.

"Quick, apprehend her!" Nullen cried out to the villagers, while pointed at Rilv. "Before she takes another child hostage!"

Tens of villagers picked their weapons off the ground and rushed toward Rilv and Kitoh. Some threw projectiles at them, but Rilv forced them all away via telekinesis. She was trembling more in the process of doing so, however. Weakened from Nexi use, Rilv wouldn't be able to use the Hader much longer.

"We have to flee!" Kitoh yelled above the cries of the encircling villagers.

"No!" Rilv replied. "Not before we've obtained the Haders!"

"It's too late..." Kitoh said.

Rilv forced aside a couple more knives and a pitchfork, but about a dozen armed villagers had gathered around the two, closing off any path of escape. Lanek considered rushing in to help Kitoh and Rilv, but Nullen specifically ordered the villagers to merely apprehend them—perhaps thinking of Lanek when he gave the order.

But at the same time, this was going exactly according to Kechi's plan. The red-haired man stood a few meters from the attacking villagers, a smug expression etched on his face. Lanek couldn't let him take all the Haders. In fact, he probably needed to be taking action against the man—but what would Lanek be able to do if Kechi could control his mind? He realized he would need a Hader himself if he were to stand a chance against Kechi. Rilv had one, and Nullen had one...

Just as a villager was about to swing a sword at Rilv, a figure rushed into the scene and stabbed the man in the stomach, then shoved him back into another villager. The rest of the villagers nearby ran away, shocked by the speed of the attack.

At the worst possible moment, Lynx had returned. Lanek had hoped to find him unconscious at the bottom of a hill, where Lanek could kill hill him once all the fighting at the shrine had ended. But it was far too late to amend anything here now. If Lanek didn't do something right away, things would likely only get worse for this village.

Lynx stood in front of Rilv, his bloody sword raised toward Nullen's direction.

"You two head to the airship," Lynx said. "I will obtain the Hader from the village leader."

He didn't realize the full situation—he had just regained consciousness and forced his way back into the fray, so he didn't know about Kechi.

Kitoh took Rilv's hand and helped her run with him down the village path. The eigni boy created a whirlwind of water around them, keeping any of the nearby villagers from attacking them. It didn't look like Rilv had the energy to resist at this point, but Lanek wondered if they were going to wait for him. Did they need him to pilot the airship? It was possible Kitoh understood how to do so—he was certainly smart enough to figure it out, at the very least.

None of the remaining villagers at the scene approached Lynx, though Nullen's guards made it clear they weren't going to let Lynx near their esteemed leader.

"Now what is the Brotherhood doing here?" Kechi screamed. "Augurc is working with the Fiefs Kingdom now?"

Lynx turned his head slightly, but whether or not he could see Kechi through the thin slits of his mask, Lanek couldn't know. But Lynx seemed aware of his presence, and perhaps the presence of two more Haders.

"So you're the man with two Haders," Lynx said. "I don't care who you work for or what your goals are, but suffice it to say I *will* be confiscating your Haders."

Kechi looked furious, gripping his Haders tighter. "Just another fool wanting all the power he can get. I'll tear you to pieces."

Blood rose from the ground near Lynx, and for a moment Lanek thought to warn him—but stopped short. Though Lanek wanted to be the one to kill Lynx, he wasn't about to get in the way of others killing Lynx for him. And a part of him wondered if Lynx really was still needed for something more, though Lanek wasn't certain if he was going to be involved in the mission for the Haders at all anymore, at this point.

Lynx avoided the burst of blood, which had formed into a long, thin needle and shot off toward his neck. The masked man was aware of Kechi's control of blood, at the very least, and was in good enough shape to be able to dodge the attack in time. Kechi forced some more blood nearby to rise from behind Lynx. The blood quickly solidified and shot off toward Lynx's back. Lynx turned and sliced his sword through the sharpening crimson projectile, forcing the blood to turn to liquid and pass around him.

A portion of blood deflected off Lynx's blade. Kechi caused this trickle of blood to gather back together while still in mid-air, and flung it at Lynx's neck. The needle of blood barely missed him, as Lynx spun while stepping to the side. Without even a moment's pause, Lynx was suddenly rushing toward Kechi, his Brotherhood weapon raised forward.

Furious, Kechi stepped back and thrust his Hader forward, forcing the stream of blood he had used earlier to rise and rush forward. The large blood splatters gathered back together and flew away from Fenley and her relatives, rushed past Kechi's left, and dashed even more quickly toward Lynx's chest. With one hand gripping his sword's hilt, Lynx slipped out a light blue Nexi with his other hand and held it forward. While aiming his blade directly for the giant blade of blood in front of him, Lynx activated his Nexi stone, forcing arctic air to rush out to either side of him. The long, thick weapon of blood split in two in front of Lynx, but Kechi immediately forced the crimson liquid to sharpen and curve back toward Lynx from the left and right. The Nexi altered the air around Lynx, and the blood instantly froze as it rushed for him from his left and right. Lynx pushed his blade through the rest of the blood and charged toward Kechi.

There was a bit more blood on the ground near where Kechi stood, and the Shire servant was quick to form it into a thin needle and fling it at Lynx's heart. Since Lynx was just finishing his push through the giant blade of blood, he had no time to swing at the small needle, aimed with an inhuman precision and speed no ordinary fighter could hope to avoid.

Lynx dropped to the ground and rolled forward, losing his sword in the process. Lanek realized that Lynx had managed to avoid the blood needle entirely, its splattered remains leaving a thin hole in an old wooden signpost.

As Lynx was getting on his feet, Kechi thrust forward his other Hader, activating its power against him. Lynx stumbled, failing to stand up all the way. For a second, it looked like Lynx was going to rush toward Kechi and attack with his ice Nexi, but Lynx stopped himself. Or rather, it seemed Kechi was forcing Lynx to stop. Was Kechi controlling Lynx's body, then?

Gripping the Hader tight, Kechi took a careful step toward Lynx, who fell to both knees, trembling. Lynx couldn't stop shaking, and he crouched back from Kechi in fear. When Kechi took another step forward, Lynx shuffled back a bit, cowering.

This was obviously not in character for Lynx, who never expressed much emotion other than anger and sullen moodiness. And now Lynx was starting to sweat, and take shallow, frantic breaths. Kechi pocketed his blood Hader, unsheathed a knife, and took another step forward. Lynx turned and trembled further, nearly out of breath. Lanek wondered if he could take the opportunity to run over and kill Lynx for himself, but he didn't want to engage with Kechi sooner than he had to. He looked to the village leader, and saw Nullen was still clutching the Stone of Truth. Perhaps this was his opportunity to take it from him—but that would turn him into an enemy of the village. He needed the village against Kechi—not him.

Just before Kechi could force his knife into the side of Lynx's head, Lynx scampered away on his hands and knees, pushed himself to his feet, and ran away screaming. Kechi threw his knife at Lynx's back, but Lynx was too quick. The knife missed him entirely, and Lynx continued to run down the village path and out of sight, his cries muffled beneath his mask.

"Scared him... too much," Kechi muttered between deep breaths. It seemed Kechi had drained himself of a fair amount of energy by relying on the two Haders as much as he had. And it was obvious this hadn't turned out the way he planned. If this second Hader was used to control people's minds, Kechi could have simply forced Lynx to sit still while Kechi killed him. Instead, Lynx was exhibiting traits of someone who was utterly afraid. From what Lanek could tell then, Kechi's second Hader was used to heighten emotions of fear and dread in a target. This would explain Kechi's frustration when facing Rilv—he was expecting her to cower before him and give up her Hader, begging him to spare her life.

Kechi sighed and looked out to all the villagers gathered in the vicinity. Many who had run away earlier and sneaked back to watch the fight between Lynx and Kechi—they appeared relieved to see Lynx defeated. Kechi was still what he had claimed to be upon arrival in their village—a man coming to save them from the government agents.

Once he finished catching his breath, Kechi spoke out to the people. "That appears to be all of them... I only see elves left here, so I take it the village is safe now."

"Praise the gods," one villager said.

"It's finally over," another said.

"You've saved us!"

"Thank you so much..."

Some villagers were gripping each other tight, relieved the fighting had finally come to an end. Others were crying, dismayed by the deaths of their five or so fellow villagers. A few stared aghast at the destruction of their beloved shrine. And a couple others were keeping their eyes on Lanek, curious to see if he was going to do anything more. One looked like she was going to speak out against him, but stopped when Kechi spoke up once more.

"I am in a bit of a hurry, as I wish to pursue the enemies who have wrecked havoc on your village," he said. "So I ask that you allow me to borrow the tool I have come here for. In repayment for saving you village, I would like to use the Hader currently in your possession."

He stared his wide, wild eyes straight toward Nullen, who sheepishly clutched the Stone of Truth a little tighter.

"I thank you for saving the village," Nullen said. "With all my soul, I thank you. But the Stone of Truth is our most sacred relic. It must only be used for rituals of peace and righteousness. We can never allow it to leave the village, or be used for any purpose other than for the rituals it was intended for. I'm sorry, Sir Kechi, but I can't allow you to use it. We will be glad to repay you for your service any other way we can, however..."

Lanek had to admit it was rather brave of the village elder to stand up to a man who could control both blood and fear. It was obvious Kechi wasn't going to settle for anything less than the Hader, however.

"I'm afraid I must demand temporary use of your Hader," Kechi said as he began walking toward Nullen. "It's the only way to stop those government officials, and make sure they don't come back to terrorize your village."

"I'm... I'm sorry," Nullen said. "It's just not possible."

Kechi's eyes widened ever further, and he quickened his pace. "Do you not understand the situation you're in, old man?" He shoved his knife back into its sheath and took back out his other Hader, so he was holding the blood Hader in one hand and the fear Hader in the other.

"No... stop..." Nullen said, backing away. His bodyguards stood in front of him, ready to fight back Kechi—but Lanek knew they wouldn't last a second against the power of the two Haders.

"I can't stop, you fool!" Kechi screamed. "Not until I have enough Haders. Not when I'm so close to obtaining them! You will regret this lack of cooperation, old man. With two Haders, I am unbeatable. With three Haders, I will be invincible. With four Haders, I shall become omnipotent. Each and every one of my master's wishes shall be fulfilled. The world will belong to Mareba Shire!"

The two bodyguards trembled, struggling to keep standing before Kechi's approaching presence. They each dropped their weapons, unable to withstand the fear being forced upon them. Kechi immediately controlled blood from the ground nearby, and forced two stakes of blood to jab through their hearts. The blood weapons liquified and melded into the killed bodies. The bodies then burst apart from the inside, their blood controlled from within them. The corpses exploded, splattering blood on everyone around them, especially Kechi.

Villagers screamed from the sudden development. Kechi only grinned wider.

"I can't wait to test the power of three Haders on this pathetic village," he said. "The power to kill anyone and everyone I wish... It fills me with utter bliss, just thinking about it. The more I kill, the more alive I feel!"

With both Haders in one hand, Kechi stepped toward Nullen and used his free hand to pull a sword from the sheath tied to his back. As long as Nullen had the Stone of Truth, Kechi wouldn't be able to use the Haders against him. But if Lanek attacked, Kechi would easily be able to kill him.

There was no time to wait. Lanek ran toward Kechi, unsheathing his rapier. "This man only came for the Stone of Truth! He'll kill us all to get it!" Several other villagers rushed toward Kechi, who turned and forced blood from the killed bodyguards to gather together and attack them like razor-sharp tendrils. While Nullen slipped back, a few more villagers came after Kechi, brandishing weapons. Kechi drove his sword through the neck of the nearest villager, then forced a torrent of blood to erupt out of the man's severed head. The blood solidified and tore through several other villagers, providing even more blood for Kechi to utilize against the rest of the villagers who attacked alongside Lanek. There were at least a dozen other villagers who attempted to assist as well, but they all fell to their knees, cowering in fear.

Kechi caused a giant wave of blood to rush toward Lanek and the team of villagers charging with him. The blood wall blocked the projectiles thrown or shot at Kechi, and then swept up several villagers off their feet, sending them flying back. Lanek barely dodged the wide, rushing torrent of blood, and saw Kechi slicing apart several guards and villagers gathered around Nullen. There was no time to try attacking Kechi—the Stone of Truth was nearly in his grasp. If Kechi obtained a third Hader... perhaps there really would be no hope for this village.

Gritting his teeth, Lanek rushed toward Nullen. A guard turned to Lanek and raised a sword against him. Lanek didn't even need to raise his own blade, however, as a scythe-like blade of blood severed the guard's head just as Lanek reached him. Blood was rushing toward Lanek from his left. He kept running, avoiding a thin spike of blood lunging toward his chest. Lanek plowed into a villager, shoving the man aside and grabbing Nullen's hand. With no time to explain, Lanek forced the Hader out of Nullen's grasp. Lanek clenched the Hader with his free left hand and immediately turned to face a behemoth of blood, its many writhing tentacles finishing off all the other villagers all around Lanek. Kechi was screaming something, but Lanek heard nothing more as the environment all around him vanished.

He found himself in a graveyard. It was daytime, and there was nobody around him at all. It was a different location entirely, as even the mountains were gone. It was just one extensive graveyard all around him, as far as his eyes could see.

Stunned, Lanek simply stood still, trying to grasp how he ended up in a completely different place all of a sudden. He was just about to face Kechi, but now he had a Hader at his disposal—the means for him to keep Kechi from filling him with fear and turning him into an easy target to slice apart with hardened blood. How did Lanek end up in some random graveyard?

He stared down at the Hader in his hand. Did it somehow send him to this place? It was as if Lanek had traveled far across the country in an instant.

The graves around him were old and decrepit, many of them cracked, others moldy, some covered in cobwebs and leaves, and most layered in dust and grime. Everything was packed tight together, leaving very thin paths between each row of graves—if they could be called rows. It was all rather haphazardly arranged.

But what was he doing here? He needed to be at the village. Was Kechi still killing everyone at this very moment? Without the Hader he came for in sight, he would only be more furious and dangerous. And Fenley was still there. Was she locked in shock by Kechi's fear-inducing Hader? All the elves in the village had little hope against Kechi's Haders, overwhelming in their abilities, especially when utilized in twisted harmony.

"What is your name?"

Lanek nearly jumped in surprise, but instead forced himself to turn toward the speaker. He found a woman sitting on top of a large gravestone just a couple meters behind him. Where did she come from?

He had his rapier ready, but the woman didn't seem to be doing anything other than sitting there. She was an elf dressed in a black and white dress, likely in her late twenties. There was something familiar about her... Did she look like one of the villagers? Lanek felt certain he had seen this woman before.

"I'm Lanek. Who are you? And what is this place?"

"You should know me," the woman said. "You and Fenley were worshiping me not too long ago."

Lanek stepped back, but kept himself from gaping in awe once the realization set in. This was Reali, the goddess whose statue knelt in the shrine, her hands outstretched toward the invisible Stone of Truth. The goddess who enlightens the villagers' minds, helping them feel at peace, helping them feel calm with their decisions and difficulties, helping them find answers to their deepest questions.

"You... you're a goddess?" Lanek asked, unable to believe his eyes.

The woman nodded. "I am reverenced as one, at the very least."

"What do you mean?" Lanek asked.

"Well, I'm a goddess to the people of the village you're visiting," Reali said. "Not really to anyone else, though."

She faded away and vanished.

"Wait!" Lanek yelled. He walked toward the gravestone where the goddess had been sitting. "The village is in danger. Everyone needs help!"

"Don't worry," came a soft voice behind him. "I'm still here. And we are inside the Stone of Truth—a plane of reality that exists outside the confines of time. You will soon return to the exact moment you left your world."

He turned around and found Reali standing directly behind him. Lanek stumbled back a bit, gripping his rapier tighter.

"You disappeared," Lanek said, his heart racing.

"This is my power," Reali said. "To make things immaterial material, and things material immaterial. To make elements fade in and out of existence."

"Including yourself," Lanek said. "So you're like a ghost."

"Yes," Reali said. "My power was originally used to deal with those abusing the power of the Elpis. Eventually my power became legendary amongst many of the elves, and I found myself likened to an ancient goddess. This village was the center of worship for these elves, and I likewise became a central object of their devotion."

"You enlighten everyone at that pool in the shrine," Lanek said.

"It's the least I can do," Reali said. "Turning specific thoughts and emotions immaterial, others material... If the villagers seek my help, I am happy to oblige as best I can. The ritual was set up with a system of magic that has long fallen out of use, but it will last as long as that shrine and pool exist."

"The shrine is falling apart," Lanek said. "Can you use your power to make Kechi disappear? He is killing all your people."

"I am aware," Reali said. "And I am willing to use you to save this people. If you will devote yourself solely to worthy causes, I will allow you full access to my power, Lanek."

"For now, I only want to save this village," Lanek said. "After that... I..."

He wasn't sure what to say. Did he really care for the mission to bring down the Brotherhood? Of course he did. But was this Hader actually going to allow him to do so? And what of his more immediate goals? He wanted to kill Lynx. His goal was revenge. Was that a worthy cause? Technically he wanted to bring down the Brotherhood in revenge, as well. At least, that was a big part of it. He didn't want more innocent people like Suran to die at the hands of the Brotherhood... But he mainly just wanted Suran to be avenged.

"What else do you wish to do with my power?" Reali asked.

"My sister..." Lanek said. "She was killed."

"My power can't bring her back," Reali said.

Lanek hadn't even been considering such a possibility. That was simply too much to have ever hoped for—and he wondered if he should feel bad for having such little hope left in him.

"I know," Lanek said. "But I know the man who killed her. There is an entire organization responsible for her death. This organization is responsible for the devastation in your village as well, to some degree." At the very least, if it weren't for the Brotherhood, this mission to find the Haders would have never been conjured up.

"I will allow you to use my power as you see fit," Reali said, "though I doubt you will find gratification in revenge. The need to seek out destroying this organization is questionable, as is the need to kill the man you speak of."

"You can't say that," Lanek said. "You don't know anything."

Reali held her arms outstretched to the sides. "But of course I do. When you rested in my waters of enlightenment, I gleaned quite a bit from the quietest stirrings of your heart."

"What do you think I should do, then?" Lanek asked. If this really was a goddess, she would know what's best for him—right? Though she was certainly real, and certainly had great power, Lanek wasn't certain if he could actually believe in her as a divine being.

Reali folded her arms and stared into Lanek's eyes a few moments, as if looking into his very soul. "You have a very intelligent mind, Lanek. You are contemplative. You know how to analyze situations. You're a decision-maker. You see a cause, and you ascertain its logical effect. In your mind, everything has its place in the world, and your moral code is based on achieving the best possible outcome in every condition you're in."

Reali smiled. "But you don't know your own place in the world anymore, do you?"

There was a long silence. Lanek didn't want to have this discussion. Not now. This wasn't the time for it. "It doesn't matter."

"It matters a great deal," Reali said. "If you don't know how you feel about your own self, how can you know how to feel about anyone else? Including people you're planning to kill?"

"I may not be much better than the people I'm planning to kill," Lanek said. "I go about my life, and this world... It's a world that took my sister away from me. And I've lost not only her... But I've lost a piece of myself as well. I don't know if I can ever get it back at this point. I thought I could replace it at least, with some feeling... Any feeling. But I'm never going to actually become whole again, am I?"

"What would your sister say if you asked her that question?" Reali said.

Lanek frowned. "She was always hopeful. She never felt it was too late for someone to change. She always saw the best in people."

"Perhaps you could afford to think of your sister a bit more," Reali said. "You've kept your memories of her alive in you—but what about her heart? I believe this is the piece of you that is missing, Lanek. And this isn't a feeling you need to go searching for. It's very much inside of you. You know what you should and shouldn't be doing. If you want to honor your beloved sister, wouldn't you want to live your life in a way that would make her smile?"

"Of course," Lanek said. "It's not such a simple thing, though... I'm still me, and I still have to make difficult decisions."

"Just give it some thought," Reali said. "Only you can choose your own path, but when the time comes to make those important decisions—remember to think with your heart, as well as your mind. You will know what to do, then."

Lanek nodded. Reali and the graveyard vanished, immediately replaced by the mountain village, the dying elves around Lanek, and the construct of blood converging upon him.

But he knew the blood couldn't touch him now. Lanek clenched his teeth, raised his rapier, and ran straight through the swarming wave of blood blades. The crimson liquid-turned-metal twisted around Lanek, who caught a glimpse of Kechi amidst the rushing streams of blood and frantic villagers. Lanek knew he wouldn't be able to use his Hader against Kechi, so it was going to be a matter of swordsmanship between them. There was no telling what Kechi would try to do though, so Lanek needed to dispose of the Shire servant as quickly as possible.

Lanek charged through the bloody waves without a single drop of the altered matter landing upon him. Kechi was controlling blood to slice apart a villager wielding a water Nexi. At the last moment, Kechi turned in time to take his sword and beat aside Lanek's jab to the heart. Lanek stumbled forward, but avoided the swing of Kechi's sword.

"Hand over the Hader!" Kechi screamed. "Hand it over, or I'll kill everyone in this village!"

Lanek swung his rapier at Kechi's neck, but the man blocked the attack, then pushed Lanek back. "You were planning on killing everyone anyways. You have no choice but to die."

A couple villagers rushed for Kechi, who activated his fear Hader to keep them from approaching any further. The courage of most of the remaining villagers in the area had dwindled at this point, and Lanek knew he wasn't going to be able to rely on overpowering Kechi through strength of numbers.

A massive fireball rushed toward Kechi—too fast to even notice until it was already upon him. It was so large, Lanek had to jump back to avoid the edge of the sphere of concentrated Nexi flames. There was an explosion of fire, blood, and bloody flames all about Kechi's location.

Lanek glanced to the shrine entrance, finding Chei lying on the floor, red Nexi stone raised forward. His arm slumped to the ground, the energy fully drained out of him. But before Lanek could go help him, he looked back as the flames slowly dissipated.

Several layers of boiling black liquid oozed to the ground, revealing Kechi in the middle of it all, covered in blood splatters and smoking patches of singed clothes and hair. He had protected himself with all the available blood in the area at the last moment. Breathing heavily, his eyes wide, and struggling a moment to stand, Kechi turned toward Chei and ran.

Lanek lunged toward Kechi and swung his rapier as hard as he could. Kechi blocked Lanek's blade, but lost his sword in the process. Lanek swung again. Kechi dodged, but Lanek kept swinging. As Kechi wearily and narrowly evaded Lanek's attacks, Kechi slipped out one of his knives with his free hands. In one sudden motion, Kechi was forcing the long blade of his knife against Lanek's rapier blade, barely spun in time to block Kechi's sweep.

A villager in front of the shrine readied a bow and arrow, but Kechi directed some of his fear Hader's power toward the aging man, who shakily pointed the arrow toward the ground. A few other villagers were attempting to rush at Kechi again, but also found themselves struggling against the Hader's power. At the very least it was whittling away Kechi's energy, though it surprised Lanek that the man was able to keep fighting in this condition so proficiently.

Lanek fought off Kechi's frantic knife swings, barely able to keep up with the madman's frenzy. Grinning wildly, Kechi began to swing faster, his zeal growing with every swoop of the blade.

"Die! Die! Die! Die!" Kechi yelled with every swing.

Lanek had to keep stepping back to keep from getting overwhelmed by Kechi's unpredictable attacks. Even without the power of the Haders, Kechi was an incredibly talented fighter. He was likely the strongest royal servant the Shire government had, considering the fact he had obtained two Haders.

Someone a ways down the village path sprinted toward Kechi. Lanek could only afford the briefest of glances to notice. Was Kechi's hold over the villagers beginning to wane?

Lanek took heart and countered Kechi's attack with one of his own. Kechi jumped back and turned to face the man rushing toward him from behind. Lanek turned and found Lynx swinging his sword at Kechi's head. Kechi held both Haders toward Lynx, but the fear Hader wasn't stopping the Brotherhood fighter anymore. Had Lynx somehow managed to overcome the artificial fear Kechi had forced upon him? The very thought that somebody could overcome the powers of a Hader through sheer willpower...

It was astounding—but also unnerving, considering the source of that uncanny strength. Lanek still intended to take down Lynx as soon as Kechi was dealt with.

Kechi dodged Lynx's swing, then forced several spikes of blood to fling out of the ground in front of Lynx. Though Kechi couldn't fight Lanek with the blood, he could hold Lynx back with it—and at this point, there was plenty of it at his disposal.

Lynx dodged the solidifying strands of blood, while Lanek swung his blade at Kechi—who guarded with his knife. While fighting off Lanek, Kechi formed a wall of blood to keep Lynx back. Lynx hacked away at the blood, chopping off chunks of the shifting formation and splattering blood all about him. The pressure from two fronts was enough to force Kechi to take defensive measures against Lanek, whose anger only boiled stronger by the fact he was needing help from Lynx to get this far.

There was no chance Lanek could let up now. He had to be the one to kill Kechi. He had to be the one to obtain those Haders. If Lynx took them for himself, Lanek wouldn't be able to kill him. Lynx would flee with the power of two Haders, likely using them to further Augurc's experiments with the Elpis.

Lanek pushed against the blade of Kechi's knife as hard as he could, and Kechi stumbled backward. The Shire servant regained control and ran backward, reforming the breaking wall of blood to shift into writhing spikes that swarmed toward Lynx. Lanek leaped forward just as Kechi threw his knife at Lanek's face. There was just enough time for Lanek to reposition his rapier, deflecting the knife and flinging it to the side.

A tendril of blood flew past Lanek's side, but he ignored it and continued to run toward Kechi. Just before Lanek could jab his rapier through the man's chest, Kechi accessed control over a puddle of blood beneath his feet. The blood solidified and pushed him back, giving Kechi the boost he needed to avoid the extent of Lanek's attack.

"Lanek! Look out!" a voice cried out. It was Fenley, still standing on the village path with her brother and his wife.

Lanek turned and found the tendril of blood that had passed him by, now looming above him from a couple meters behind. At the end of the blood strand was a knife—the one Kechi had thrown at him earlier. Lanek leaped to the side just as the tendril of blood threw the knife at him with a speed even greater than that of a fired arrow.

Just as he landed, he found Kechi in front of him, throwing a second knife by hand. Lanek ducked beneath it and leaped toward Kechi, only to find Kechi was already running to the left. Lynx broke his way through the mass of blood Kechi had been controlling. Before Lynx could turn to face him, Kechi was already performing a running jump kick. Kechi hit him square in the stomach, sending Lynx flailing back to the ground several paces away. Lanek ran after Kechi, expecting the man to turn around and attack him—but instead Kechi kept running past Lynx. He wasn't trying to take Lynx down, and he wasn't doing anything to fight Lanek either. Was he trying to escape?

Lanek realized Kechi's plan just as it was too late. Kechi sprinted straight toward Fenley, likely picking her out from the crowds from when Fenley yelled her warning to Lanek. In one swift movement, Kechi punched Fenley's brother and his wife in their faces simultaneously, turned in place as he unclipped a dagger from his arm, and grabbed Fenley's arms while pushing the edge of the dagger against her neck. Other villagers nearby gasped and screamed, and several immediately ran for Kechi.

"Stop!" Kechi yelled, pushing his way back from all the villagers. "One move and she dies! It'll be easy to slit her throat. It'll be easy to kill all of you! But I don't have to, and I don't have to fight *you* anymore, *Lanek*. So stop the fighting and hand over the Hader already." He was doing the same thing Rilv did, but there was no doubt Kechi would be willing to kill his hostage. And this hostage was of direct concern to Lanek personally. There was no way he was going to let Kechi kill Fenley.

Lanek stopped a couple meters in front of Kechi and dropped his rapier to the ground. He had done enough harm to this village already... He couldn't let Fenley die, too. He couldn't let anymore of these villagers die. But he couldn't just hand over the Hader, either. Not to this madman.

"I'm not going to give a countdown like that woman did," Kechi said. "Just toss the Hader to me, and I'll let this girl go. Now."

There was no time to think of a plan. He had to act immediately. Kechi was already pushing the blade a little harder against Fenley's neck. Was he drawing blood?

No. Not Fenley. Not again. Not again!

Not again!

Lanek pulled his arm back to throw the Hader to Kechi.

Lynx tackled Lanek to the ground before he could release the Hader.

"What are you doing?" Lanek screamed. In a jerk reaction he punched Lynx in the face, slamming his knuckles against the hard mask—much harder and sturdier than Lanek expected.

Blood streaked across Lynx's mask from Lanek's knuckles. Lynx head-butted Lanek, using his mask to inflict significantly more injury on Lanek. The pain only made Lanek angrier, and he shoved Lynx off his body, then proceeded to tackle Lynx and shove him as hard he could into the ground.

Kechi swore, and Lanek glanced to see Kechi shove Fenley to the side and drive his dagger down the length of her right leg. Fenley screamed and fell to the ground, clutching her leg, and Lanek immediately pushed aside Lynx so he could take down Kechi.

The Shire servant used the blood drawn form Fenley's leg to form a lance, which he immediately flung straight at Lanek—with a white Nexi in tow, Lanek realized. Just as the lance of blood passed Lanek by, Kechi activated the white Nexi, creating a blinding flash of light. A moment later, sharp metal slammed into Lanek's side. He fell back, screaming. It was the dagger. It hadn't punctured any vitals, but the agony was excruciating.

He'll kill Fenley. Just as Lynx killed Suran!

Lanek pushed himself to his feet, his eyes still adjusting from the light flare, and tore the dagger out from his side. Kechi was running toward him, sliding out the metal rod tied to his leg in the process. Some kind of weapon... At the same time, he heard Lynx approaching. Lanek instinctively reached for his sheath, and remembered he had dropped his rapier to keep Kechi from killing Fenley outright. He had already tossed the dagger aside as well, and there was no time to pick it back up.

Lynx reached Lanek first. The masked man swung his sword at Lanek. He was going for the kill—all pretenses of cooperation had vanished—he wanted the Hader for himself. At the last second, Lanek activated the power of his Hader. Lynx's sword passed straight through Lanek's neck, but Lanek felt nothing.

He had become immaterial.

The next moment, Kechi was approaching Lanek from the other side, swinging his extended pole at Lanek. Knowing his Hader wouldn't work against Kechi, Lanek leaped back, and Kechi's weapon collided with Lynx's. Kechi shoved Lynx back, but Lynx immediately forced his way upon Kechi. Lanek used the opportunity to slip out a red Nexi stone and fire it at Lynx.

Lynx dodged the blast and turned to swing his sword at Lanek. At the same time, Kechi rushed at Lanek. To avoid Lynx, Lanek leaped into Kechi, slamming his shoulder against Kechi's chest. Kechi tried swinging his rod at Lanek, who grabbed it with his free hand and pointed the end of it toward Lynx, who was running straight at Lanek. Lynx crashed into the pole, coughing up blood, but kept on his feet and swung at Lanek once more. Kechi swung his pole against Lanek, knocking him just out of Lynx's reach.

The pain coursing through Lanek's body was all-consuming, regardless. Lanek wanted to collapse and die, but he couldn't give in—not at this critical of a moment. Not when the two men he wanted to kill most were right here, both trying to obtain the Hader.

Kechi swung his rod at Lynx, who swung his sword at the same time. An explosion accompanied the collision, the fires guided directly against Lynx. Lanek found a red Nexi stone connected to Kechi's weapon, hidden just below where he gripped the metal pole. The man could power a highly-concentrated explosion with each swing, as long as he had the energy for it.

Lynx fell back, gasping as the fire encompassed him. Water covered him nearly a moment later, as Lynx was quick and calm enough to take out a dark blue Nexi stone and douse the flames with it. Kechi was already turning toward Lanek by then. Lanek aimed his fire Nexi at Kechi, but the man was too quick for him. Kechi slammed his pole against Lanek's outstretched arm. An explosion didn't ensue—perhaps he didn't have the energy to do another one so soon—but it was still a metal pole regardless. Lanek stumbled to the side, losing the red Nexi in the process, but at least keeping a hold of the Hader. He stumbled to the ground. His arm didn't feel broken, fortunately—just badly bruised, and left with a large, stinging lump. Lynx was struggling to get back up, and Kechi was already swinging his pole down to Lanek's head.

Lanek rolled to the side, then slipped an ice Nexi out from his pocket. Just as Kechi turned, Lanek released needles of ice from his Nexi stone. Only one managed to hit Kechi, but it sunk straight into his right eye.

Kechi quickly stepped back, screaming. Lynx was suddenly upon Kechi, nearly about to drive his sword through Kechi's chest. At the last moment Kechi forced blood on the ground to erupt at Lynx, shoving him back with another violent push—straight toward Lanek. By then Lanek had pushed himself to his feet, and aimed his light blue Nexi at Lynx. As Lynx fell backward, he turned and swung his sword at Lanek, who decided at the last moment to form a shield of ice. Lynx's attack shattered the ice and knocked Lanek back, and Lynx immediately swung again. Lanek exerted what strength he had to jump back further, barely evading Lynx's swing.

"Die, both of you!" Kechi screamed.

As Lanek stepped further back from Lynx's attacks, he found Kechi had taken out a tan Nexi. The ground beneath Lanek's and Lynx's feet erupted, blowing apart into pieces and sending both of them crashing into opposite directions. Lynx rolled toward Kechi, who was already gathering more blood together into a giant wave behind him. As Lynx struggled back to his feet, the solidifying blood slammed down against him. The partly liquid mass shoved him into the earth, sending him rolling some more. Kechi didn't let up on the attack, however, and continued to shove more hardening blood against Lynx, who was still fighting to escape the trampling.

Lanek fought off his own pain as he fought to get back on his feet. Somehow Kechi still had this much energy at his disposal, even while fighting both him and Lynx. He had to focus on Kechi. He had to kill him quickly.

Despite the exhaustion of the battle, Lanek ran straight for Kechi and exerted all the energy he had on his ice Nexi, releasing as much frozen air as he could muster from the stone.

Kechi screamed at the top of his lungs, his tan Nexi glowing all the more brighter. The ground beneath Lanek's feet erupted, and Lanek leaped from rock to rising rock, forcing himself to keep from falling over. A fountain of partly solidified blood arose around Kechi, lifting him in the air a couple meters, bringing him straight toward Lanek's side. At the last second Lanek managed to turn and direct his ice Nexi energy toward Kechi. The Shire servant instantly caused most his airborne blood to transfer in front of himself, forming a shield. The wall of blood froze, and suddenly Kechi was twisting himself to the side of the shield. He had a small knife in hand, and was already throwing it at Lanek. Lanek let himself stumble over the bursting rocks in order to evade the attack, and crashed into the ground below, pain searing through his entire body.

He had to get back up. Despite the agony, he forced himself to stand—but Kechi was already returning to the ground via the mass of blood he guided himself with. With the tan Nexi in his hand, Kechi caused the earth about Lanek to break apart and weaken, causing his feet to sink into the ground. Hands of dirt formed from the ground around him, and immediately latched on to Lanek's legs before he could escape.

Kechi ran, raising his metal rod toward Lanek, the fire Nexi embedded at the end of it glowing brightly. There was no way Lanek was going to be able to dodge it, and he was too weak to escape the Nexi-strengthened earth gripping his legs. The earth continued to tighten, to the point where he felt the circulation of blood was being cut off below his knees. There was no using the Hader in this situation—the earth binding Lanek was connected to Kechi's tan Nexi, and the Hader couldn't be used against other Hader users. And Lanek didn't even have the energy to use his ice Nexi again.

A few paces away, Kechi readied his swing. Lanek took his ice Nexi and chucked it at Kechi's head as hard as he could.

The stone slammed into Kechi's forehead, and he fell down, screaming. The red Nexi in his weapon was still being powered, so it released a concentrated explosion upon impact with the ground, directly between Kechi and Lanek. The earth binding Lanek broke apart, and he was sent flying back in the furious heat of the fire Nexi blast. At the same time, Kechi was violently scraped backwards across the ground, losing his metal rod in the process. Both Lanek and Kechi had held on to their Haders, and as far as Lanek could tell, they were both still alive, shakily gasping painful liquid breaths.

Kechi was an utterly bloody mess, and Lanek imagined he didn't look much better. The sheer amount of blood involved in this fight was horrific, and it still wasn't over—not until Kechi was dead.

Lanek tried to stand up, but it had turned even more difficult to do so. The blast had battered him severely, and it was hard to tell how much more injured he was at this point. Every fiber of his being was in pain, and just the thought of fighting further was almost unbearable. And yet Lanek fought to stand.

He saw Kechi had lost control over the blood that was beating down Lynx, but the masked man hadn't gotten to his feet yet. Was Lynx dead? Lanek found it unlikely, knowing his luck. He'd have to kill Lynx as soon as Kechi was dealt with. And then... would it all finally be over? He couldn't think about it now. He had to stand up. He had to find a weapon. He had to kill Kechi.

Lanek's vision went blurry, and for a moment he wondered if he had lost consciousness. Something kicked him in the face.

He looked up and found a crimson figure standing in front of him, screaming something. Lanek couldn't make out what he was saying though. The world had turned silent for a few moments. Or had it been minutes?

"...like that?" Kechi screamed. "I'll make you pay ten-fold for these injuries you've given me!"

Blood flew across the air, and Lanek heard villagers screaming. People were running, but they weren't getting far. Lanek's vision and hearing returned, but an overwhelming nausea took its place, and he struggled to keep from throwing up. As he did so, he found villager after villager getting killed by Kechi's Hader-guided blood. There was blood everywhere, and with every villager Kechi killed, more blood became available for his disposal.

An old man was beheaded. Blood writhed from his head, its bladed tentacles slicing apart a young man a few meters away from him.

A tendril of blood wrapped around a small girl's neck, strangling her. Nearby, spikes rose from a puddle of blood beneath a teenage boy, impaling his feet and legs. The boy fell to the ground, impaling himself further on more rising spikes. The blood that burst from his back gathered together and rushed toward an older woman, bludgeoning her in the back of the head.

Thin streams of blood rushed toward a man trying to escape the carnage. The blood flowed straight into his mouth, ears, and nose. Once all of it had entered his body, he fell to his knees and began shaking uncontrollably. Kechi's Hader blood melded with the man's blood, and seconds later, the man blew apart into two halves, separated at the waist. The blood that exploded from within him soared from his body toward two women escaping down the village path. The blood ribbons formed into crimson blades and proceeded to chop off their hands and feet, then slice into their bodies at least a dozen times before finishing them off outright with slices through their necks.

And all the while, Kechi laughed. The blood covering his body vibrated with ecstatic glee. He lived for this torture. This madness. This inhumanity.

Lanek could barely grasp the sheer terror this man was inflicting. Kechi was literally a one-man army, capable of bringing an entire village to its knees with the fear Hader, and then torturing them to death with the blood Hader.

Lanek stood up, but immediately Kechi kicked him in the stomach.

"We're not done yet!" Kechi yelled. "There's still your friend here left. I'd like to deal with her personally! Let me position you in a way so you can get a good view."

Kechi wiped the blood off a nearby Nexi stone, finding it to be a green one. He pointed it at Lanek and caused vines to wrap around Lanek, binding his arms and legs together, and covering his entire body tight. The ends of the vines dug into the ground and lifted Lanek up a bit so he was standing up, staring straight toward Fenley. There was no way for him to move, especially in this weak state, and the only weapon he had on hand was the immaterial Hader. He felt some energy left in him, but he couldn't access the power of the Hader—Kechi's energy was linked to the binding vines of this Nexi stone. All Lanek could do was watch as the monstrous figure of Kechi walked over toward Fenley.

No... Not Fenley. He couldn't let him torture Fenley. He couldn't let Kechi kill her. He wanted to yell out to her—tell her to run. To just forget him. Use all her might to escape this madman.

But there she lay on the bloody earth, crying from the pain and terror her beloved village had suffered. Had all her friends and family members died? Lanek hadn't been in a state to notice who was being killed and who was escaping—if there was anyone escaping.

Kechi's fear Hader glowed a little brighter, and Fenley cowered further, her cries crumbling into barely audible whimpers.

"These weak, pathetic elves!" Kechi screamed. "Strange to think it was the elves who played the central role in creating the Haders! Not that it matters anymore. The world will come to learn the source of the greatest power the world will ever behold—the mind and strength of the royal Shire line, with Mareba Shire the star that will eternally shine brighter than all the rest! And I will forever be his most precious servant!"

Kechi knelt down beside Fenley and lifted her up so she'd lie across Kechi's lap, her back and head resting in Kechi's bloody hands. He still had his two Haders clenched in his hands.

"L... L... Lan...ek..." was all Fenley was able to get out. Whether it was concern for Lanek's safety or a plea for help, it was impossible to tell.

"You poor girl," Kechi said. "You don't need to worry about him... Let me give you something else to focus on!"

Kechi grabbed Fenley's right index finger and wrenched it back, dislocating it. Fenley screamed and writhed in pain—but could only move a little. Kechi kept a tight grip on her, and was still flooding fear into her via the green and black Hader.

"Stop..." Lanek said. It was difficult to say anything more, and he was trying to focus on breaking free of Kechi's vines. He couldn't let Kechi keep hurting Fenley... But it was too difficult to move, let alone fight.

Kechi grabbed Fenley's middle finger and wrenched it back. Fenley screamed louder, but Kechi didn't flinch. He simply smiled and moved on to the next finger. Once he broke her ring finger, he took her pinky and pulled back as hard as he could. One by one, Kechi broke each of Fenley's fingers, and her cries continued to ring more desperately across the silent, bloody village.

"Stop it, Kechi!" Lanek yelled, finding enough strength to at least struggle against the vines. Even if he somehow managed to break free, he had no idea how he'd stop Kechi. "I'll give you the Hader! Just stop!"

Kechi pointed at his still-impaled eye, the icicle dripping with blood. "You make me suffer, and I will make you suffer ten-fold! You can not stop the work of Mareba Shire, any more than you can raise a hand up to stop a waterfall from crashing down on you! Resist and suffer. Resist and perish."

Worms of blood congregated toward Fenley and Kechi from all across the bloody field. Dozens of them squirmed into Fenley's screaming, gagging mouth, while others crawled into her ears, her nose, up her dress, through her blouse, and into her eyes. At the same time, blood covering Kechi's body began to converge toward his free right hand, forming a curved, sickle-like blade.

Above Fenley's muffled cries, Kechi screamed, "As a servant of the one true power, I condemn this village and everyone who walked its grounds this day!" Kechi proceeded to carve a long, deep slice down the length of Fenley's right arm. Blood poured from her wound, forming into jagged spikes that turned and sliced across her arm in all random directions. Kechi then cut her other arm, and the process repeated.

He tore through her skirt and sliced deep into her thigh, and on down the length of her leg. Blood poured freely—more blood for him to control, more pain for him to inflict. Still grinning, Kechi cut up her other leg, then turned her over onto her side so he could carve into her back.

Lanek screamed, his cries melding with Fenley's torturous anguish and Kechi's glee and laughter.

Suddenly the vines binding Lanek loosened. Something was cutting them from behind. Lanek didn't pause to figure out how he was being freed, or who was freeing him. He simply shoved the vines apart and sprinted toward Kechi. Though Lanek was pushed past the point of exhaustion, he willed himself to run with every fiber of his being.

Kechi's frown immediately disappeared. With the sickle of blood, Kechi quickly slit Fenley's throat and shoved her aside before turning and running away.

"No!" Lanek screamed.

Kechi killed her. He killed Fnely. And now he was running away. Why was he running away?

Kechi stumbled to the ground, his mind at a complete loss at this turn of events. He fell to his hands and knees, just in front of Fenley's limp, bleeding body.

"F... Fenley..." Lanek coughed. "Fenley... Fenley..." He crawled toward her, barely able to breathe. Her body was covered in deep, blood-filled gashes. She wasn't moving at all—not even breathing. Her eyes were filled with blood.

There was nothing left to her but a lifeless, desecrated corpse.

It was too late to save her. She was dead. There was nothing more he could do. She was gone. Lanek had wondered if he'd be able to meet with her again, even if he had to steal the Stone of Truth. Even if he had to betray her village. He still hoped he'd be able to return... To speak with her again. Explain why he had to do the things he did.

But what did any of it matter now? Just like Suran, Fenley was murdered. All because of some powerful Nexi stone. All because he had to get entangled in the world's power struggles. All because this world was filled with deranged killers.

There was blood everywhere. As far as Lanek could see, there was blood. He was covered in blood himself. This wasn't only Kechi's fault. This was his fault too. Tears filled his eyes, but he couldn't bring himself to feel any deep remorse. It was too difficult to feel anything at this point. It was all just too incredulous... As if this had all been some kind of strange, unexplainable nightmare.

But he didn't want this. He didn't want any of this.

Kechi. Rilv. Augurc. Lynx. These terrible people. These terrible, unforgivable people.

There was movement a ways behind Lanek. A muffled cough, and the metallic ring of a sword shakily sliding into its sheath.

Turning around, Lanek found Lynx standing a couple meters away. He was a bloody mess too, quite possibly at the brink of death. No... Recalling all the injury Lynx sustained in that battle, there was no way Lynx was well-off right now. Of course, Lanek was in terrible condition as well. There was little hope for him to kill Lynx right now.

And besides... it was Lynx that freed him from Kechi's vines, wasn't it? Lanek saw a green Nexi stone in Lynx's hand, and a small knife tied to the end of the vines connected to the stone. After Lynx had been pummeled by Kechi's massive blood attack, Lynx must have somehow found the energy to use a green Nexi and control some vines with a knife tied to the end of them. Lynx cut the vines and freed Lanek, allowing him to try stopping Kechi.

Kechi ended up killing Fenley as he escaped, but had Lynx not helped Lanek... There was probably no way for Lanek to escape on his own. Kechi would have killed him once he was through with torturing Fenley, however long it was he planned on continuing that. Kechi must have run away because he saw little hope in continuing to fight both Lynx and Lanek, both of whom he may have underestimated in regards to perseverance. Kechi may have been very low on energy at that point, and didn't want to risk getting killed by a vengeful, furious Lanek and uncannily persistent Lynx.

So Kechi ran away, likely heading to his own airship, wherever it was. This technically meant Lynx had saved Lanek's life. It was infuriating to think about, but Lanek wasn't going to thank him. Lynx had tried to kill Lanek, after all. And Lynx had only helped him so that there would be two of them to fight against Kechi. Lynx was only concerned with himself. He wanted the Haders for himself. He was as selfish as he was sinister.

Was he going to try to kill Lanek now? Lanek glanced to the ground and found an abandoned knife. He picked it up and clutched it wearily, but Lynx didn't make any attempt to approach Lanek. It was difficult to tell what Lynx was thinking, of course, thanks to that mask. The smiling face was obscured with blood, as was everything else that had stood within twenty meters of Kechi's bloody rampage.

"I'm sorry," Lynx said.

And what did he mean by that? Lanek clenched his weapon tighter. There was no way Lynx was actually apologizing. It made no sense.

"I have trouble controlling myself," Lynx continued. "I need the Haders... More than anything in the world, I need them. All this blood... it triggered these emotions that have been placed in me... I really need the Haders..."

Lanek pocketed his Hader, feeling Lynx's eyes gazing at the movement of his the last person who needs the Haders."

...thing, Lanek wanted to kill this man. Right here and now.

...sn't true. More than anything, Lanek just wanted Fenley alive ...entirely wrong for her to die. If she had never met Lanek, none ...d have happened.

...because of people like Lynx that these tragedies kept happening. ...ley probably wouldn't have died if Lynx hadn't caused a stir in ...e in the first place.

...airship was approaching. Lanek recognized the sound before he saw his ship coming. Apparently Kitoh was able to pilot it after all... And apparently Rilv still wanted to make sure they left with this village's Hader. She was coming for him, and there was going to be no way for him to resist. Lanek would have to deal with her somehow, but for now he had to figure out what to do about Lynx. He couldn't just continue this mission with Lynx as if nothing had happened.

A rope ladder lowered from the airship, and Lanek unconsciously grabbed onto it. Why was he grabbing onto it? He couldn't just leave this village now... And yet he was holding onto it. Deep down, he did want to leave. He couldn't bear to gaze at Fenley's corpse any longer. He didn't want to know who had lived and who had died amongst the villagers he had come to know and love this day. Were Fenley's relatives alive? Had Nullen survived? What about Chei? And all the other elves he had spoken with? Perhaps they were all dead now.

Lanek kept his eyes on Lynx. He didn't want Lynx to come aboard the airship too. But he didn't want to leave Lynx behind in this village, either. There were still survivors, and Lanek didn't want Lynx to kill any more of these innocent people.

Lanek started climbing, and he could feel someone climbing up after him. He didn't look down—he didn't want to see Lynx following him, like an insidious shadow.

Somehow Lanek had become part of a league of murderers, and his own airship was its base. And even after witnessing the deaths of dozens of people he cared for, he still had a desire for murder in his own heart. How much better was he than the likes of Lynx or Kechi?

•

Kechi jogged down the steep, rocky hill, cursing between his breaths. With his energy nearly expended, he decided it was prudent away from the elf and the Brotherhood member who were fighting a They were both formidable enemies, each of them somehow away fighting well after they were practically pummeled to death.

Perhaps it wouldn't have been difficult to finish them off right the there, but Kechi couldn't afford to take any risks greater than what necessary. He had obtained two Haders for his master—all that matte was that he find at least two more, and bring them back to Lord Maret Shire.

I can't die now... Kechi thought. *Whatever I do, I can't die yet. Once my master has four Haders... Then I can die.*

Once he was well enough away from the village, Kechi let himself sit on the ground, his whole body stinging in agony. This pain was terrible, but he knew he'd survive. This was certainly the worst off he had ever been in after a fight, but all that mattered was that he was still alive, and could continue his mission to find Haders.

For master, I can keep going. I can keep fighting for master...

The ice embedded in his eye had melted away, leaving behind a torn, bloody mess. The very fact the elf had managed to impale his eye like that was infuriating. Kechi had been careless. Or perhaps the elf was truly stronger than Kechi, and it was simply fortunate that he was still alive. One thing was certain—he wasn't going to underestimate the elf if they ever met again. Same with the Brotherhood member. Kechi would be sure to kill them both if they stood in the way of his Haders.

It was certainly a possibility. The uniformed woman from the Fiefs government had a Hader, and so did the elf. It seemed they were all working together, along with the Brotherhood member and the eigni boy.

Kechi looked up to the sky, trying his hardest to ignore the pain of all his injuries. His eye stung the worst, enough that he wanted to tear away at it, burn what was left of the useless organ. He would need to find a doctor to deal with it, as the pain would just hinder him in any future fights. With his good eye, Kechi spotted an airship in the distance, flying away from the village. It soon faded into the ghostly clouds, heading southeast. Kechi needed to hurry... The airship would likely be heading to another place where a Hader was located, and Kechi would need to get there before his enemies. Perhaps he could find the Hader there before them, and once they got there, he could use his three Haders to take their two Haders. Then he'd have five... The very thought of using five of the stones filled him with glee. With that much power at his disposal... there wouldn't be anything he wouldn't be able to do for his master.

Kechi's small one-man blimp was hidden further down the hill, tied to some rocks in a small enclave. As he expected, there was nobody there, and there was no sign of anyone tampering with the airship. It was a delicate vehicle, but it was fast. Once Kechi untied the ship and got the engine and appropriate Nexi stones activated, he entered through the hole in the metal floor of the ship and walked into the bridge, which was just large enough for him to sit in and operate the controls with. He didn't need anything else— the time would go by quick enough just by focusing on his mission for Lord Mareba Shire.

Once the ship was airborne, Kechi turned so he would go in the same direction the enemy airship was heading toward. The Shire Kingdom was in that direction, and it made Kechi wonder if the next Hader was there somewhere. It would be convenient for him, considering his master was there, waiting for him.

His master was expecting to hear good news right now. It was going to be shameful to report that the enemy got away with not one, but two Haders now. Kechi took out a teal Nexi from his pocket and activated its power. He'd have just enough strength to speak to his master for a minute or two, which was all Lord Mareba Shire normally warranted anyways.

"Report, Kechi." Lord Mareba's voice was strong, vigilant. There was never any weakness in his voice, regardless of the man's age. Though Master was in his late fifties, there was no hint of frailty to him—only royal Shire pride. Unlike the quiet void that was Augurc Shire, this was a man whose very presence—whose very voice—commanded obedience and subservience.

"I apologize, Master," Kechi said. "I failed to obtain the Hader in the elf village. The enemy has escaped with it, and they still possess the telekinesis Hader."

"Follow them," Lord Mareba said. "Kill them. Take the two Haders from them. Return to me once you have finished."

"Yes, master," Kechi said.

Lord Mareba didn't say anything more. He was not a man who cared to give reprimands or rousing speeches. He simply gave orders, and expected them to be fulfilled. Kechi knew he had failed—he was filled with an overwhelming guilt for coming up short.

But it was a temporary failure. He could still succeed in the mission. He simply had to do as his master instructed. Kill the enemies. Take their Haders. Return to Master. It was simple. And all Kechi had to do was not die in the process.

It was time to restore the Shire Kingdom to its full glory. Ever since Delkol died and Augurc took his place, the kingdom had been in shambles. With the power of the Haders, Lord Mareba Shire would be able to become ruler over the land, and bring the Shire Kingdom into a new age.

Lord Mareba Shire... You will soon rule in absolute fear and authority. With the Haders to back you up, nobody will be able to oppose you. Even Augurc with his Elpis, and his experiments, and his Brotherhood—they will all fall before you. All enemies of the Shire Kingdom will fall. The lands of Shire and Fiefs will be reunited once more, with you as the true king with true royal blood flowing through your veins. You shall be a ruler for all to look up to and reverence... for ages to come.

I will stop at nothing to acquire all the Haders you need, Master. I am willing to kill for your cause. I am willing to die for your cause. I need nothing more.

It was easier for Borely to readjust to the light than it was for everyone else. Out of the four of them, he had been a vampire for the least amount of time. Though Nivakil was blind, he still shuddered whenever light poked through the trees and reached his skin. And though Analicia hadn't been a vampire much longer than Borely, she was young and had more trouble handling the light, or at least was quicker to complain about it.

They had traveled the forest for about a day now, the city of Istal now far behind them, left in the hands of Augurc, Hidif, and the rest of the Brotherhood and vampire elites who overthrew it. And Areo. Borely couldn't stop thinking of her—how he had finally found her, and how he had been unable to do anything to rescue her. Her fate was worse than he had ever feared. She wasn't just a prisoner in a cage—she was a prisoner in her own body. Augurc's experimentation with the Elpis was likely responsible, and it pained Borely to think that Areo was one of Augurc's enhanced soldiers assisting in the Brotherhood's terrorism. Over the years in Fiefs Kingdom and surrounding territories, there had been many high-scale robberies, delicate assassinations, and precise acts of wanton destruction designed to inspire fear in the corrupt organization. How many of these had Areo been forced to participate in?

And all this time, Borely hadn't been able to leave Istal long enough to find her. To save her from getting so much blood on her hands. It still felt wrong to be leaving Areo behind, but he was finally part of a plan that would lead to freeing her from Augurc and the effects of the Elpis. The royal head servant of the Fiefs Kingdom—Rilv, Borely recalled—communicated with Nivakil via teal Nexi stones, informing them too late about the possibility of an attack on Istal. But fortunately, there was also a plan formulated to put an end to the Brotherhood, and at long last, Borely was going to be able to do something about it. With the fall of Istal, he was able to obtain a Rite Nexi without having to wait many years to go through the Rite, and Nivakil was finally pushed to take action.

The fact he promised to assist Borely and Jenba in rescuing Areo helped persuade him to assist the Fiefs Kingdom in its ambition to obtain materials called Haders. They were apparently powerful Nexi stones crafted for the sake of fighting against the Elpis. Precisely what Borely needed to help bring down Augurc and free Areo.

Borely knew Nivakil, Jenba, and Analicia all had doubts on this mission, and he had to admit to himself that it was going to be very risky, but he wasn't going to let Nivakil and Jenba back down now. Of course, he would have preferred Analicia stay somewhere else while they searched for the Haders, but there were no good places to leave her. Not many people would take in a vampire child, and Jenba felt it safer for her to stick with them, despite the danger they were likely walking into.

After all, they were heading to Limbo, the port city notorious for its piracy. Based on the research of Rilv's operatives and a team of Nexi researchers, one of the Haders was believed to be near Limbo. They somehow were able to tell that the Hader was moving over the sea, implying it was being used by someone who traveled on a boat. And considering how there were so many treasure-hunting pirates that docked in Limbo, it seemed likely some pirate captain had the Hader.

Borely had no qualms with taking down a pirate and apprehending the Hader from him. He had had plenty of experiences with pirates in his life before becoming a vampire. Pirates were generally just thugs that happened to be crew members on a ship. Thieves and despots, just looking for a way to stir up trouble. Whenever they went too far at the pubs Borely had frequented, he was always quick to beat some sense into them. It was going to nice to do that again.

Of course, just being in the light again was going to be nice. He and his companions were traveling through the forest, well past the artificial lighting of Istal and the surrounding area. Now bits of natural light were starting to slip in, and it was making Nivakil, Jenba, and Analicia uncomfortable.

In a physical way it was making Borely feel ill at ease—an unfortunate reminder of what he had become—but in his mind he was pleased to be approaching the daylight sun once more. He had only been in the light on a few occasions the past few years, and each time he came in contact with it, he felt a little more human again. He missed that feeling, and looked forward to getting out of this forest and taking a boat to Limbo. He hadn't been on a boat once since becoming a vampire, nor had he set eyes on the glimmering sea. Just to breathe in that crisp ocean air... Borely couldn't wait. It was going to be like stepping back into his past life. At least a little bit like it.

Everyone traveled in silence for the most part. The previous day was one long series of terrible events, and it was going to take a while for all of it to settle in their minds. They weren't going to be able to return to their homes until the Brotherhood was dealt with, and from what Borely gathered, the Fiefs Kingdom did intend to assist in freeing what was left of Istal from the banished elites. They simply needed to succeed in finding all the Haders, and then they'd have the power necessary to right all the wrongs plaguing the land at the moment.

It all felt very reminiscent to Borely's time with Terico, Areo, Kitoh, and the others, back when they were searching for the Elpis fragments. Borely would never forget how everything ended with that life-changing adventure, but he felt things would work out better this time.

They had to. After all, how could things get worse than they already had?

•

The next day brought less trees and more light, but Borely was the only one who felt better about it. Granted, it was giving him a headache, and his body shuddered from time to time, but he felt this was progress. They were going somewhere. They were doing something about the Brotherhood, and about Areo.

Thanks to their enhanced hearing ability—particularly Nivakil's—they were able to hide whenever other travelers were approaching. Though Borely and Analicia didn't look too much like vampires yet, Jenba and especially Nivakil exhibited all the physical signs of vampirism quite clearly. Once they reached a town, Borely planned to go buy hooded cloaks for the two of them so they could avoid any trouble with passers-by.

When they were about an hour's walk away from a riverside town, traversing an open field, Nivakil heard quiet footsteps in the distance. There was no good place to hide, so there was nothing to do but travel casually and try not to bring themselves to anyone's attention. Analicia had grown used to the light enough to keep from squinting constantly (though she still complained about it), but Jenba could barely keep his eyes open at all, and Nivakil walked wearily, like a man sick with the flu. Borely hoped they would adjust to the light soon. It wasn't the first time for either of them to be out in the sunlight, after all—they were both there during Delkol's attack on Setar.

The traveler in question soon came into view, walking alone down the grassy trail. A shorter man in his thirties, wearing drab, muted clothes. A drifter, perhaps.

The man stopped in front of Nivakil, who chose to stop a few meters away. Borely and the others stopped as well, and Borely wondered if this meant they had been found out.

"You walk as quietly as Rilv informed me," Nivakil said.

"Figured that'd be the best way to let'cha know I was comin'," the man said, placing his hands in his trouser pockets. He leaned back casually, then leaned to the side, presumably cracking his back.

"She didn't mention an accent though," Nivakil said.

"Best I try to blend in when I can," the man replied. Apparently this was an operative who worked for Rilv, and was described in Rilv's conversation with Nivakil.

The man walked up to Nivakil and handed him an envelope. "Don't spend it all in one place."

"I'll try to restrain myself," Nivakil said. He was probably the last person Borely would have pegged as an impulse spender, though. Apparently the old vampire had a bit of dry wit to him.

"Good, I'll be goin' then," the operative said.

"Rilv said you'd assist us in acquiring passage to Limbo," Nivakil said.

"An' I have," the operative said. "I'm sure you can handle the rest on your own. 'Sides, I don't really like travelin' with vampires."

Borely couldn't blame him. He watched the operative walk on down the path, nobody breathing another word.

"Let's keep going then," Nivakil said. They resumed their journey, likely none of them quite sure how to feel about the operative, or the mission in general. How much hope was being placed in them right now?

And was it just a begrudging alliance? Borely thought about his situation a little more deeply. He was a vampire now, after all. Most everyone in the world wasn't going to be looking forward to his company anymore.

He looked to Nivakil, Jenba, and Analicia. These were his lone allies right now. Just him and a bunch of vampires. A bunch of *other* vampires.

•

Once at the riverside town, they found an unassuming boat leaving for Limbo that evening. After Borely got cloaks for Jenba and Nivakil, they all boarded the vessel with a few dozen other people. Most of them were humans and elves who worked as merchants, but there were a few people planning to visit towns a ways away from Limbo. It didn't seem anyone intended to stay at the city any longer than they had to, and from what Borely could hear from conversations on deck, there were rumors of more pirate trouble than usual stirring at the port.

There were several guards aboard the ship, which itself was armed with three cannons on each side. It was a decent-sized ship, certainly larger than the one Borely ran. But despite the measures given to the ship in order for it to transfer goods successfully across dangerous waters, the traveling civilians didn't appear to feel entirely safe.

Borely wondered how much was being done to deal with these pirates. Was the Fiefs Kingdom's armed forces spread thin, needing to focus on the greater threat of the Brotherhood at this time?

It was pointless for him to worry about it, at any rate, since he was traveling to Limbo with the *intention* of finding pirates. It was likely that most of them at least knew about the Hader, and chances were good that one of them *had* the Hader. Whatever the stone did, it surely gave that pirate a great advantage over all his enemies.

Once the boat set off, Borely and most of the other civilians took the time to stand outside on deck to enjoy the brisk ocean air. Nivakil, Jenba, and Analicia were quick to go to their reserved room below deck, however, not wanting to be in any amount of light any longer than they had to. It was dark—past twilight—but they were still recovering from the journey beneath the sun, and were anxious to be in as dark an environment as they possibly could.

Borely could hear any conversation he wanted to, he realized. Back in Istal, vampires knew how to hide their voices so distant bystanders couldn't hear them. But these humans and elves didn't know Borely was a vampire—a blessing, considering how most of them would react if they did know. He didn't want to eavesdrop, so he stood by the side of the ship, resting his arms on the wall separating him from the depths of the restless sea. He focused on the sounds of the waves, angry and loud, spraying water toward his face, but never quite reaching him.

In a way, he felt like the waves, never quite able to reach what he wanted. How exactly was he going to save Areo? Rilv and the Fiefs Kingdom at large were just concerned with Augurc and the Brotherhood. And while he also hoped to put an end to their violence and cruelty, he was much more concerned with finding Areo again. Rilv probably just wanted the Haders in order to kill experiments like Areo. Most, if not all, of the royal operatives would be willing to kill Areo in a heartbeat as soon as they had the means to do so. She was an incredibly dangerous weapon now, not to mention a vampire. Borely tried not to think of how much destruction Areo must have caused in her rampage through Istal, her consciousness dulled by the Elpis, and her emotions stirred by the ambitions of the banished vampire elites and the Brotherhood.

Why was he so concerned about Areo though, in the first place?

Borely shut his eyes and thought back to all the time he spent with her. It wasn't like they ever got along that well. She had hidden the fact she was a vampire from the start, but she never sought out his blood or tried to turn him into a vampire.

Well, until he offered his blood to her. And then she did turn him into a vampire.

It was a miserable memory. The battle may have ended in victory for the Fiefs Kingdom, but it ruined Borely's life, as well as Areo's.

Borely certainly hated Augurc for everything he did in that battle, but Borely didn't feel the need to dwell on him. He just wanted to save Areo. She didn't deserve the fate handed to her. Even after what she did to Borely... Even after turning him into the thing he despised most of all.

She knew how much Borely hated vampires. But she turned him into a vampire anyways, perhaps expecting him to hate her for the rest of his life. And she was probably fine with that. She just wanted him to survive. She just wanted him to live.

And Borely was still alive, unable to change what had happened. Had she made the right decision in making him a vampire? Perhaps she wouldn't have been captured by Augurc if she hadn't taken the time and effort to inject her blood into Borely's body. Perhaps it would have been best to just let Borely die.

But everything that happened wasn't going to change.

I just have to keep reaching, he thought.

Nivakil had payed for a room with four cots, so each of them could sleep comfortably after their draining trip in the sunlight. It wasn't so comfortable for the others, but Borely felt right at home, rocked to sleep by the subtle movements of the ship.

He awoke in the middle of the night, however, when his bed shifted, rolling him from his side to his back. Something brushed up against him.

Borely opened his eyes and turned to find Analicia lying beside him, snug beneath the covers. She tried wrapping an arm around Borely's arm, at which point Borely promptly shoved her aside.

She whimpered, her eyes still closed. It was hard to tell how awake she was, but she was able to pull the blanket around her tight—a feeble resistance.

Borely pulled the girl out of the blanket and tossed her off his bed. She landed on the floor with a loud thump, then let out a muffled whine.

"Stay in your own bed," Borely muttered.

"I'm cold," Analicia said.

"It's not that cold," Borely said. "Just go to sleep and you'll be fine."

Analicia whimpered.

"Come on," Borely said.

Analicia stood up and balled her hands into little fists. "*You* come on, you stupid pointless useless dumb lazy worthless not even worth calling a vampire totally ridiculous worthless loser!"

"Quiet, you'll wake everyone up," Borely said.

Analicia jumped onto Borely's bed, and flopped her knees down into Borely's stomach. He held back a scream, and took pained breaths as he wearily drooped his head back. Meanwhile Analicia crawled back into the covers, then scrunched her body up near Borely.

He immediately picked her up again and tossed her off the bed.

"Hey!" Analicia cried. "Why are you so mean?"

"I'm trying to sleep, obviously," Borely said. "I can't sleep with *you* lying in my bed!"

"I don't..." Analicia stopped short. She turned away and lay on the floor, gripping her legs up to her chest. She whimpered pathetically, like some kind of kicked puppy.

Borely wasn't going to fall for this charade. He rolled to his side so his back was to the child. All he had to do was ignore her, and she'd grow bored of trying to annoy him. Kids like her just enjoyed getting attention, and always had to be doing something when they were awake. And it wasn't hard for them to be awake and full of energy, even in the middle of the night.

After several minutes, her melodrama finally passed, and Borely felt himself starting to fall back asleep again.

Until his bed shifted, ever so slightly.

Borely sat up and grabbed Analicia before she could slip under the covers again.

He gripped Analicia's arms so he could stare his eyes straight into hers. "Go. To. Bed."

She turned her head away and made a pouting face. "I'm *trying* to."

Borely sighed. "How about you go bother Jenba? Don't you like him better anyways?" He didn't want Jenba to be bothered and woken up, but he couldn't put up with this girl any longer.

"He's not here," Analicia said. "He can't sleep."

Borely looked to Jenba's bed. It was more difficult for him to see in the dark than it was for everyone else, since he was the newest of the vampires. After staring for a few seconds though, Borely could get the sense that Jenba wasn't there—just a disheveled sheet.

Perhaps Jenba was on deck to get some fresh air, or was planning to sleep during the day when everyone else was up. This would make sense, since he wouldn't want to be out in the sun anyways, and didn't want people to find out he was a vampire.

Borely got up and walked out to the hall, then made his way to the stairs leading to the deck. Fortunately, Analicia didn't follow him—if he was lucky, she'd be asleep by the time he got back. And if she fell asleep in his bed, he could just take her bed.

Standing on deck were a few sailors, going about their tasks wearily. There were always things to do to keep a ship running smoothly at all times of the day and night, and Borely understood well enough what these people had to deal with. There would be only more tasks on a boat this size, and the number of people aboard the ship would require a number of people serving as guards in case some kind of trouble erupted.

Standing at the edge of the port side of the ship was Jenba, staring out at the stars reflecting off the waves of the sea. Borely stood beside him and asked how he was doing.

"Decided I could just sleep in the daytime," Jenba said.

"Don't want to be wearied by the sunlight?" Borely asked.

"Don't feel I deserve to be in the sunlight," Jenba responded.

Borely kept his eyes out on the sea and tried to imagine what was going through Jenba's head. The Rite didn't go well for him. It was admittedly likely Jenba would have been killed had Augurc not used that moment to attack the arena, while everyone's attention was on the fight. The Rite was something Jenba had worked hard toward for many years, and to fail after giving his all for such a long time... It had to be a grievous pain, and it wasn't something that was going to go away any time soon.

The fact that Jenba had failed the Rite and yet was still alive had to be disconcerting as well. Failing the Rite was supposed to entail death—Jenba probably felt like he "got off easy." On top of this, he ended up gaining a Rite Nexi, despite his failure. As long as Jenba had this Rite Nexi, he would be constantly reminded of his failure.

"Don't look at it that way," Borely said. "Everyone deserves to be in the sunlight."

"I've been a vampire a long time, Borely," Jenba said. "And I've accepted all the practices in Istal over the years. I can't just change my feelings overnight. I lost the Rite, but here I am... still living, still breathing. I shouldn't be. I should be dead. I failed myself, and my master."

Borely frowned and turned to Jenba, who kept his eyes on the waters. "Technically you didn't lose the fight. The Rite was cut short by that little invasion. The one you helped fight off, you might recall."

"I hardly contributed anything," Jenba said. "And in the end, the city fell into the hands of our enemies. I'm not strong enough of a vampire to ever play a significant role in these sorts of things. I probably never will be, despite all my best efforts."

Borely shook Jenba by the shoulder to get Jenba to glance at him. "Hey. You know that's not true. If you're going to be comparing yourself to vampires like Nivakil, then of course you'll feel incompetent. But that hardly matters—you're a lot stronger than you think. You wouldn't be as strong as you are today without all those years of hard work, after all. And if you remember, you did help out in the invasion. If you hadn't been there, I might have died, and so might have Analicia. I wouldn't call that 'hardly contributing anything.'"

Jenba closed his eyes and sighed. "I just wish... none of this had happened."

"Same here," Borely said. "But some good will come of this. In the end, we're going to save Areo."

Jenba opened his eyes. "I hope so..." He didn't look like he believed this mission would lead to such a result. Of course, Borely wasn't certain himself if it would. He just had to hope it would.

They looked back out at the dark waters again. Borely's thoughts wandered from Jenba to Areo, and then to vampires in general, and how Borely had become a vampire. He didn't ask to become one, but he couldn't change what he was now. He needed to work as hard as Jenba, and become as strong as he could in order to save Areo. How was Borely ever going to be able to defend against Areo, when she had the power of the Elpis on her side?

"How long have you been a vampire, Jenba?" Borely asked. He was curious to know how long it took Jenba to be ready enough to participate in the Rite.

"Over forty years," Jenba said. "I hibernated on a few occasions, though not nearly as long as Areo had, of course. I've been alive as a vampire for about fifteen years."

"And you became a vampire some time in your forties?" Borely asked.

"I was thirty-nine," Jenba said. He didn't say anything more.

Borely realized he had never found out the circumstances behind Jenba's transformation into a vampire. "Were you attacked?"

"No," Jenba said. "I was the one who wanted to attack."

"What do you mean?"

Jenba gripped the railing and pursed his lips. Perhaps it was wrong of Borely to ask a question like this, but he wanted to know more about Jenba. Maybe he'd be able to help Jenba out better if he knew what Jenba had gone through in becoming a vampire.

"When I was human, I was a farmhand in the countryside," Jenba said. "I lived a simple life. Had a wife, a son, and twin daughters. One day they were all killed."

Borely had never guessed any of this from Jenba—the man certainly never hinted at any of these things before. He wanted to ask how this happened, but he wasn't going to push Jenba to give any more details than the man wanted to.

Jenba shook his head. "It's not something I try to dwell on. It all happened in a past life, you know? And yet I can remember it all so vividly. I return home and find them all dead, blood everywhere. My entire world, gone. No warning whatsoever."

He looked to Borely for a moment. "You think it was vampires who did it?"

"It crossed my mind," Borely said.

"At the time, it crossed my mind, too," Jenba said. "There were rumors of vampires lurking in the forest, so I went straight there that very night, armed with stakes and knives. In the end I found four vampires, but I was no match for them. They beat me down and took my weapons away without me even landing a scratch on them."

"And they turned you into a vampire?" Borely asked.

"No, they told me to go home," Jenba said. "It turned out they were in the forest hunting monsters, and were searching for one in particular—a creature that could take the form of a human, or any other being. They discerned with their vampiric senses that the monster had taken my form, and went to my home on the outskirts of town while I was away. It killed my wife and children, its power strengthened with every gleeful murder."

"The vampires wanted to hunt this monster?"

"This monster's blood was very powerful," Jenba explained. "And they didn't want more innocents getting killed by it. These were vampires much more charitable than I had ever heard from the stories."

Of course, Borely knew at this point that there were good vampires in the world, but he didn't expect this story to turn out like this. It didn't seem to make sense, considering the end result was Jenba turning into a vampire, presumably.

Jenba continued. "I asked the vampires to let me help them on this hunt. I wasn't going to just sit at home—not when this monster was still lurking in the forest, the blood of all my loved ones on its hands. Seeing how strong these vampires were, I sought their power in order to kill the monster. They were reluctant to inject any of their blood into me, since those who lack the will can die in the process, and there's always a chance the body will reject the foreign energy and go insane.

"But I persisted, and they relented, deciding they'd stand a better chance against the creature with a fifth vampire assisting. One of them bit my neck, and I received the blood that turned me into a vampire... It was painful, excruciating. But it was all worth it. I helped the vampires track down the monster, and we killed it. I had my revenge, and I vowed to become as strong as I could in order to keep others from suffering the same fate I had. Deep down, I never wished to be a vampire—but I needed that power. Without strength, I'm hopeless, and people suffer because of my inadequacies. And that's why I keep pushing myself.

And that's why I can't accept this failure of mine. The Rite was my chance to prove I had grown all these years—that I was finally capable of being the kind of vampire who could help other people. Save them from the evils of this world. And yet I've continued to fail. I couldn't protect Areo at the battle in Setar five years ago. All I did was get in the way. And now, I shouldn't even be alive, considering how much more powerful my opponent in the Rite was. I don't see how I'll be able to help save Areo in this state."

"Just keep working at it," Borely said. "Just keep struggling, keep fighting. You'll improve."

"Those words ring a little hollow from you, to be honest," Jenba said. "You're always reluctant to use your vampiric abilities."

"I use them when I must," Borely said. "I just prefer to rely on my own strength as much as I can."

"Your vampiric strength is your strength now, though," Jenba said. "One day you'll have to take Nivakil's advice to heart, and accept everything about yourself as a fighter, including your vampiric nature."

Borely didn't want to go down this road in his conversation with Jenba. He already knew all this—he just didn't want to give in to his vampire side. It was a difficult truth to swallow, even after five years, and he didn't want to be accepting of something so terrible.

"What about Nivakil?" Borely asked. "He's clearly one of the most powerful vampires there is. But there had to be a time when he became one. Some time in his fifties, it seems."

He became a vampire when he was fifty-five," Jenba said. "He's been one for over 140 years now, though again, he hibernated for some of that time."

"Do you know how he became a vampire?"

"He's never given me many details. All I know is that one day he was attacked by one, and that he had to struggle for several years in order to maintain his sanity. It was a long, hard road for him, getting to the point he's at today."

Borely doubted Nivakil would tell him any details, considering how not even Jenba had been told much. The old master was the kind of man who would tell of such things when he was good and ready to do so—which Borely supposed may not be any time soon, if ever.

"I guess everyone has had to adjust to becoming a vampire," Borely said. "I'm glad I didn't go insane, at least. I was... definitely afraid of suffering my brother's fate." He had told Jenba and Nivakil about the fateful day his brother was turned into a vampire, and how his parents were subsequently killed by his brother.

"It seems to be random, who is able to complete the transformation soundly, and who isn't," Jenba said. "And though it's possible to overcome the insanity, the intensity of the condition can vary. Your brother may have suffered a severe case of it... There was probably nothing you or anyone could have done."

"There was no reasoning with him whatsoever," Borely said. "He was... no longer himself. It all reminds me somewhat of Areo, actually."

There was a long silence. Borely hadn't made the connection before, but the analogy felt apt. How was Borely going to be able to free Areo's mind? Perhaps it was impossible—just as impossible as it would have been for him to save his brother.

Perhaps he was going to have to kill Areo, the same way he had to kill his brother.

"I know what you're thinking," Jenba said. "It may not have to end that way. Perhaps the Hader will be the key to freeing Areo's mind. We still have time to save her."

Borely thought over what that was going to be like. He hadn't given much thought to what he would need to do if he did somehow manage to rescue Areo from the Brotherhood, and restore her mind back to normal. Would Areo remember all the atrocities she unwittingly brought to pass? She would likely blame herself for everything—and what would Borely do then? What would he say, and what would he do for her? He wasn't even quite sure how he felt about her.

"Yeah..." Borely said. "Time isn't really the issue, though. It's more a matter of power right now. I don't think any of us can stand up to Areo at the moment."

"No," Jenba admitted. "We'll probably need the Haders in order to stand up to the Elpis, regardless of the kingdom's plans."

•

Leaving Jenba on deck, Borely walked back down to the room he and the others were staying at. Analicia was sleeping in his bed, her face tense, and her body squirming at times, as if reacting from a nightmare. Borely had to wonder if she was actually afraid. It made sense... She was still just a kid, and had just witnessed a massacre. She probably cared for Istal a lot more than Borely did, and was still recovering from the fact it had been overrun and taken over by despots. She didn't even know if any of her friends were still alive. And now she was on a boat, hardly even understanding where they were going. She probably had never been on a boat before. Everything that was happening had to be strange and unfamiliar to her.

Borely sat on Analicia's abandoned bed. He had felt it a bad idea to bring the child along—she was probably just going to get in the way of the mission.

But what were they supposed to do with her? He needed to just accept that she was going to be involved from here on out.

He turned to Nivakil, who continued to sleep silently in the bed furthest away. All these years, Borely had never gotten along very well with the mentor. Nivakil always came off as a grumpy old man to Borely, too different to ever understand him. But the old man did know what it was like to turn from a human to a vampire, and even went through a period on the brink of insanity. Nivakil's transition had to have been much worse than Borely's, at least in some ways.

And the fact was, the old master did know what he was talking about. Borely's skills as a vampire had potential, and he could feel deep down there was much more he was capable of if he didn't hold back whatsoever.

If he was going to save Areo, he was going to have to rely on every power he could obtain, be it the power of his fists, his Nexi stones, his vampiric abilities, or the Haders. He could take these strengths and make them his own, and simply leave out everything bad associated with them. He knew he could use his vampiric powers without becoming a bloodthirsty madman. He just had to take things a step further.

I'll use all my strength to find the Hader, Borely thought. *And then I will use that power to defeat and rescue Areo. And then... I'll find something else— some other strength or power—to restore your mind and soul.*

•

Day and night passed, and it was the middle of the next day by the time the ship reached Limbo. The city looked a lot like how Borely's companions felt—tired, beaten down, and just a mess in general. Borely, however, was excited to be in such a large port town. His ventures as a sailor never led him to Limbo very often, which was probably for the best, considering all the rumors he heard of pirates ransacking the goods of merchants. He had never had any really big trouble each time he passed through Limbo, so the rumors were likely exaggerated for the most part. But that didn't change the fact there was some piracy, and likely a number of big-name pirates who lurked in the region. The hope was that they'd find out about the one who had the Hader, be it Yeaf or some other pirate.

Of course, Borely had heard stories of Yeaf over the years. Descriptions of his appearance varied greatly, so there was no certainty even of how he looked. Even his personality seemed to change from story to story—some said he was as quiet and serious as a vengeful ghost, while others said he was as loud and wild as a raving lunatic. And then there were so many stories of his wicked deeds, it seemed he had stolen every valuable good on the continent's northern shores.

Nivakil and Jenba decided their best course of action was to start prying for information at some of the local inns and taverns, though Borely was pretty sure they mainly just wanted to get out of the sun as best they could. They wore their hooded cloaks for now, and fortunately they didn't stick out at all in this city. There were all kinds of people on the streets of Limbo, many of them poor, many of them sick, and many of them maimed in some form or another.

It was a crowded, noisy city, its docks filled with creaky boats, and its dusty streets filled with half-broken tables covered with half-broken wares. Borely's companions all seemed flustered by the crowds, but Borely found it all rather exciting.

Nivakil decided they could split up in order to get more information on the whereabouts of Limbo's most feared pirates. He'd go down one street with Jenba, while Borely would go down another with Analicia. After deciding on a time and place for them to meet back together, Borely put a hand on Analicia's back to guide her in front of him. He was going to have to keep an eye on her now, unfortunately.

As they walked down the road, Analicia asked questions about every little thing they passed by. Apparently this was her first time in a really large city. And since Istal was so much better organized and much more ancient-feeling than Limbo, everything on these jostling streets was new and intriguing to her. Borely was glad all the sights and sounds were taking her mind off her fears, but it was getting a bit tedious, putting up with all her questions. *What's that? What's that do? Why are they yelling? How much does that cost? How come they're walking so slowly? Do people actually live in that? Why are they dressed so strangely?*

They eventually found a good tavern, which brought a wave of memories crashing into Borely's mind. He always went to a pub each time he docked at a new port, and enjoyed scoping out the cities and towns in order to find the most interesting-looking ones. It was always fun to just relax, have a good drink, and play a few games with sailors like him, who were also in the mood for some new company after a long voyage.

He wasn't going to be able to enjoy any of those things now, though. He didn't have enough money to gamble with, or the time for any games. And since he was a vampire, he couldn't even enjoy any of the establishment's drinks anymore—though even if he could, this wasn't the time to get drunk. Not when he needed to find some critical information from potentially dangerous people, and not when he needed to keep an eye on Analicia. It probably wasn't a good idea to be bringing her into places like this, but things wouldn't be so bad in the daytime.

After chatting with some people in the bar, Borely got a few more vague stories about some pirates in the area, but nothing concrete about where any of them were, or when some may be coming to port.

They went to a couple more taverns, and Borely was able to learn a bit more about Yeaf. A slick, twisted man who preyed on the weak, and killed everyone he ever met. An exaggeration obviously, but it fit with the general description of a heartless criminal.

After speaking with some more people on the street, Borely was able to glean a few more stories about Yeaf and some of the other pirates in the area. Most hadn't been heard from in some time—it was only Yeaf who seemed to be making any headway in this region lately.

The sun was beginning to set by the time he found another pub—this one with many more people than the others he had visited. He was getting a little exhausted from the sunlight by this point, and for a little while had to carry Analicia to keep her going. She was very bored with this information gathering, and had to keep pestering Borely in little ways in order to entertain herself. It was getting very annoying putting up with her, but Borely forced himself to keep focused on the task at hand.

After speaking to several people in the pub, he caught wind of a few rumors of Yeaf returning to port that night. A few of the sailors looked genuinely worried, while a few others waved off the comments as groundless worries. The rest were already too drunk to really grasp what everyone was discussing.

“I think we're done,” Borely told Analicia. He didn't want her to be in the restless bar any longer, and it was about time to meet back up with Nivakil and Jenba anyways.

Once they gathered back together, they shared all the information they learned.

“Yeaf is returning to Limbo in the dead of the night,” Nivakil said. “It was the only specific detail I could get consistently. The sailors don't seem to have any other pirate captains worth talking about these days—most of the rest have been dealt with by government forces, apparently.”

“That simplifies matters then,” Borely said. “But it means we need to act right away if he'll be riding these waters tonight. Should we wait for Yeaf to arrive at the dock?"

"His ship might not actually come to port," Nivakil said. "If he's planning a heist, he won't come barging in when there are everyday people who seem to know of his presence in the area. Some of his crew will be sent in smaller boats, most likely. And we don't have a consistent description of Yeaf to go by, though I imagine he won't come to land at all. If there are no solid details about him, it means he's a secretive man, and his crew has been trained to spread a variety of conflicting tales about him. We'll have to tread carefully."

"The port is at the inside end of a long inlet," Borely said. "If his ship is to come in sight of Limbo at all, he will have to enter the inlet. If we go out in a small boat with some decent-looking goods, he may pause to confiscate our wares."

"Several sailors specifically said Yeaf preys on the weak," Jenba said. "A boat with only a few people manning it would look like an easy target."

"They would have to be goods worth his time to take, though," Nivakil said. "I suggest Borely command a small boat, while the rest of us hide in some of the barrels. Once the barrels are brought on board, we can take down Yeaf and find out if he has the Hader in question."

"You believe he has it then?" Borely asked.

"It seems likely," Nivakil said. "According to Rilv, the Hader's location is always drifting over the seas, so it has to be on a ship. It would make sense that a valuable treasure would end up in a pirate's hands, and that the Hader could be used to make said pirate very powerful. The reason Yeaf is the only pirate left in the area worth talking about may be largely because he has used the Hader to take down all of his competition."

"Makes sense," Jenba said. "So we'll all be on a small boat tonight. What will happen to Borely when Yeaf's crew steals the goods?"

"Yeaf may make Borely a slave on his ship," Nivakil said. "Or, he may simply kill Borely."

"Neither of those are very healthy options," Borely said.

"Don't worry," Nivakil said. "The better option of course is to make yourself look valuable—perhaps with your skills as a sailor—so that you'll be made a slave. When the time is right, we'll rescue you, and we'll escape the crew by taking back our boat. Or we may just kill the whole crew. They're pirates, after all."

"But what if he decides to just run me through with a blade?" Borely asked.

"You're a vampire," Nivakil said. "Just avoid a fatal blow to the heart, and you'll be fine. You can let yourself fall into the ocean, and drink a vial of blood to recover from any injuries Yeaf deals you."

It sounded very risky, but Borely wasn't about to turn the plan down. There were a hundred things that could go wrong with it, but now was the time to act. If bringing down this pirate captain would yield him a Hader, he was going to go through with the plan, despite any of the dangers. This power could very well be just what he'd need in order to save Areo.

"Okay, let's do it then."

•

Fortunately Nivakil was given more than enough money to buy a small boat and enough goods to fill up a dozen barrels. Three of them weren't filled up all the way however, in order to leave room for Nivakil, Jenba, and Analicia to hide in. The plan was to try to get Nivakil and Jenba near Yeaf enough for them to take him down before the rest of the crew could do anything. Chances were a large fight would escalate, but Borely was confident he and Nivakil and Jenba would be able to deal with a bunch of thugs, especially after startling them with the death of their infamous captain.

The plan was to just have Analicia stay in her barrel, which she was fine with, since it would be nice and dark inside. There was no reason for her to get involved in the danger that would escalate on the pirate deck. Borely left his fighting gloves and metal headpiece with Analicia, not wanting the pirates to take them away from him. To make himself look at least a little armed though, Borely had a fire and water Nexi on his person—which he would be fine with giving up following the pirate ambush.

The barrels were filled with trinkets that looked valuable, and would prove of interest to any pirate captain. However, Nivakil made a point of placing all the goods in very ordinary food barrels, not wanting Yeaf or any of the other pirates to suspect this was a trap. If they made it blatantly obvious that a single man was transporting valuable goods across dangerous waters, it would easily give away their plan to take Yeaf by surprise. Nivakil, Jenba, and Analicia each used an inner circle of wood to keep themselves hidden beneath the pile of goods above them, so anyone opening the barrels and rummaging inside a bit wouldn't see them.

Once preparations were completed, Borely checked on each of his companions to make sure they'd be all right in case they had to be stuck in the barrels all night. They each gave a muffled okay, so Borely went ahead and launched the ship out to sea.

It didn't take long for Borely to reach the point Nivakil wanted him to guide the boat to. It was an ideal spot to watch from, but as the hours passed, Borely found himself increasingly tired. Only one ship passed by the entire time, and it was just a little one. There weren't going to be many boats leaving and entering at night, especially with talk of pirate activity in the area. Borely walked from point to point on the boat, gazing out at the thousands of waves bobbing up and down in every direction around him. There was a chance the pirate ship wouldn't come at all—rumors were nothing more than rumors, after all. But Borely really wanted to find this Yeaf character right away. The sooner Borely got the Hader, the sooner he'd have the means to save Areo.

But in the back of his head, there was doubt. Even if he did succeed in defeating this dangerous pirate, and even if he did obtain a Hader—that didn't mean the stone's power would actually be useful in rescuing Areo. There was very little chance everything would work out as smoothly as he hoped.

Even this plan was filled with unpredictable factors. At any given moment, it could all go falling apart, and Borely could very well die. He felt capable of taking down any regular pirate—but he had no idea how powerful Yeaf could be with the Hader. Plus he and Nivakil, Jenba, and Analicia were all walking straight into enemy territory. What if Yeaf's Hader allowed him to see through their plan?

Borely focused on a speck in the far distance. Perhaps it was just some bigger waves...

No, this is a ship approaching, Borely realized. *And a big one.*

He hurried back to the ship wheel and maneuvered the small vessel so that it looked like his boat was leaving the inlet, just as any boat normally would. If this was the pirate ship in question, he couldn't let it look like he was just sitting there, waiting for them.

The ship flew across the water, heading straight for Borely. This was most certainly a course to intercept—and though the ship looked very plain and ordinary, it had to be the pirate ship Borely was waiting for. He felt both nervous and excited—but mostly excited. This was his chance to finally get things moving for the mission to free Areo. He wasn't going to lose to a bunch of pirates.

As the large, tall ship loomed closer, several rowboats lowered from the closer side of the ship, each filled with three or four men. With his vampiric eyes, Borely was able to see their weapons—crossbows, Nexi stones, and swords. Once they came closer, within a normal human's sight, Borely made a point of panicking, and attempted to maneuver his boat away from the approaching pirates. As Nivakil suggested, he made a good effort of it, in hopes of getting the pirate captain to notice his seafaring skills.

Several times the shouting pirates attempted to surround him, but each time Borely made quick decisions at the helm and guided his boat through each narrow opening he could find. The pirate ship the rowboats came from had formed a wall in front of where Borely was headed, however, and though he could have kept up the struggle had he wished, he decided to give in to the pirates. He raised his hands in the air to surrender, and the capturing rowboats were quick to surround him close enough for some of the pirates to board his vessel.

The pirates didn't cheer or make a show of anything—this was simply business as usual for them. A couple of them shoved Borely to the ground and confiscated his red and light blue Nexi stones, while a few others began looking through some of the barrels.

"Rich merchant here," one of them said—a bald man in his twenties. "The captain will like this haul."

The ship brought down a series of ropes and nets to help the boarding party bring the barrels up to the deck. Once Borely's hands were tied behind his back, he too was brought up, along with each of the pirate rowboats. Borely's new boat was brought up as well—easily able fit on the giant deck of the pirate ship.

The pirates were rough with Borely bringing him up, and some suggested they just kill him here and now. A couple others voiced that the captain would be able to use Borely, however, so nobody made a move to end his life. None of them seemed to think he was a vampire yet either, and fortunately Nivakil, Jenba, and Analicia were all silent when they were brought up to the ship in their barrels.

All was going according to plan. All Borely had to do now was ascertain who on the deck was the captain, and hope that it would be Yeaf. And hope that Yeaf would reveal where his Hader was. Presumably it would be on his person, but this wasn't something Borely could count on as a certainty. And there was no way Borely could even be sure if Yeaf had the Hader. Or even would help him achieve his goals. Or even if he would make it off this ship alive.

He landed between two pirates onto the deck, jabbed forward with a lot more force than he thought necessary. The men liked to make a point that there was no way out of this situation, and continually mocked Borely for being foolish to man a small boat by himself at Limbo, of all places. Borely played along with them—he'd be able to tear them apart the moment it was time to make his move. He just had to get the captain near the barrels.

The pirates guided Borely to a man hanging from a mast pole upside-down by rope, dangling a meter or so above deck. His feet were tied together, and he lurched slowly back and forth, his arms hanging limp toward the floor. He looked to be in his thirties, had short black hair, and was dressed quite nicely—almost like a seafaring aristocrat. Long black boots, purple trousers, a collared shirt, and a belted red jacket, all of which was lined with silver ornamentation. It was quite a different look from the rest of the crew, most of which were rough men dressed in shabby cloth and leather accessories.

The man glanced over at Borely and grinned, his smile looking like a twisted frown from Borely's point of view. The two pirates brought Borely right up to him, so the man's upside-down face was about a meter in front of Borely's.

"They say you've got a knack for handling a ship," the man said.

"I've been a sailor ever since I was a child," Borely said. He imagined this man was the captain, but why was he hanging upside-down?

"That's wonderful," the man said. "This ship is your new home then. Keep yourself useful to me, and I'll let you live."

A sword appeared in Yeaf's hand, the tip of the blade suddenly against Borely's neck. He flinched, but the pirates to either side of him kept him from stepping back. Borely held his breath. Where did the sword come from? It just appeared out of nowhere...

"What's your name, by the way?" the man asked.

"Rengel," Borely said, using his brother's name.

"I'm Yeaf," the man said. "You may have heard of me."

Borely chose not to respond, not wanting to reveal any fear in this situation. He simply waited for Yeaf to lift the blade from his neck. Was it the power of the Hader that allowed Yeaf to create this sword out of thin air? One moment

Yeaf's hand was empty, the next moment he was holding a sv
Borely's neck. How was Borely going to deal with an opponent wi
of power?

"Let me assure you one thing," Yeaf said. "If you ever try to leave th
you will be killed. In fact, if there is even an inkling of a possibility o
kind of trouble, I'll kill you."

Yeaf swung back his sword, making Borely flinch from the suddenness o
the pirate captain's movement. With one swift swing of his long thin blade,
Yeaf cut the rope tied to his feet. The man was quick to grab the cut end of
the rope—and Borely had to blink and stare a moment to realize Yeaf
grabbed the rope with the hand that had been holding the hilt of the sword...
which was now gone. Vanished right before Borely's eyes. Yeaf let his feet
down so he was hanging from the rope right-side up, then let himself drop
onto the deck.

The man's smile faded and he untied the rope around his feet so he could
walk freely. He looked over to the barrels on the other side of the deck—too
far away for Nivakil and Jenba to make their surprise attack.

"I can help any way you wish," Borely said. "I can start by showing you the
value in all my wares, and suggest good places where you could sell some of
the items."

"Good idea," Yeaf said. "But first things first. I can never be too careful these
days, considering how every operative in the kingdom wants me dead."

Yeaf raised a hand toward the barrels, and suddenly a shining purple Nexi
appeared in his fist. Without any warning, all of the barrels burst apart in a
blast of purple energy.

Borely gritted his teeth—Yeaf was apparently paranoid enough to blast
apart the wares to check for traps.

Nivakil, Jenba, and Analicia all fell out from their hiding places, battered by
the wave of purple Nexi energy targeted directly at the barrels. Pieces of
wood and metal trinkets crashed about their battered frames. In one
moment, the element of surprise was entirely lost, and the fighting force
nullified by the painful attack of the powerful Nexi stone.

"Huh," Yeaf sighed. He spun around and swung his arm straight toward
Borely's face.

The purple Nexi stone in his hand vanished, instantly replaced by a giant axe.

•

Borely elongated his claws to about a half-meter long, instantly tearing through the ropes that bound his hands. As the axe descended for his face, Borely lunged forward and flung his claws at the long pole of the axe, slicing straight through it. Yeaf immediately leaped backward, stunned by Borely's inhuman reflexes.

"Vampires!" Yeaf yelled. "Kill them all!"

All the men on deck drew weapons, some of them rushing toward where Nivakil, Jenba, and Analicia lay, the rest coming to assist Yeaf against Borely.

Borely swung his claws toward Yeaf, elongating them a little further to try to take him by surprise. Yeaf leaped back again as a thick shield appeared in his hand. The captain held it so Borely's claws deflected off it, rather than slicing through it.

The two pirates who had kept Borely in check each drew weapons, but Borely had to keep his focus on Yeaf—the man's shield disappeared, only to be replaced by an ice Nexi. A long, thin icicle lurched out of the stone. Borely sliced it apart with his claws, then had to turn to the nearer of the other two pirates. With only a moment to catch the attack, Borely deflected the pirate's sword with his claws. The second man used the opportunity to run at Borely with two daggers. Borely pushed back the first pirate, turned, and flicked away both daggers from the second pirate. Yeaf lunged at Borely with a lance, which Borely had to dive away from.

Borely rolled down the deck and once back on his feet, glanced over to his companions. Jenba was on his feet, tearing apart one pirate with his right hand's claws, while shooting off a violent cloud of dust with an earth Nexi in his left hand, slowing down a few other pirates. Nivakil was struggling to get up—the old master apparently got the brunt of Yeaf's random attack with the purple Nexi. There was blood all over his chest and stomach... Fortunately Analicia didn't appear too injured, save for some bad scrapes and bruises. She had run off, carrying Borely's weapons.

Nivakil needed blood, and fortunately there was some on the deck from the shattered vials he and Jenba had brought. Once Nivakil was healed, this fight would get back under control.

"Freeze the blood!" Yeaf yelled to his crew, immediately realizing what Nivakil was about to do. The pirates acted quickly—several pulled out ice Nexi at once, and Nivakil and Jenba had to jump out of the way to avoid getting frozen. The blood-stained portions of the deck turned to ice, and the pirates kept after the two to keep them occupied, to keep them from finding a way to heal and rejuvenate themselves with any blood. Nivakil was on his feet now, but hunched over, his hand clasped over his wounded torso.

Borely turned back to Yeaf, who had a pirate to his left and another to his right. There were three other pirates approaching from the stairs leading from below deck, and then two more a ways down the deck, raising Nexi stones for some long-distance attacks. Borely glimpsed Analicia hurrying across from the opposite direction, but it was too late to wait a moment longer. He ducked beneath a blast of water, leaped forward, hacked his way through a series of vines, stepped to the side of a thrown dagger, then sprinted at the nearest pirate. The bearded man raised his sword a second too late—Borely ran his claws through the pirate's neck, beheading him.

Borely didn't stop. A second pirate was already swinging a sword at his back, and a brief glimpse showed this blade was powered by an orange Nexi. Only needing to hear the attack, Borely leaned to the side, kept his balance as the blade passed him by, then leaned back in to jab his claws through the man's chest.

A massive weapon swung toward Borely. He leaped over it, discovering it was a ridiculously long poleaxe. It was swung by Yeaf, keeping a safe distance away from Borely. The weapon disappeared the moment it passed Borely by, only to be replaced by a brown Nexi. A large burst of swamp material flew at him, and Borely had to really push himself to avoid the entirety of the attack. The moment he escaped, an arrow flew straight for his face. He tilted his head just in time to avoid it, and wished he had his headband so he could blast the pirate away with its dark blue Nexi.

There were too many pirates to deal with all at once, and for the most part they all seemed to be competent fighters. These were the best of the best, Borely realized. The men Yeaf deemed worthy to live on his ship. And Yeaf was right there with them, using the abnormal power of the Hader to utilize virtually any weapon he wanted, whenever he wanted.

Borely knew he wouldn't be able to take down Yeaf while there were all these other pirates to deal with at the same time. He had to thin out their ranks a bit if he wanted to stand a chance against a Hader-user. Range was his greatest weakness at the moment—he had to deal with the pirate wielding a crossbow first. Borely sprinted toward the man, startling the pirate as he was readying his next shot. Another pirate got in the way with a sword, but Borely was too quick for his attack. In one swoop, Borely ripped a hole through the first pirate's side, then continued the lunge into the second pirate's neck. Borely turned, slicing the man's head off.

Another pirate came at him with two daggers. Borely flicked away one dagger from the man's grasp, then slid his other hand's claws into the enemy's face before he could even react.

But at the same time, a hand axe flew toward him from behind, and he could hear two other pirates approaching from his left. He ducked beneath the hand axe, turned to the nearer of the other two pirates, and moved his claws to block the assailant's attack. As Borely did so, he realized the other man was Yeaf, chucking a lance at him.

It was too late to get out of the way—he hadn't seen or heard the lance coming. Of course, it must have appeared in Yeaf's hand just as the man was in the process of throwing it. There was no way to prepare for Yeaf's attacks, especially when Borely was preoccupied with the man's crew.

Borely took the lance to the chest, having just enough time to avoid a blow directly through his heart. Screaming, Borely swung an arm and took off the nearer pirate's head. But before he could do anything more, a weapon slammed into the back of his right shoulder—another hand axe. The pirate who attacked from behind had a second one, apparently.

And already, Yeaf had another weapon in his hand—a yellow Nexi. And then a rapier. He could summon more than one weapon at a time. Yeaf charged at Borely with his yellow Nexi stone activated, smart enough to be cautious of Borely's claws.

Borely forced the lance out of his chest and stumbled forward, his body going into shock from the incredible pain. He couldn't just let himself fall to the floor and die, though—not at this moment, not when Yeaf was in the process of attacking him again.

Clutching his wound with one hand, and gripping the bloody lance in the other, Borely forced himself to step forward—quicker than he thought possible in this condition. Suddenly Yeaf was upon him, jabbing his rapier toward Borely's heart, fast enough to alter his movement to make up for Borely's rush. Borely lifted his arm from his wound and took the thin rapier blade directly into his hand. The rapier pierced down the entirety of his arm. The pain was excruciating, overwhelming, barely even imaginable—but Borely used the moment to slam his lance into the side of Yeaf's face. The captain's yellow barrier of energy barely held, but the impact sent Yeaf flying to the side, tumbling across the deck.

Screaming, Borely immediately turned to the pirate who had thrown a hand axe into his shoulder—the pain there barely registering when so much more agony was now coming from his arm, as well as the gaping wound in his chest. The pirate stepped back, surprised by the sight of this vampire—this monster—still standing despite all these tremendous wounds. Despite the blatant fear in the pirate's eyes, the man still managed to throw another hand axe at Borely. Standing still, Borely let the axe fly just to the right of his face. Then before the pirate could reach for a fourth hand axe from his back, Borely chucked his lance straight in the man's chest. Without the resilience of a vampire, the man simply fell to the ground, dying in a bloody heap.

With his uninjured arm, Borely reached into a pocket to pull out a vial of blood. He popped open the glass lid and downed the entirety of its contents in one gulp. It gave him the strength he needed to pull out the rapier from his arm and the hand axe from the back of his shoulder, and the wound in his chest was healed enough to keep him from dying right away. Desperate for more blood, Borely slipped out the other vial of blood he carried on his person—a strong dose of monster blood.

Two more pirates were already rushing for Borely, however, buying time for Yeaf to get back to his feet and shake off the powerful blow Borely had dealt him. Borely pocketed his vial of blood to keep from losing it, and ducked beneath a knife thrown at his head. It was painful to move his body at all, let alone to keep fighting a bunch of well-armed pirates—but they were barely leaving him time to even react to their attacks. The second pirate flung a series of icicles at Borely from one Nexi stone, and a long, thick vine from another. While Borely dodged the flying icicles and sliced away the large, heavy vine with the claws of his good arm, the other pirate sprinted toward Borely, unsheathing a thick, stocky sword in the process. It was more like a chunk of sharpened metal than an actual sword—and now it was glowing orange, powered by a Nexi stone embedded in its hilt.

Barely able to withstand the pain of his injuries, Borely lifted his mangled left arm and jabbed his claws into the running pirate's stomach and hip. The man stumbled to the ground, but forced himself back up and swung his giant blade at Borely's side. At the same time, the other pirate's vine pushed Borely back, too strong for him to withstand in his current state. Screaming again, Borely dropped to the floor so the blade passed over him. The vine was sliced by the blade in the process, and Borely had a brief moment to push himself off the ground and dash toward the pirate with the two Nexi stones. The man released a burst of freezing air just as Borely was upon him. Borely spun to the side and jabbed his claws into the back of the man's head. Borely snatched the green Nexi from the corpse's hand and flung vines at the other pirate, who was limping toward Borely. In one swift movement, Borely guided vines to wrap around the man's leg, and flung his body straight to Borely's claws, still sticking out of the front of the other man's face.

Borely ripped his claws out of the pirates and turned to Yeaf, who had formed a massive floating sphere of hardened dirt via an earth Nexi, surely summoned by his Hader.

Borely had to drink more blood—he was about to collapse from sheer pain and exhaustion. He reached for his vial of blood, but Yeaf was already launching the large ball of earth at him. It was too late to hesitate. Borely ran as hard as he could to his right, while drinking the blood at the same time. He was too weakened to use his full strength, and Yeaf's command over the tan Nexi was too superior to be taken lightly. Borely was going to be hit again.

But just before the sphere of dirt could crash into him, a strong jet of water blasted head-on into it, knocking it just to Borely's left. Borely fell to the ground, forcing himself to gulp his blood in the process. He glanced to where the stream of Nexi water had come from, and found Analicia a ways down the deck, running from a pirate. She was wearing Borely's metal headband, and had somehow managed to activate Borely's water Nexi embedded in it. There was only a second for Borely to get up again and make his next move against Yeaf, though—the captain wasn't going to be surprised by Borely's survival for very long.

On his feet again, Borely rushed toward Yeaf. The blood had reacted quickly, healing his wounds and filling himself with an intense vigor. And with the pirates in this vicinity taken down, Borely only had to concentrate on Yeaf. Unfortunately there were still a bunch of pirates fighting Jenba and Nivakil, and things weren't looking good for them in their injured state—especially for Nivakil. There was no time to assist them, though—the sooner Borely retrieved the Hader from Yeaf, the sooner they'd be able to leave the ship and escape for their lives.

Yeaf summoned a long sword in his hand and swung at Borely the moment he was within range. Borely leaped back to avoid the blade, which instantly vanished and was replaced by an armed crossbow. Yeaf fired the moment it materialized in his hand. Gritting his teeth, Borely twisted his body to avoid the arrow, barely able to use his vampiric speed and senses to keep up with the man's weaponry.

Before even another second had passed, Yeaf had replaced his crossbow with another purple Nexi, which he blasted right where Borely was stepping toward. Borely bent down, dug his long claws into the wooden deck, and pulled himself forward with all his strength. The blast of Nexi energy exploded just behind him, but by positioning himself just right, Borely used the shockwave to send himself flying toward Yeaf.

The pirate didn't look fazed, however. Instantly his purple Nexi was replaced by an ice Nexi, and before Borely had stepped back onto the deck, a thick shield of ice had formed in front of Yeaf. A giant icicle emerged from the wall of ice as Borely landed, and he had to slam his claws into the side of the sudden formation and pull himself up onto the icicle. Amidst the crackling of the growing icicle, Borely was able to hear the creeping growth of vines. Yeaf used a vine Nexi to raise himself on top of the wall of ice, but now the captain had a lance in his hand—and it was glowing a bright silver. Was that the power of a Nexi stone? What did a silver Nexi do?

Borely leaped into the wall, digging his claws into the ice to hang on. Yeaf laughed, and Borely waited for the last moment to swing himself as hard as he could, flinging himself upward and to the side of the thrown lance. A tendril of silver feathers lunged out the side of the glowing lance, digging into Borely's side. It hooked into his skin and latched on, pulling him down with the lance. Borely crashed into the deck, screaming. A couple more tendrils of silver feathers emerged from the lance, spiraling for his chest and face. Fighting past the pain, Borely pulled the lance from the deck and slammed the expanding silver formations into the wall of ice.

Already Yeaf was attacking again, now throwing knives at Borely. Barely having time to even glimpse the weapons, Borely swiped his claws at the spinning blades. Just as his claws impacted the first two knives, he realized they were powered by orange Nexi stones. The knives tore straight through his claws, breaking them. Borely pushed himself back to his feet and leaped away from the next several knives.

When was he ever going to get an opening? This pirate had an infinite disposal of powerful weaponry, and there was no way for Borely to form a plan when the weapons kept changing every half-second. Yeaf's Hader constantly gave him the element of surprise, and no matter what Borely did, Yeaf would be able to summon the perfect offense or defense to counter Borely's attacks.

Yeaf continued throwing knives at Borely, keeping him from approaching the wall of ice Yeaf stood atop of. Borely clutched the gaping wound in his side, and gritted his teeth against the stinging pain of his broken claws. It was too difficult to fight an opponent this powerful in this injured of a state. And yet he had to keep pushing himself. He knew fighting a Hader user wasn't going to be easy. Of course the road to freeing Areo wasn't going to be an easy one. And if he had to fight a dozen enemies like Yeaf, he was going to do so. He didn't even need to think about it.

A couple glances of his surroundings revealed to Borely that Yeaf had lodged about a dozen knives into the deck around Borely. The constant throwing had to be exhausting for Yeaf, but it was difficult for Borely to keep up with him as well, especially when he was out of blood to rejuvenate himself with.

"You're tiring me, vampire!" Yeaf said, continuing to throw summoned knives directly to where Borely would run toward. "It's time to bring this monster hunt to a close."

A white Nexi appeared in Yeaf's hand, and Borely realized what the captain was planning. But before he could escape, Yeaf released a flash of lightning at the knife closest to Yeaf, embedded into the deck a few meters in front of Borely. Sparkling white Nexi energy instantly connected with all the knives on deck. All the streams of Nexi lightning linked to Borely, standing in the direct center of all of Yeaf's thrown knives.

•

Pirates kept coming, and Jenba could barely keep up with them. In normal circumstances, he was certain he'd be able to take down these thugs much more easily, but he was injured and had no blood to regenerate with. Though he was able to kill several of the pirates ambushing him and Nivakil, there wasn't enough time for him to drink any of their blood. The pirates coordinated attacks from a safe distance, using Nexi stones and other weaponry to keep him constantly moving.

Jenba was also afraid to leave his master behind and just go all out against the pirates. Nivakil was very badly injured by the purple Nexi blast that blew their cover, and was having trouble standing, let alone fighting. If anyone needed blood, it was Nivakil.

And at the same time, Analicia was out there, trying to keep away from the pirates that chose to go after her. And then there was Borely, having to fight without his normal weapons, and locked in combat with the man using the Hader—presumably Yeaf.

Relying on his claws, his speed, and his sensitive senses, Jenba took down each pirate that got near him, to the point that the remaining pirates were keeping their distance, and trying to get Jenba away from Nivakil. It was up to Jenba in Nivakil's time of need to protect his master—and yet he was struggling to keep up with a group of mere pirates. He couldn't fail now. Not again. Not when he had failed his master so many times already. Not when Nivakil was truly counting on him. Perhaps for the first time in a very long time, Nivakil was truly in danger of getting killed.

Two pirates used green Nexi to send vines toward Nivakil while Jenba was occupied with a slinking snake of dirt from a third pirate's tan Nexi. Jenba clawed away at the hardened earth, wincing from the pain encompassing his entire body. Glancing back at his master, Jenba saw Nivakil was managing to avoid the Nexi plants, still capable of hearing the growing vines and sensing when they drew close to his arms and legs.

Jenba lunged toward the nearer of the two vine-wielding pirates, avoiding a burst of hardened earth in the process. The pirate unsheathed a sword, but Jenba managed to claw the man's hand off. A knife flew toward Jenba from another pirate. Jenba turned and dodged the weapon, then heard the sound of water from a dark blue Nexi. He ducked in time for the watery jet to pass over him, then rushed hunched over toward the second pirate with a green Nexi. Before the pirate could redirect some of his vines, Jenba slammed his claws into the pirate's stomach and tore through the man's side.

Jenba glanced back to Nivakil, who was being rushed by a couple other pirates. Panting but desperate, Jenba sprinted to Nivakil's position, noticing the difficulty his master had in landing an attack on the two sword-wielding pirates. They were both capable of using both an orange Nexi to power their swords with strength, and a yellow Nexi to temporarily protect themselves with a thin layer of energy. Nivakil barely managed to avoid a lunge from the nearer of the two pirates, but stumbled back when the second swung toward his neck. The old master suddenly flung himself forward and slammed his claws straight into each of their hearts, still able to tell precisely where they both were. Unfortunately he wasn't strong enough in this state to puncture through their Nexi shields, but he managed to send them crashing across the deck.

"Make noise!" a man yelled a ways away. "That vampire's blind, so he listens for our movements!"

More pirates were coming onto deck from below, and a number of them caught wind of the message. They brought up musical instruments—drums, a flute, and bagpipes—and they started playing as loud as they could, simply blaring random notes. It was an extremely noisy distraction, and one that would prove difficult for Nivakil to put up with in his current state.

Pirates armed with an assortment of weapons rushed toward Nivakil, who was shakily recovering from his exhausting attack on the two previous pirates, who were also pushing themselves back to their feet. Jenba ran in front of Nivakil and jabbed his claws at the closest approaching pirate. The man was huge, and wielded a large, thick hammer. As the man swung his giant hammer, Jenba retracted his claws to keep from losing them, realizing this man's strength was likely enough to snap them off even without the assisted energy of an orange Nexi.

As Jenba avoided the second swing of the man's hammer, a beam of hardened earth formed beside Jenba, from which flung out large rocks in random directions. Several battered against Jenba, and he was barely able to hear the snake of earth from another pirate who had been attacking him earlier. Jenba ran from the attack, checked back on Nivakil, and turned back to another pirate—this one about to land a spear directly into Jenba's face. As Jenba avoided the sharp weapon, he realized that in his brief, frantic glance of his master, the old man was struggling with ice formations rushing out of the frozen deck beneath him.

There were too many pirates to deal with all at once. Jenba had to kick things up a notch if he was going to survive this. If Nivakil was going to survive this. His master needed him to become the vampire he was trained to be. And not only Nivakil needed him, but Analicia and Borely too. Jenba was struggling so much just keeping himself alive, that he hadn't even been able to keep tabs on his partners. Was this entire mission falling apart? Did they just need to escape with their lives? What chance was there of them getting the Hader in these conditions?

Jenba focused on the situation at hand. He had to kill these pirates. He had to kill all of them. Immediately.

With all his might, Jenba launched himself at each and every pirate, avoiding their attacks, working out appropriate counter-attacks, clawing, beating, pushing, and shoving. He clawed apart one man's neck, then turned to another man and tore through his heart, not even taking the time to rely on his sight. His vampiric senses overflowed within him. He unleashed his full terror upon his enemies. There was no need to hold back. He simply had to kill, and kill, and kill.

His life was on the line, and so was Nivakil's, Borely's, and Analicia's. Jenba couldn't keep failing everyone. He had to pull through for once. He had to use his power and succeed. He had to persevere.

A knife cut against the side of his face. He clawed at the pirate's arm, barely scraping the man's shoulder. The pirate stabbed again at Jenba, who slammed his head against the pirate's forehead. In the process of the clash, the knife didn't quite reach Jenba's heart. The moment the pirate was knocked back a bit, Jenba slammed his claws through the man's heart, then sprinted at a pirate releasing a large formation of ice at him. With his claws still through the first pirate's body, Jenba rushed through the razor-sharp ice shards, letting the corpse take the majority of the attack. It was difficult to hear where the ice-wielding pirate was amidst the overbearing noise, but Jenba could sense his location by focusing on where precisely the ice was originating from. Jenba's claws shattered through a wall of ice and punctured the stomach of the assailant.

Immediately Jenba turned to Nivakil, only to find him getting overwhelmed by dirt wrapping around him. Nivakil flung himself away from the tan Nexi attack, but the earth hardened and crushed his leg. The old man fell to the ground, screaming in agony.

"No!" Jenba screamed. He rushed toward Nivakil, but was stopped by a pirate armed with a large axe. The man was fast, and Jenba took a bad gash across his abdomen. Jenba nearly fell to the floor, but kept himself going, swiping his claws at the man's chest. The pirate dodged and swung again—Jenba used the moment to just run for it, hurrying toward Nivakil.

Blood-curdling screaming and a burst of light exploded from the other side of the deck. Jenba glanced at the scene and saw Borely getting electrocuted by a powerful white Nexi attack.

First Nivakil, and now Borely. Everyone was getting beaten. Jenba was failing them. His strength wasn't enough to save them. He wasn't fighting well enough to assist them effectively. These were just ordinary pirates, and he was failing to make a real difference. Again and again and again, he was failing the few people he cared about.

First his wife and children. Then Areo. And now everyone else who had been a large part of his life.

Jenba swiped his claws at the pirate wielding the tan Nexi stone, but the enemy was quicker than him. A tendril of dirt whipped against Jenba's back, hitting him so hard he thought his spinal cord had broken entirely. He collapsed on the ground, but immediately tried to force himself back to his feet. He had to keep fighting. Despite the pain. Despite the terrible odds.

Suddenly he was on his feet, bleeding and screaming. He couldn't let himself die yet. Not when his master needed him. For the first time in history, his master needed him! And he could not fail him!

Jenba burst through a whirlwind of dirt and sliced off the head of the pirate wielding the tan Nexi. A pirate was about to stab Nivakil in the face with a lance, but in an instant Jenba was at the man's back, ripping him in half.

Someone else was approaching. Jenba turned, only to find the captain himself, suddenly swinging a giant sword at him. He had noticed Yeaf too late—the noise of the music-players had thrown him off. Jenba leaped to the side, gasping from the strain he was forcing on his battered, bleeding body. Yeaf sliced Jenba's left arm clean off.

Jenba fell to the deck, screaming, screaming, dying, screaming.

But Yeaf now had a crossbow pointed at Jenba's head. Jenba rolled aside just before the arrow could pierce his face at point-blank range. He swiped at Yeaf's legs with his right arm's claws, but the pirate suddenly had a green Nexi, which he used to create vines that pushed himself into the air. The world turned blurry, a cacophony of agony and madness. There were more pirates. And Yeaf was somewhere else. Who was attacking whom? It didn't matter... He was dying...

Blood. He needed blood. But there was none, save for his own. He couldn't drink his own blood. And the pirates he had killed were out of his reach. And there were other pirates on deck... Not too many left, but they were much better off than he was.

No, he couldn't stop. He had to get up. He had to save Nivakil.

With his one good arm, Jenba pushed himself back to his feet, lightheaded and exhausted. He had little time left.

Nivakil screamed. Yeaf was behind him. A lance was poking out of Nivakil's chest. Nivakil spun in place, screaming, and swinging his claws at the pirate captain. Yeaf had already activated a yellow Nexi stone, and the weakened master's claws only managed to push Yeaf back, rather than tear through his torso.

Yeaf landed on his feet, an armed crossbow appearing in his hand again.

Jenba pushed Nivakil aside, taking the arrow to his own chest. Nivakil yelled something at Jenba, but he couldn't tell what the old master was saying. It was too loud, and there was too much going on, and he was losing too much blood. Yeaf was attacking again with another weapon, but Jenba couldn't tell what it was, his vision blurry and darkened.

"Sorry, master," Jenba whispered. "I always fail you."

Nivakil yelled something again, and was pulling Jenba back. The two of them tumbled to the deck. Something blew apart, releasing dirt everywhere. Something sharp and cold nicked Jenba's side. Then someone was standing in front of him and Nivakil.

It looked like Borely.

•

After his senses slipped out of the pitch black silence, Borely felt his entire body tremble uncontrollably. How long had he been knocked out by the light Nexi attack? The white lightning had jolted his heart, shocked his mind, and nearly knocked the life right out of him. Had Borely not been a vampire, Yeaf's concentrated white Nexi energy guided by the metal knives would have surely killed Borely right then and there. But how much time had passed? He had to get on his feet. He had to find the others. How was Nivakil and Jenba faring? And was Analicia still evading the pirates that were after her? Where was Yeaf?

Borely's senses came back to him all at once, overwhelming his mind, still slipping in and out of recognition of the current situation and surroundings.

"Find them," Borely told himself, his own voice sounding distant—barely audible, barely breathing. "Find them. And Yeaf. And the Hader. And Areo."

Even now he was still thinking of Areo. Was this infiltration of the pirate ship worth the effort? He could hardly think straight, and there were pirates coming. They looked surprised—no, furious. Maybe both. They wanted Borely dead—he wasn't supposed to be alive. Yeaf was somewhere else...

Borely looked past the approaching pirates and spotted Nivakil, struggling to pull Jenba away from a pirate firing a blast of water. Behind the pirate a few paces was Yeaf, summoning a long poleaxe. Borely blinked and realized Nivakil and Jenba were both injured, but it was difficult to tell how badly. Borely shoved past the pirates ganging up on him and sprinted toward his companions, ignoring the nerve-wracking earthquake splitting his mind apart. He wanted to just fall back to the ground and lie there for a few hours. The pain throughout his entire body was overwhelming, but there was no time to stop for blood. A pirate behind him was firing icicles, and it took all of Borely's might just to keep from getting impaled from behind. One of the icicles nicked one of his legs, but he managed to reach the closest pirate attacking Nivakil. Borely severed the man's head and turned to Yeaf, taking the captain by surprise. Yeaf swung his weapon, but Borely turned in time and clawed through the pole, severing it in half. Immediately Yeaf summoned a knife and jabbed the blade at Borely's neck. Borely leaned down and grabbed the blade with his teeth, then flung the knife right back at Yeaf. The captain barely managed to avoid a fatal blow to the face, but cut his ear, blood trickling down his neck.

Yeaf dove backward, summoning a sword in the process. Borely clawed at Yeaf's chest, but the captain was too quick, and Borely too tired and injured to reach him in time. However, Yeaf's sudden dive caused a golden necklace around his neck to slip out from behind his shirt and jacket. At the end of the necklace was a stone glowing a strange mix of yellow and silver, shifting back and forth like oil and water.

Borely swiped again at Yeaf, despite the man already swinging his sword straight for Borely's neck. Though weak to the brink of death, Borely pushed himself to snatch the Hader from Yeaf's control. Borely extended his claws just enough to slice through the links of Yeaf's necklace, releasing the Hader. Yeaf still had his sword, however. Borely snapped his claws together around the Hader. The stone held together tight in his grasp. Yeaf's blade reached Borely's neck.

The boat vanished beneath Borely's feet, replaced by the multicolored leaves of a bright maple-filled forest. He wasn't on the pirate ship anymore. This really was a forest. Was he dead? Or had he simply gone mad?

Collapsing into a pile of leaves, Borely lay on the forest floor, gasping slow, painful breaths. The smell of crinkly leaves was overwhelming. The stinging, shaking, resonating pain throughout every bone and organ in his body was overwhelming. Even the sunlight was overwhelming.

I'm dead or dying, Borely thought. He let his claws retract back into ordinary fingernails, bringing the Hader into the grasp of his hand. It continued to shift and glow, a mysterious entity emanating power of a magnitude Borely could hardly imagine. This was what he had come for—perhaps died for. Would Jenba, Nivakil, and Analicia die as well? Was it worth all that, to possibly have a chance to save Areo? Summoning weapons wouldn't actually free her mind, would it? And he wasn't even alive anymore to use it... Or had the Hader actually magically sent him to a forest somehow?

"Don't die before we've even started," a voice called out. Borely tried to lift his head, but he was simply too exhausted. The lightning attack had fried him from the inside-out. His vampire body was strong enough to survive, but not to function after such a powerful, concentrated burst of energy like that. Borely simply lay there, wondering if the voice he heard was even real.

"It seems the wielder of my power has become quite a competent fighter," the voice continued. It was a man's voice—a man Borely's age, and very normal-sounding. This wasn't a gruff pirate speaking to him, nor was it Yeaf's all-knowing, crazed tone. "You've taken quite the beating."

Borely couldn't respond. He could open his mouth, but he didn't have the strength to speak. He just wanted to slip out of consciousness and sleep... sleep until he died, and hope this dream world would bring him the results he had sought from the very beginning of this Hader search mission.

"It looks like you're a vampire," the stranger said. "A pretty recent recruit, since you're ears and skin tone haven't changed much. But it's barely noticeable."

Something cold was pushed into Borely's free hand. It felt like a large glass vial. Movement against the object implied that the man was taking off the topper to the vial.

"If you can just drink some blood to heal yourself, we can move things along quickly," the stranger said, his voice soft yet not what Borely would call kind.

It was difficult to keep a grip on the vial, but Borely managed to get it to his mouth and force hard, painful swallows of the thick blood. Where it had come from and why this random stranger in this random forest had some, Borely didn't know. Regardless, it was a powerful dose, quickly lessening the pain inflicting his body and healing the electric shock he suffered. All other injuries were patched up in a matter of seconds, Borely's regenerative body working its magic with the catalyst of the foreign blood. Within a minute or so, even his weariness felt nullified—he was more than ready to get back to the pirate ship and finish his fight with Yeaf, and all the others left in his crew.

Borely stood up and found the stranger sitting on a cleanly-cut log a few meters away. The man looked to be an elf, but what stood out most were his bright yellow eyes. He had long yellow hair—not blond, but dandelion yellow. The man was dressed in blue robes covered in shining, swirling green ivy patterns. He sat barefoot, leaning forward casually with his elbows against his knees.

"Thanks," Borely said. "But where am I, exactly?"

"In my world," the man said. "I am the Hader of Material Displacement."

"You're the Hader?"

"Yes."

Of course, this didn't make any sense. The Hader was supposed to be a Nexi stone, not an elf. And wasn't this the Hader right here, in Borely's hand? On top of this, the man's claim didn't actually explain where Borely was.

"Well, how do I get out of here?" Borely asked. "I need to return to that ship I was on."

"You don't want my power?" the elf asked. "It's unusual for someone to lay hands on the stone, and not attempt to gain access to my power."

"I don't know what you're talking about," Borely said, getting to the point. "But I really need to hurry. My friends are in danger, and need my help."

"Don't worry," the elf said. "My world exists outside of time. You're about to get your head lobbed off, though, so you'll want to be careful once you return to your reality."

"So is this just some kind of dream, or something?" Borely asked.

"Something like that." The elf stood up and formally placed his hands behind his back. "In order to access my power, you will need to prove yourself worthy of it. I can't let just anyone use the ability to summon whatever objects he pleases."

"So you're saying you're the Hader, not this stone?" Borely asked.

"The stone provides access to magical energy, just like any Nexi stone does," the elf said. "But this stone is special. It provides access to *my* magical energy."

Borely thought this over a few seconds. "You mean you yourself are the source of this Hader's ability?"

The elf nodded. "A very long time ago, my siblings and I chose to sacrifice ourselves for the sake of protecting the world from the wicked uses of the Elpis stone. We perfected the greatest magical techniques in the world, and with the assistance of the extreme Nexi energy resources of the eigni, the Haders were created. Centuries have passed, and our essences have continued to exist within these stones."

"And you let people access this power, as long as they prove worthy of it?" Borely asked. "You let one of the worst pirates in the world use this stone, so apparently you don't care if people use the Hader for good."

"It's impossible for me to judge a person's character," the Hader said. "How much a heart will change, for better or worse, is entirely uncertain. There's no telling if you'll use my power any better than Yeaf has."

"I just want to save a friend of mine," Borely said.

"I don't care what you intend to use my power for," the Hader said. "That can change at any time, and you could end up using it for all sorts of terrible things in the long run. But I at least must ensure that you're capable of wielding the power before I grant you access to it. Otherwise you'll just get yourself and many other people killed for no reason. The power of a Hader is very difficult to contain in the hands of a weak spirit."

"So I just need to prove my strength? Is that it?"

The Hader turned and started walking away. "Defeat me in a fight, and my contract with you will be formed. You will be able to summon hundreds of physical objects that have been displaced in this invisible reality. Most of the objects are weapons, but you may find other useful items, such as that vial of blood I gave you."

"So you can summon things, just as Yeaf did," Borely said.

The Hader turned around to face Borely again, standing a good ten meters away now. "Please understand this. I am the Hader, and Yeaf's power was *my* power. Without the stone, he can no longer access my power. And though you have the stone in your hand right now, you won't be able to use it properly until you've proven yourself worthy to me. So now... I will give you five seconds to prepare yourself, and then I will begin my attack."

All at once, tens of weapons appeared around the elf, all of them floating in the air. Swords, axes, knives, crossbows, lances, and every color Nexi stone imaginable. This elf had somehow summoned well over a hundred weapons, and was able to keep them levitated. He raised an arm forward and pointed at Borely.

"One... Two..."

Was this crazy elf going to fling all these weapons at him?

"Three... Four..."

What was Borely supposed to do against so many weapons? There was no escape from something this ridiculous!

"Five."

Tens of gleaming weapons flew at Borely, all rushing toward him simultaneously. At the same time, arrows flew from crossbows and elements burst from their appropriate Nexi stones. Taking this madness head-on was impossible—Borely ran as fast as he could behind the nearest, thickest tree he could find.

Weapons slammed into the tree, pummeling it, sending splinters and strips of bark flying to either side of Borely. The ground shook beneath him, and he glanced to his left to right to find a nearly constant stream of blades and arrows flying by. The tree erupted in flames, and Borely was forced to run before dirt lurched up around his feet. He ran behind another large tree, barely quick enough to avoid the Hader's attacks in the process. In seconds this tree was destroyed as well, and Borely had to sprint to a third, despite being out of breath.

Have to find an opening, Borely thought. *Have to get through these weapons... Have to get to the Hader.*

He wished he had some Nexi stones he could use on his person. Something to protect himself from the summoned weapons, even if it was just for a few seconds. Or something to attack from a far distance—that would have been helpful. His metal gloves or headband would have especially been nice—good, useful weapons he had grown accustomed to over the years, nearly as familiar to him as his own limbs. But he had nothing at his disposal. Nothing but his claws and teeth, and his vampiric speed and senses. These were all very useful skills, of course, but Borely wasn't an expert at fighting as a vampire.

He didn't even want to fight as a vampire. But there was no choice at this point. He had to get to the Hader and defeat him, relying solely on his abilities as a vampire. If he was going to save Areo, he was going to have to use every power he could access.

Even if he had to become a monster—a bloodthirsty vampire, just like the ones that turned his brother mad and killed his parents.

The tree Borely stood behind split apart at the constant beating of swords, axes, and lances. He couldn't just keep hiding anymore—he had to go for it. Borely had to take down this Hader, take his power, and return to the ship prepared to defeat Yeaf and the rest of the pirates.

I won't be able to run all the way to the Hader without getting hit, Borely thought. *But that's okay. I just need to not die.*

The rest of the tree blew apart from a burst of lightning. Borely rushed out from behind the tree, watching and listening for each and every weapon approaching him. He lifted his claws and swiped at the swords and daggers flying for him. With every open spot he could find, he took another step, swiping away at every weapon flung toward him in the process. Fire, ice, and earth converged upon him amidst the blades and arrows, and Borely had no choice but to accept getting hit by several of the attacks. His right leg burned severely, and a large rock slammed against his right shoulder. An arrow pierced his stomach, but he kept pushing his way forward. He had no time to stop to remove the arrow, as he continued to claw away at all the projectiles he could.

The Hader was still far away, constantly summoning and flinging more weapons at Borely. He needed to go faster—the Hader could just jog backward while Borely struggled through the crashing waves of weaponry.

With all the strength he could muster, Borely ran headlong into the weapons, focusing his senses as hard as he could on the movement of approaching blades and arrows. It was difficult to turn accurately amidst so much chaos, but Borely found himself getting closer to the Hader, who struggled to bring in more weapons and aim them effectively at Borely's unpredictable trajectory. Borely had to keep running, letting some of the attacks hit him. With each passing moment, the Hader had to be expecting Borely to just collapse and give in to the overwhelming odds.

Instead, Borely kept going.

A dagger lodged into Borely's chest, just beneath his collarbone. A blast of lightning burned the side of his right arm. A lance cut through his side. An arrow shot into his right foot. Borely kept running, and kept himself from screaming. Every iota of concentration was focused on reaching the Hader, on avoiding as many of the summoned weapons as physically possible. He nearly tripped several times, but managed to recover each time and keep himself going. The Hader was closer... closer...

Borely let his vampire nature take over, not caring about the pain, knowing with a certainty he would live on. All he needed was blood. He would live on with the blood. He only needed to drink blood.

His prey stood just before him. He only needed to accept becoming the same kind of bloodthirsty monster that had destroyed his family, and altered his life forever.

More weapons hit Borely, the Hader far too capable with his summoning to slow down for even a moment. But Borely kept running, clawing away a path straight to the Hader.

Just be a vampire, Borely repeated in his head. *Fast and silent, merciless and ravenous. Defeat your enemy and drink his blood. Become a monster.*

He reached the Hader and latched his fangs into the elf's neck. Borely shoved the elf to the ground, oblivious to the weapons sticking out of his body. He gulped down the Hader's blood, thoroughly overpowering the elf. There was nothing the Hader could do the moment Borely began to suck his blood. The elf struggled to push Borely away, but the act of Borely latching on to his neck and drinking his blood weakened the man significantly.

Borely pulled out weapons from his body and continued drinking the Hader's blood. Borely's wounds disappeared, and an unparalleled vigor filled his very being. He could keep sucking the Hader's blood as much as he wanted. He didn't want to stop. He was a monster, and this was his victim.

Borely opened his mouth and pushed the Hader away, letting the elf drop to the ground. Borely stared down at the limp figure, blood dripping down his face. The elf was still breathing, but Borely knew he had sucked so much blood, the Hader was at the brink of death. If the Hader was as powerful as he claimed to be he would be fine, but the fact Borely had allowed himself to suck his prey's blood—just like a vampire would—was horrifying. He had nearly killed this elf, the very same way a vampire would.

He was a vampire. There was no denying it now. He had committed the unforgivable act of attacking a person and sucking his blood.

And yet, Borely didn't feel entirely despicable for it. This was his nature, now. He had become just like his brother.

How much further was he going to go, though? Would he be willing to kill people for the sake of obtaining their blood, now? Would he go mad for the blood? Would he ever want to stop drinking blood the next time the opportunity arose? He should feel terrible. He should hate himself. He should never forgive himself for letting himself become the very monster he had always despised.

It took several minutes for the Hader to regain his senses and sit up on his own. Borely sat on the log the Hader had been sitting on before the fight, waiting, watching, wondering. He had managed to keep himself from killing the Hader, but would the elf allow access to the summoning power to a monster? That was what Borely had become, and in some strange fashion he felt ashamed for not feeling horrendous for his moral downfall.

"That was surprising," the Hader said. "To think you would be so crazy as to just plow straight through my attacks..."

"I didn't see any better options," Borely said. "I couldn't just keep running away from you."

"I can't keep summoning weapons like that forever," the Hader said. "My plan is generally to intimidate the enemy and lead him into a trap before my energy wears out. Since you're a vampire, I had to lead you to the trap as quickly as I could, knowing you'd be able to outlast me. The very idea that somebody would come at me headlong is... absolutely insane!" The elf laughed. "Absolutely unthinkable! And yet you barged right through."

Borely sighed, upset to realize he didn't need to put himself through all that misery he subjected himself to. All he had to do was weather the storm of weapons a bit longer, and he would've been able to defeat the Hader through much simpler, less painful methods. "Guess that's just my style."

"You seem the headstrong type," the Hader said. "But regardless, you've most certainly proven yourself worthy of accessing my power. I hope the madness will not affect you as badly as it has Yeaf."

"What do you mean?" Borely asked.

"Access to great power can change people dramatically," the Hader said, his yellow eyes never blinking. "It can make people zealous. Overly ambitious. Proud. Arrogant. Vengeful. Hateful. Treacherous... And sometimes it just messes people up."

Yeaf certainly didn't seem all right in the head, though his paranoia proved accurate in this instance, and his unpredictable behavior did give him the element of surprise. Had he really gone mad though, from the power of the Hader? Or was he just a mad pirate to begin with?

"I just need the power to help a friend," Borely said. "Once my mission is done, I won't need your power anymore."

"If you find the means to destroy the stone, feel free to do so," the Hader said. "I have lived on long enough, and so have my brothers and sisters."

"Are you trapped in this stone, then?" Borely asked.

"I'm not even real, to be technical about it all," the Hader said. "And my concept of the passage of time is tenuous at best. Even much of my sense of self has eroded over the centuries, so there really isn't much left for me to lose. My power remains strong and vibrant, but my memories slowly fade away."

Borely nodded, feeling extremely tired from this entire surprise encounter with the being within the stone. The entire situation came and went so abruptly, it really did feel like a peculiar dream—one he wasn't quite sure he had actually experienced.

"I will let you return to the ship," the Hader said. "I suggest you take some kind of weapon or shield with you, since you're about to get your head lobbed off."

"Ah, right," Borely said. He stood up and took the Hader stone from his pocket. It glowed just the same as always, but he felt as if some kind of connection had been made between him and the smooth rock. Perhaps it was just in his head—but perhaps this entire forest and all its scattered weapons were just in his head, as well.

To his surprise, all Borely had to do was think of the item he wanted—a long, sturdy poleaxe. He had seen Yeaf use it, so Borely imagined he'd be able to summon it as well now.

And just as he hoped, the exact weapon he thought of appeared in his hands, straight out of thin air. There was no poof of smoke, or flash of light. It simply *was*.

"This will do," Borely said.

The Hader nodded. "May you find success before your journey's through."

"My journey will be through once I find success," Borely said.

The Hader looked up a bit and smiled. "Life tends to keep going, even after we've achieved a significant goal in life. Your journey in this mortal existence will be through once you've died—nothing more, nothing less. Though I imagine you will live a long time, seeing how you're a vampire."

"Thank you for lending me your power," Borely said. "I will use it well."

And with that, the forest disappeared, instantly replaced by the pirate ship Borely and his companions had boarded. And standing directly in front of Borely was Yeaf, swinging a sword straight for Borely's neck.

Borely pushed his poleaxe against the pirate's sword, keeping the blade from reaching him. Yeaf stumbled back in surprise, clearly not expecting a weapon to appear out of thin air in Borely's hands at the exact moment the he was about to lob Borely's head off.

Before Yeaf could recover, Borely slammed the axe into the pirate's face, killing him.

There was no time to feel at ease, however. Borely pulled the axe from Yeaf's head and turned to where Nivakil and Jenba were located, still fending off a group of frenzied pirates.

Borely caught a better look at their current state. One of Jenba's arms was clearly severed, and Nivakil was impaled by a lance, square in the chest. There was no way either of them were going to survive without blood, but there was no time for them to drink any—not with so many pirates gathered around them. A blast of ice was launched at the two, and Jenba and Nivakil were struggling just to keep on their feet. At the last moment, Jenba appeared to have regained some of his strength, and managed to push the old master out of the way before the blast could overtake them. Part of Jenba's leg was frozen, but he tore it out of the ice, screaming. There were already a few more pirates with weapons charging at the two, and Nivakil looked ready to pass out.

A high-pitched scream stopped Borely in his tracks. He turned and found Analicia, stumbling back from a couple pirates. She shot another jet of water from the dark blue Nexi on her forehead, but she missed the nearer of the two pirates, and ended up flinging herself backward in the process. It took practice to get accustomed to controlling the metal headband—something Borely doubted she had ever done before. The fact she was able to fire the stream of water at all was an impressive feat, but she was no match for these pirates, as inexperienced with combat as she was.

Borely sprinted to Analicia's position, summoning a water Nexi in the process. He shot off a jet of water at the pirate closest to Analicia, knocking the man in the side of the head hard enough to snap his neck. The other pirate turned and fired an arrow at Borely, who quickly replaced his water Nexi with a metal shield, deflecting the projectile at the last moment. Borely kept running and slammed the shield into the pirate's face, knocking him out cold.

Borely looked down to Analicia, checking to see if she was injured. "Are you all right?"

"I'm fine," Analicia said, her eyes wide, and her small body trembling. "But Jenba... And Nivakil..." The child looked as white as a sheet, noticeable even when accounting for the fact she was normally rather pale to begin with.

Borely looked across the deck and found Jenba and Nivakil surrounded even tighter by gathering pirates. A giant explosion burst from Jenba and Nivakil's location, sending several burning pirates flying around them. It looked like one of them had used a red Nexi—and then another explosion erupted, quickly followed by a third and fourth. Fire Nexis were bursting apart the ship, spreading its flames up and down the wooden planks and posts of the vessel.

Borely swore. He couldn't see through the smoke, or hear through the dying screams and crackling flames. The pirates wouldn't have been the ones to use the fire Nexi stones—it must have been Jenba or Nivakil, using last-ditch tactics to fend off the rest of the pirates.

The fires spread to Borely and Analicia's location. They had to get off this ship right away. This wasn't a mere defensive maneuver by Jenba and Nivakil—this was a final tactic to buy Borely and Analicia time to escape with the Hader.

•

Jenba set off the last of his fire Nexi, using up what little was left of his energy to spread the fires as far as possible across the ship. If Borely was smart, he'd be off the ship by now with Analicia, and swimming away to safety. The fires raged all around Jenba and Nivakil. The heat was overwhelming, but the burning paled in comparison to the pain of his injuries. He couldn't move a muscle anymore, and from what he could tell, neither could Nivakil. They had utterly wasted themselves in this battle.

Some of the pirates were trying to quell the flames with their water Nexi, but Jenba had put all his energy into those flames, spreading them all across the boat far too quickly for the remaining pirates to keep up with. Jenba wasn't sure if Borely had managed to obtain the Hader, but hopefully this fire had assisted him in some way. Borely knew about these final measures being a possibility in this mission. The fires were a signal for Borely to get out of there—even a vampire's regeneration wouldn't survive a rush through such deep, billowing flames. The body would burn and melt away in seconds.

So there was no hope for Jenba or Nivakil to survive, lying in the center of it all. Even if they had the energy to drink each other's blood, they wouldn't have been able to get through the fires.

It's up to you now, Borely, Jenba thought. *I hope I was able to help at least this once.*

Jenba was too weak to shut his eyes. He stared up at the stars, the world turning silent despite the roaring flames around him.

"You did well," Nivakil said, his voice barely alive, barely audible.

Jenba couldn't respond. He wasn't even sure if Nivakil had said these words. It seemed unlikely, and yet Jenba's mind had registered them. Perhaps it was just his own thoughts.

In his head, he thanked Nivakil. It was thanks to the old master that he was able to find any kind of purpose in life. He wished he could have properly repayed Nivakil for the years of training. He wished he could have saved his mentor in his hour of need.

But in the end, this was the best he could do. There was no way to know if it was enough, or if he had made any difference at all. But if Nivakil felt he had done well, that was the best Jenba could have ever hoped for.

Ever since he lost his family and became a vampire, he had hoped for some way to make up for his failures. Ever since he began training under Nivakil, he had hoped to become the type of person who used his power to save others.

Hurry off this ship, Borely, Jenba thought. *Keep watch over Analicia, and save Areo.*

Finish what we started.

•

In the end, there was no way for Borely to reach Jenba and Nivakil. The smoke was too thick, the flames too rapid and destructive. Once it was clear he wouldn't be able to find them before the ship was destroyed, Borely tried to get to the small boat he had sailed out of port, but it was already too late to access it—the fires had already spread to that part of the deck.

"What do we do?" Analicia asked.

"Can you swim?" Borely asked.

"A... a little..." Analicia said. She looked scared out of her wits.

"Hold your breath," Borely said. He grabbed the child and ran to the end of the deck, carrying her in his arms. Analicia screamed in surprise at how high of a jump this turned out to be, but remembered to take in a gasp of air before crashing into the sea. Borely sunk deep into the waters, finding it difficult to keep a hold of the child as the waves battered them around. As Borely swam toward the surface, he lost his grip on Analicia, who was spun around violently by the waves. Borely opened his eyes and searched for her, frantic and desperate.

He spotted her, floundering her way deeper into the sea, flailing her weak arms and legs without any rhythm or focus. Borely pushed himself to reach her as quickly as possible, then helped pull her up toward the surface of the waters. They both gasped for breath the moment they cleared the surface, but Borely was quick to pull Analicia with him and swim away from the burning ship, not wanting them to get pulled in with the sinking wreckage.

Analicia struggled to swim at all, let alone quickly, so Borely got her on his back and gripping his shoulders. As hard as he could, Borely swam toward the distant shore, knowing he wasn't going to reach it anytime soon. This was going to be a long, difficult swim, made all the more strenuous with having to help Analicia across as well.

Once they were a safe distance away from the ship, Borely treaded water so he could watch for any sign of Jenba and Nivakil. Analicia repeatedly asked if they were going to be okay, if they were going to get off the ship in time—but the slow, tiring minutes passed, and there was no sign of any rowboats or swimmers escaping the dying ship. The vessel soon fell apart and crumbled into the ocean, overwhelmed by the fury of the red Nexi fires.

Jenba and Nivakil never got off the boat. Borely watched intently, straining his eyes to see through the darkness, across the thousand waves of the sea. Minute after minute passed, and still he hoped that somehow Jenba and Nivakil would show up, swimming in their direction.

But it soon became too tiring for Borely to keep treading water like this, and he realized there was no way he was going to make it all the way to shore in this exhausted state. There was no sign of Jenba or Nivakil surviving, and Borely had seen the fatal injuries they had sustained. Without access to blood, they were good as dead.

"I'm sorry," he told Analicia. "They're gone."

The girl didn't respond. She simply took slow, shallow breaths, struggling to keep from sucking in salt water. Borely turned and started swimming toward shore again, quickly straining himself against the strong, constant waves. There was no way he was going to make it at this rate.

"I need some of your blood, Analicia," Borely said. It was the last thing he wanted to do, but there simply wasn't a choice in the matter. The waters were bitter cold, and he was going to wear himself out before even making it halfway to shore. He was a good swimmer, but the distance was just too far, the waves too strong.

Analicia didn't respond, so Borely treaded water and took her arm, deciding it would be easier to draw blood from there rather than try to reach for her neck. The girl didn't resist, and Borely worried for a moment if she was going unconscious or even dying. She was just overwhelmed by the series of events she had just gone through, however. Once Borely had a few gulps of blood, he repositioned Analicia and started swimming again, now able to exert much more strength and vigor.

He wasn't sure if Analicia was crying, and Borely didn't want to think about the tragedy of this mission any more than he already was. Jenba and Nivakil were gone now. It wasn't right. They were strong. They were decent vampires—great ones, in fact. They were there for him when he had no clue what to do with his life. He didn't even know if he wanted to live anymore after becoming a vampire, but they were there to help him through the harrowing transition.

And now they were dead, just when Borely had gained the power of the Hader. He had been too slow, too weak. Perhaps if he hadn't pushed for going on this mission, they wouldn't be dead now.

He kept swimming, and kept wondering if Analicia was crying. It was too hard to tell with the constant splashing of waves all about him. She was too quiet.

Eventually Borely stopped to give Analicia some of his own blood, realizing the waters were turning her deathly cold. She drank weakly from his neck, but once she got a few gulps down she was much better off. Borely had to drink some more of her blood in return, as there was still a ways to go before they reached shore.

There's still a ways to go before we reach shore... Borely focused on this thought. How much more would he have to go through before finally finding Areo and freeing her? Would he be able to keep fighting like this for much longer? And now without Jenba and Nivakil, the fighting force of his team had dwindled significantly.

There was nobody but himself left to save Areo now. And he wasn't sure if he had the strength to go at it alone.

•Part X•
A GATHERING OF IMPOSSIBLE POWER

He was stuck in a log cabin room with arguably the two most powerful fighters in the world, but Trilir wasn't worried. At least... not too worried. As long as he did as Augurc commanded, there would be no problems with him. And as long as he ensured Subject VI continued to function as expected, the Elpis-enhanced vampire would never do any harm at all. Except, of course, to those Augurc commanded.
Which, from what Trilir understood, were a great many people. From the sound of things, Subject VI was more powerful on her own than an entire platoon of Brotherhood members. And these were elite soldiers to begin with...

Right now Trilir was wrapping up an analysis of some of VI's achievements over the past week. She had managed to kill several more of the Fiefs Kingdom's top spies and assassins. The system of royal servants was a dying one at this point, and there was little hope of the Fiefs Kingdom gaining any more insight on the Brotherhood's plans. Soon enough, Augurc would likely start destroying some of the kingdom's major cities, potentially leading to a full attack on the capital of Setar.

"Subject VI is in perfect condition," Trilir said, setting down a summary of his readings and analyses. He sat at a small round table covered with papers and medical instruments. Augurc sat to his left and VI to his right.

Augurc nodded, and Trilir continued. "There isn't a single scratch on her body, and she's as healthy as a vampire can get. She is still susceptible to pain, and her mind continues to fight against your will to some faint degree. As long as you continue to give her targets to kill on a regular basis, she will continue to be a powerful servant."

"Good. The Brotherhood will soon destroy Niez," Augurc said, straightforward as always. Niez was one of the continent's largest cities, and was only about an hour's walk from this tiny village. Augurc had already directed most of the Brotherhood to gathering points closer to the city, from what Trilir understood. "VI will assist alongside all other ready subjects. It will be a final test of the Elpis's capabilities."

Of course, Subject VI was not the only successful Elpis-based experiment at this point. Subject EV had proven himself just as worthy of Augurc's approval, having taken down a whole troop of Fiefs soldiers, as well as several of the kingdom's top servant spies. As far as Trilir was concerned, there wasn't a force in the entire planet that could kill EV, even if he wasn't yet as capable of a fighter as VI.

And preparations were finally set for MI, potentially the most powerful experiment of them all. Embedding the Elpis energy necessary for Augurc to be able to summon MI was an incredible challenge, but the process went smoothly enough. It would take a while for Augurc to recover from the painful procedure, but the transfer of energy would enable Augurc to will a third experiment to destroy anyone and everyone he pleased.

"I will leave VI to you then, if that is all," Trilir said.

"Continue tests on MI's power," Augurc instructed. "If there is anything more I should know, you will convey the information to Viecint for speedy delivery."

"Yes, of course," Trilir said. He didn't care much for the Brotherhood guards Augurc had assigned to constantly breathe down his neck, making sure Trilir never performed any experiments contrary to Augurc's demands. And Trilir especially didn't care for Viecint, one of the Brotherhood's more ornery higher-ups. Of course, Trilir didn't care much for Augurc, either—but he was the man with the world's greatest Nexi energy. There was no way Trilir was going to turn down the chance to work with him.

Augurc got up to leave, and VI instinctively got up to follow him out the door. The two stationed guards locked it behind them, leaving Trilir to continue research on the Nexi seal he had placed on the center of Augurc's chest. The Elpis energy built up inside of Augurc had reached the point where the man could summon an Elpis-crafted monster potentially capable of destroying an entire city.

Or perhaps an entire country. The sky really was the limit where the Elpis was concerned. Trilir could only imagine what he could learn if he had the full Elpis.

Of course... if Augurc had the full Elpis, there probably wouldn't have been any need for Trilir. Augurc would have simply been able to do whatever he wanted. And perhaps would have destroyed the entire world ten times over by now.

Though Augurc never showed any pleasure on his face, he had made it clear that he did indeed view Trilir as the greatest mind the eigni race had ever produced. Nobody in the world had experimented with as many Nexi forces as Trilir had. And now Trilir had helped create the three most powerful beings in the world. Of course, Augurc himself was likely the most powerful being in the world, thanks to the fact he was capable of wielding half of the

Elpis itself—but thanks to said Elpis fragments, Trilir had learned to enable Augurc to turn powerful beings into unstoppable ones.

Subject VI was a vampire who could kill anyone. Subject EV was an elf who couldn't be killed by anyone. And Subject MI... was a god, just waiting to be born.

And none of it would have been possible without Trilir's intellect. If it weren't for his many years of extensive research on the various Nexi energies of the world, including the Elpis, Augurc wouldn't have been able to wreak even a tenth of the havoc he had wrought since the death of his brother Delkol. The Brotherhood would have been nothing more than a dying rabble, if it weren't for Trilir. Thanks to him, Augurc and his Brotherhood was truly a force to be reckoned with.

Trilir didn't care about Augurc's goals, and frankly, he wasn't quite sure what the reticent man was actually hoping to achieve. Hundreds of people in the Fiefs Kingdom had been killed at this point (with a majority of them likely being killed by Augurc and Trilir's experiments), but there was little rhyme or reason to the destruction. The insurrection in Istal at least gained Augurc some allies amongst the scheming vampires, though Trilir questioned how much Augurc should trust any of them.

It was all none of Trilir's concern. All he really cared about was Nexi energy, and the possibilities the magical science presented him. And right now, he needed to ensure his employer would be able to keep control over the most destructive monster the world had ever seen.

•

Borely considered returning to the sea so he could retrieve Jenba and Nivakil's corpses, but he had a lot of injuries to recover from, and he didn't want to leave Analicia alone for very long. She was still worn out from the whole fiasco, but more so she was broken inside. After losing her home in Istal, she now lost the one person she had left who she'd known well. Now she was just left with Borely, and still having to travel in this strange, aimless quest. Borely felt it best they put as much ground between them and Limbo as they could, considering how any surviving pirates were probably out looking for them.

For as long as they could, they traveled in the darkness of night, slinking their way across vast fields of long grass. It was painful to travel, but Borely couldn't risk people finding him in this state. He was a vampire now, and the average night traveler would be quick to kill him at the first sign of trouble.

There was little for Borely to think about, other than Jenba and Nivakil's deaths. It didn't seem to make any sense... They were the experienced vampires. And now Borely was by himself, with nobody to help him deal with... anything. With finding the Haders. With finding Areo. With finding... himself. He had accepted the fact he was a vampire, and had to deal with life the way a vampire would need to.

But it was difficult. It was going to continue to be difficult. It wasn't something he felt ready for, but he really *needed* to be ready for it. What was he supposed to do now? He had the summoning Hader, but how was that going to help him save Areo?

He felt so tired... With so much on his mind, and with so little left in his heart, he just wanted to collapse on the ground and let a few months pass away. Perhaps this was a subconscious vampiric desire to hibernate. It still disgusted him, knowing he had these monstrous urges. A part of him still craved blood, even after the chaos that ensued aboard the pirate ship.

He had Analicia at his disposal, but he'd had enough of her blood already. He couldn't let himself lose control and suck her dry. She'd die if she lost too much blood.

Hours passed, and they walked through the countryside in moonlit silence. Borely had Analicia walk in front of him, feeling the need to keep his eye on her at all times. He certainly didn't want her around, but the fact was she was his responsibility now. She'd be helpless without him at this point, and admittedly he was at least glad that watching over her gave him something to do—something to think about other than his failures on the pirate ship, the deaths of his master and companion, and the turmoil Areo must be going through. It pained Borely to think he'd have to one day explain how Areo's master and brother figure were both killed. There was nobody left to seek out Areo but Borely now. He couldn't fail her... There was no one else to help her.

Borely could hear Analicia crying from time to time—but only a little, and in very brief spurts. The child was either trying her hardest to be strong through this tragedy, or her emotions were fried a bit. The situation had to be overwhelming for someone so young. In a way, Borely could relate, he realized... He was young when he lost everyone he loved, too.

This world of vampires was a dark, miserable one. But there was no escaping it, Borely understood. He had to simply make the world better.

Analicia stopped and sat down, her face wet and revealing just how exhausted she was. There was still a ways to go before they reached a town in the area, though Borely wasn't sure what they would do once they got there. It would probably be morning by then, though Borely would have been glad to stay at an inn for a while and sleep away some of his fatigue and misery.

Not wanting to push Analicia any harder than he had to, he sat down beside her, accepting to take a break for a few minutes. He didn't say anything, and neither did Analicia. They simply sat amidst the grass, hidden from the light of the moon, far from any trails people could be taking.

What was he supposed to do for this girl? He didn't exactly care for her—they were both simply associated with Jenba—and presumably Areo. Borely wasn't certain if Analicia had spent much time with her before.

"You going to be okay?" he asked her.

Analicia didn't respond, or even move. She just sat there, frozen in time.

"I'm sorry things turned out so badly," Borely said.

"It's not fair," Analicia said, barely loud enough to register as a whisper. She stared out blankly in front of herself, clutching her legs up to her chest.

"No... it's not," Borely said. "Sometimes you just... lose everything. That's... how it goes." This wasn't quite what he wanted to say, but he wasn't sure how to word anything better.

"Why is everyone dying?" Analicia said. It wasn't quite said like a question—it was as if she had resigned herself to this terrible fact of life. "Why didn't I..." Her words faded away, and tears began spilling out from her eyes unhindered.

Borely looked straight ahead, not wanting to watch the girl cry like this. It reminded him of all the times he had lost it all. He thought of the day he was turned into a vampire first, but his thoughts turned back to when he was a child... Just a boy on a ship, simply glad to be with his family. It only took one day to lose all of them, and suddenly his entire life was flipped upside-down. How had he moved on after that?

He simply... moved on. Just searched for something to do, something to focus on... Something to accomplish.

"It's not your fault," Borely said. "You did nothing wrong. In fact, if it weren't for you, I would've been killed." It was an embarrassing thing to admit, but Analicia did indeed save his life during his fight with Yeaf. And it would be wrong of him to not support her in her time of need in return.

The child kept crying, burying her face in her knees. She shuddered a few times, struggling against the cold of night. Borely placed a hand on her far shoulder, not sure if this was a good way to support her through this.

"If you want to leave me, you can," Borely said. "But otherwise, I'd be willing to stick with you... I'll help you get to wherever you want to go to."

"We... still need to save Areo, don't we?" Analicia said between sniffles. "That's what Jenba and Nivakil died for. And I can't just let Areo keep suffering..."

"You spent a lot of time with her?" Borely asked.

Analicia nodded. "Not as much as I did with Jenba, but Areo was always nice too."

So this mission was personal to Analicia as well. Perhaps even more so now, since there were so few vampires left that she knew at all.

"Okay," Borely said. "We'll stick together then... We'll find a way to rescue Areo."

Analicia lifted her head and tried wiping her eyes. New tears trickled down right away, so she gave up trying to hide it.

"You're not very good at comforting people," she said. "Jenba would have done a lot better."

Borely gave a faint smile. "But I probably did better than Areo would have."

Analicia smiled a little as well. "Yeah... probably."

They sat there a few minutes longer, trying to decide where to go from there. They needed to either continue the quest for Haders, or search for Augurc and Areo. Borely wondered how he would free her with the power of this Hader he had stolen. Would he be able to defeat Augurc with the power of summoning weapons? And would that be enough to save Areo? Perhaps Rilv's team had found a Hader that would be able to free her mind from the influence of the altered Elpis energies.

Analicia pulled a stone out of a small satchel tied to the side of her dress. It was the teal Nexi stone Nivakil had used to keep in contact with Rilv.

"Nivakil gave that to you?" Borely asked. It was a bit difficult to believe.

"He wanted me to just escape in case everything went wrong with the mission," Analicia said. "If everyone else was killed in the fight, he wanted me to be able to give Rilv all the information I could about the Hader."

At the very least Borely survived, and managed to succeed in taking the Hader from Yeaf. But it turned out Nivakil's caution proved beneficial—this teal Nexi would allow Borely to find out precisely where to go next.

Analicia handed him the Nexi stone, and Borely activated its power. After speaking Rilv's name, it took a few seconds to hear Rilv's voice emanating from the stone.

"Yes, Nivakil?" she asked.

"Borely, actually..." He wasn't sure what to say next.

"What is your status?" Rilv asked.

"We've killed the pirate captain Yeaf and taken his Hader," Borely said. "Nivakil and Jenba died at the hands of Yeaf and his crew, however. Analicia and I escaped, and are a few kilometers south of Limbo."

"I'm sorry for your loss," Rilv said. Her tone was probably about as sympathetic as the woman was capable of, which wasn't much—but it was perhaps a little more than Borely expected. "What is the power of your Hader?"

"I can make weapons appear out of thin air," Borely said. "I now have an unlimited supply of weaponry."

"That will prove very useful," Rilv said. "We will meet together at the location of the next Hader, which has been on the move over the past few days. It is currently situated in a small town outside of Niev. Intelligence has informed me that there are teams of Brotherhood members in the area, so you will need to be on the lookout. Augurc is also in that region. Once you are approaching Niev, inform me, and I will give you our exact location."

"It will take at least a day to get down there by horse and carriage," Borely said. Niev was a ways south, near the border of the Shire Kingdom. "When will you get there?"

"Approximately the same time," Rilv said. "It is prudent we move as quickly as possible. A man with two Haders is currently following us, and we are still recovering from a series of incidents that have transpired. We now have two Haders ourselves. Once we reach Niev, we will work together to obtain the Hader there, giving us the cumulative power of four Haders—at which point we should be capable of defeating the man with two Haders. With six Haders, we will be able to defeat the Brotherhood, and destroy the Elpis once and for all."

"And save Areo," Borely said. He wanted to make it clear this was what he was fighting for.

"Yes," Rilv said. "Plan to meet with us by morning two days from now. I will inform you later of an exact meeting-place, possibly in one of the towns just outside of Niev."

"Okay," Borely said. With the plans confirmed, Rilv deactivated her Hader, and the glow of the teal Nexi dimmed a bit.

"Once we reach a town, we'll have to take a horse and carriage," Borely said to Analicia. "Did Nivakil leave you with any money?"

She nodded. Even if she had just a small portion of the money Nivakil was given by the Fiefs agent, it would be easy for Borely to obtain speedy passage to Niev.

"Let's see if we can get to Niev first, then," Borely said. He patted Analicia's back and stood up.

The girl looked up at him, her face still thoroughly wearied. Borely tried to smile a little more sincerely, and bent down a bit to take Analicia's hand. She accepted, and Borely lifted her to her feet.

•

It was important to Trilir to always analyze his current situation, determine the best course of action, and be willing to change his plans at a moment's notice. He sat at his desk, looking over the many pages of notes he had taken on powerful sources of Nexi power he had learned about from hundreds of different books and scrolls over they years. The Elpis was certainly the most powerful source, particularly when it was in a whole, perfected state. But there were other stones that had been formed and improved upon over the centuries, and at the moment Trilir could only guess how these Nexi masters managed to shift the application of Nexi power so effectively.

He shut his eyes a moment and thought over his current situation. He was working for Augurc, which was perhaps the most dangerous employer he could ever have. But at the same time, this gave Trilir a great deal of protection—not to mention a great deal of information and tools for him to work with. His own survival would always be his first priority, he recognized. But after that, what mattered most was to place himself in circumstances that would enable him to access more powerful Nexi energies. All his life, he had felt there was no greater science in the world he could devote his life to. Every time he made a new discovery, he experienced nothing but pure, unblemished joy, and he wanted nothing more than to find ways to better the world with his findings.

He imagined Augurc shared some of these same feelings in some twisted form, though the Brotherhood leader was never going to show them. And it was still up in the air what Augurc wanted to accomplish precisely, though the destruction of the Fiefs Kingdom seemed to play a role in it all. But he may have only been attacking Fiefs cities in order to secretly appease the Shire governing body, receiving funds under the table for his Brotherhood— and more significantly, for his experiments.

And what wonderful experiments they were! Most were certainly in a moral gray area, but Trilir wasn't going to speak up against Augurc any time soon. Not until Trilir had the upper hand in power, at least.

What mattered most though was that Trilir was learning more about Nexi energies every day. He could only imagine what the ancient magicians must have felt when they first learned to refine Nexi stones all those millennia ago. Would he ever get to feel the same way? It would take an advancement in magic arts of an unprecedented level.

Trilir scratched at his left eye. It was tingling a bit more than usual, alerting him of potential threats. He had long ago replaced his eye with a Nexi stone designed to help keep him safe, sensing those around him who had a strong connection with Nexi energy. The stone was designed to look exactly like a normal eye, so nobody had ever suspected it to be anything but. Unfortunately, ever since Trilir found himself working with the Brotherhood, his eye was constantly throbbing ever so slightly. Fortunately he had learned to hide his discomfort somewhat while in Augurc and Subject VI's presence, whose gave Trilir a painful headache—at least until the Nexi stone eye triggered an energy to dull the pain. But Trilir had to explain it away as a twitchy eye condition to everyone else who asked about it, and Trilir could only imagine what these Brotherhood members thought of him. It was difficult to tell what any of them thought, thanks to their masks.

But now his eye was bothering him even more—enough to make him consciously notice, at least. Most every Brotherhood was an expert Nexi user, so to sense this much of an increase in Nexi competence was saying something. It meant someone especially powerful was in the area... And as Trilir's eye began to hurt even more, he realized the person in question was approaching this building. Or perhaps it was a group of people... No, it felt too concentrated. Someone was coming alone.

Trilir looked up to the door, where two masked Brotherhood guards stood. Then there was Viecint at another desk in the dimly-lit room, busy formulating battle plans while he watched over Trilir. These were some of the Brotherhood's top men, from what Trilir understood, and he always worried a little about making them mad. The last thing he wanted was a lack of cooperation on their part, making his work and research more difficult. But now he worried they wouldn't be enough for this potential threat...

"Make sure you're ready for any intruders," Trilir said, knowing he had to sound silly saying this.

"Don't worry," Viecint muttered. "You focus on your work, and we'll focus on ours."

Trilir turned back to the two guards at the door. There was something... off about them. Trilir squinted with the eye he could still see through, and realized there was something sticking out of the guards' necks.

Long, black needles... jutting straight out of the doorway, and on through the center of their necks. Two of them in each guard's neck.

Then in one motion, the needles pushed out through either side of the guards' necks, effectively severing their masked heads. The bloody corpses dropped to the ground. Trilir and Viecint stood up, Trilir stepping back while Viecint stepped forward, slipping a Nexi stone in each hand—a silver one, and a pink one.

The long black needles slid back through the door, vanishing.

Trilir and Viecint held their breath, listening with all their might for the hidden assailant. Was he still standing just outside the door? Or was he hidden somewhere else by now... invisible to their eyes?

Something scratched at the ceiling to their left. As they both looked up, something landed with a thump behind them. They both turned around, Viecint running forward to protect Trilir. Someone was there. Viecint raised an arm, which instantly turned silver, expanding with hundreds of razor-sharp silver feathers. Incredulously, he was transforming a part of his own body via the pink Nexi stone, accessing the power of the silver Nexi stone for the transformation form. Trilir had never thought someone could be capable of such a combination of high-level powers, particularly a human.

In an instant, nearly half the room filled with the fatal metallic feathers—the ultimate Nexi shield and weapon all in one.

Suddenly, Viecint stopped. He gagged, and Trilir looked to the masked man's throat. Two long, black needles were sticking out of his neck. The next moment he was beheaded, suffering the same fate as his two companions at the door.

Trilir knew he was at the mercy of the assailant. Running would be pointless, especially when even the likes of a top Brotherhood member couldn't keep up with the enemy's speed. The needles diminished and disappeared entirely, and Trilir followed them to their source—pale, slender fingers.

A woman suddenly stood in front of Trilir. She was tall, imposing—an aristocrat with long, light blue hair.

And a vampire, Trilir realized.

"You're one of the vampires Augurc Shire assisted," Trilir said.

"I'm one of the masters, yes," the woman said. "I am Hidif. And if my sources are correct, you are Trilir, the mastermind behind Augurc's latest and greatest experiments."

There was no reason to deny the claims. "Yes... And I imagine you're not here to assist the Brotherhood, considering how you just killed a few of them."

"Very astute," Hidif said, her smile condescending.

"You haven't killed me yet, so what is it you want me to do?" Trilir asked. It seemed in his best interest to cooperate with this woman, considering there was nothing stopping her from killing him at a moment's notice.

"Something simple," Hidif said. "I saw how effective your latest experiment was... A vampire named Areo. She killed off more of my enemies in a single day than I and my associates have ever killed our entire lives."

"I see... She'd be useful for you," Trilir said.

"Maintaining hold over Istal has already proven difficult," Hidif said. "As you should well understand, the world of vampires can be an incredibly dangerous place."

"I'm afraid handing Subject VI to you is not a simple matter," Trilir said. "You would have to break her attachment to Augurc Shire first, and to do that... Well, her mind is primarily fueled by murderous rampages. You would have to get her attention in a rather... bloody way."

Hidif squinted her eyes and grinned. "Come with me then, Professor Trilir. I believe I can quite easily arrange a rather... bloody, murderous rampage."

•

The carriage ride was about as fast as Borely could hope for, though at the same time, he wished it hadn't made for such a horrendously bumpy ride. There was no way he was able to sleep the entire way, and Analicia likewise wasn't able to get any sleep. Instead she would cry curled up in the corner of her bench seat, leaving Borely anxious and frustrated. He hadn't been able to help Analicia much through her anguish, but he supposed there simply wasn't much he could do. Anything less than bringing Jenba and Nivakil back to life would never erase the pain, after all.

The hours passed, and Borely had tried resting in every position he could to get himself to fall asleep. He didn't want to hear Analicia crying anymore, as cruel a thought as this was... Perhaps in a strange way he was jealous of the child. Jenba and Nivakil had died, and what was he concerned about? He still wanted to keep going with this mission. No time to dwell on the past.

But these were the men who helped him through his years of difficulty, as he adjusted to the miserable life of a vampire.

Borely sighed. Even now, he was still seeing it all as a miserable experience.

I've accepted what I've become... Shouldn't I be glad?

But how could he be glad, when the few people left he's cared about are either dead or might as well be dead?

The unpleasant thoughts seeped deeper into his mind. Borely didn't like focusing on any of these things. He didn't like to dwell too long on anything, really. He just preferred to keep himself busy. In the past, he busied himself with sailing, and keeping up his family's shipping business. It felt like the right thing to do... It was his calling in life, he had felt.

But then, he had lost his ship and become a vampire. Nearly everything about his past self was completely taken away from him. All he had left, it had seemed, were his weapons. And he clung to those metal gloves and headband as hard as he could. It was the last bit of his identity—fighting his own way, rather than relying on any of the vampiric fighting styles. But in the end, fighting his own way simply wasn't enough.

Not enough to save Areo, at least. He had to be willing to do whatever it'd take in order to save her.

And since he was forced into such a pensive mood, he had to wonder... Why was it he had become so focused on saving her? Was it just to pay her back for saving his own life? Was it because this seemed to be the first time she really needed someone to save her? Borely recalled being saved by Areo on multiple occasions, during their adventure with Terico, Kitoh, Lanek, and Suran.

A flood of memories came to Borely. Some of them were good, others bad. But the main feeling Borely got was... It was hard to pin down. It was a sublime feeling. A feeling that he had been part of something truly grand. Perhaps he had lost a lot of things over the course of that adventure, but he knew he had made a difference in the world. Thanks to Terico, Delkol and his armies were defeated, and thousands of lives were ultimately saved. And though Augurc and much of the Brotherhood managed to escape, the Elpis stone was not fully taken by the enemy. In time, it was still possible for the Brotherhood to be overthrown entirely—and Borely was technically still helping out on that front. In order to save Areo, he was ultimately going to need to take down Augurc Shire.

Would the Haders be enough to defeat Augurc and the Elpis, as well as the subjects of Augurc's Elpis-powered experiments? Borely wasn't going to let himself give up. Not now. Especially not now.

He looked over to Analicia, and he could feel a little of that suffering she exuded in his own heart. How was he going to help her through all this if he wasn't even sure how he was going to get through all this himself?

Eventually the driver of the carriage stopped in a town to let the horses rest, and to allow everyone time to get something to eat. Of course, Borely and Analicia weren't about to have lunch in a diner any time soon—or ever—so they had to pretend they were on their way to one of the village's small restaurants.

Borely turned from the carriage driver to Analicia. "Where would you like to eat, Sis?" He was pretending to be her brother, to keep things as simple as possible. Borely didn't want anyone to suspect anything about them, so they wouldn't get found out as vampires. He didn't want to get caught up in any more fighting than he needed to, especially when it was likely he'd have to encounter the Brotherhood upon entering Niev.

"I'm not hungry," Analicia said.

Borely placed a hand on her back to keep her moving, his heart dropping a bit at her words. It felt like she had lost all will to live.

Borely waited a minute before saying anything more. He wanted to make sure they weren't near anyone who could hear them, but he also wanted to think through his words a bit before speaking.

"I'm sorry," he said. "I can't say everything will be okay, or if they'll even get better. But I'll try to help you, if I can."

"You don't really care about me, though," she responded.

Borely kept walking, and keeping Analicia walking.

"Why do you say that?" he asked.

"You're just sticking with me because we're all that's left of the group," Analicia said. "You never cared about me. You hate vampires. Or at least most of them."

Borely sighed. "You're right. I generally haven't liked vampires. Vampires killed my family. And the day I turned into a vampire was... a very bad day. I know now that not all vampires are bad. That's obvious... I mean, I'm trying to save Areo, since I care about her, right? And if I really hated all vampires, I wouldn't be upset about Jenba and Nivakil dying. And I wouldn't be trying to help you out, either."

Analicia pushed herself away from Borely and gritted her teeth.

"You're only helping me because... because of Areo!" she yelled.

Borely placed a hand forward to try and quiet her, but she jumped back and raised her hands in the air.

"You don't want to be with me, so just go away and do what you want!"

This didn't seem to make any sense. Wasn't she saying just a while ago how she also wanted to save Areo? So why did she suddenly want to leave him? She wouldn't last a day on her own. Granted, she was a vampire, but she was still a child. She'd get found out, and it would only be a matter of time before a group of upset villagers managed to drive a stake through her heart.

"I'm not leaving you," Borely said. "Maybe I don't care a lot about you right now. But maybe I'll care more about you over time. You told me you wanted to help save Areo. And I don't want you to come to harm—perhaps primarily for Areo's sake. But it's for your sake too."

"I don't think so," Analicia said. "You just want to stick with me to make yourself feel better. You don't really feel bad about Jenba and Nivakil dying. You don't—"

"Stop it!" Borely yelled. "Of course I feel bad about them dying. I admit I haven't been able to do much to help you after Istal was destroyed, or after Jenba and Nivakil were killed. But I might understand how you feel, at least. At least a little. I've lost people important to me before." He had made this connection in his head, but he hadn't thought to tell Analicia about it.

The girl looked to the ground. "It doesn't matter if you know how I feel. You still don't... don't..." Her teeth clamped shut, and she looked ready to cry.

"You don't have to decide what you want to do right now," Borely said. "If you stick with me for now, that doesn't mean you have to stick with me forever. Just stay with me for a little bit. We can work together to save Areo. And then you can do whatever you want. It won't be long. But for now... I can at least give you someone to be with. And I can give you this."

He held out a hand toward her, placing his wrist in front of her face. "If you need blood, I can give you some." Borely had a few vials of blood on him, but he needed to save them for the future fights he would undoubtedly get involved in. If it would make Analicia feel better, he'd be willing to give her some of his own blood.

"I... I don't need your blood," Analicia said, her voice getting a little higher, a little softer.

"You're a vampire," Borely said. "And so am I. So I understand you want blood. It will make you feel better."

Analicia looked up at Borely, her eyes filling up with tears. Borely could practically see the water rising up her bright, glistening eyes.

Borely glanced around, seeing nobody was in the area. He placed a hand on the back of Analicia's head, and tilted it down toward his wrist. She clamped her fangs into Borely's arm.

His eyes instinctively shutting tight, Borely focused on the flow of his blood, slowly leaking out his arm and into Analicia's mouth. She sucked quietly on Borely's wrist, her tears dripping down his forearm.

Borely kept a hand on Analicia's head, thankful the gesture was accepted. Perhaps Analicia still didn't feel Borely cared about her deep down, but she was at least willing to stay by his side...

At least a little longer.

•

The rest of the day passed slowly, despite the frantic, steady pace of the horses. Borely and Analicia both kept quiet, and eventually their sheer weariness was enough to get them both to fall asleep in the carriage. By the time Borely woke back up, it was nighttime, and the carriage was passing at a tamer pace through another small town.

Borely poked his head out the side window to speak with the carriage driver. "How close are we to Niez?"

"Not much further," the man said. "This town is just a short ways outside of Niez."

Borely thanked the driver and sat back inside the carriage. Analicia was awake now too, but didn't look happy about it.

"You doing all right?" Borely asked.

Analicia didn't respond. She wearily turned her head toward the window and stared out with her vacant, bloodshot eyes.

Perhaps it was just going to take some time for her to accept things as they were. It wasn't like one simple talk was going to be enough for her to believe Borely would actually be there for her. She was still a child, and though she was a bit older than she looked, she was still fully a child at heart.

"We'll be at Niez soon," Borely said. "And then we'll be able to move on from there." He wasn't entirely sure what he and Analicia were going to be doing next. They were going to meet up with Rilv and her team, at the very least. Hopefully she had a plan in mind. Would they be able to pinpoint the exact location of the Hader in the city?

Borely felt healed from all the injuries he went through on the pirate ship, but felt a bit drained of energy after giving up some more of his blood to Analicia. But even more so, he just felt unbelievably sore from this grueling carriage ride. It simply was not designed for comfort, especially in terms of an all-day excursion. He stuck his head out the window again and asked the driver if they could stop for a bit so he could stretch his legs and walk around. A short walk would probably be good for Analicia too, especially considering how short her attention span usually was. This carriage ride had to be rather torturous for her, even if she didn't have the burden of Jenba and Nivakil's deaths on her mind.

They got out and starting walking down the main path through town. It was a dark, drab place, but Borely wasn't really there to go sightseeing anyways. This was just a brief stop for them on their way to Niez.

Analicia was still uncharacteristically quiet, and Borely decided it best to just let her think things out while they walked around. He wanted to ponder a bit himself, glad to be walking on his own two feet and not stuck in that shaky carriage. It was easier to hold a thought in his head when he wasn't being bounced around every which way.

There was a slight gasp. It was far away... Far behind him. He stopped and heard a stifled groan. Someone was being attacked. Even with his vampiric hearing, it was the subtlest of sounds. Borely turned around and saw the carriage far in the distance. Focusing as hard as he could with his eyes, Borely could make out a figure grabbing another. It was the carriage driver, and he had turned limp in the arms of the first figure. There was another man behind him, and then two more figures slinking out from behind the trees to the side of the road. They were stealing the carriage.

Borely sprinted toward the carriage, beckoning Analicia to keep up with him. There was no telling yet who these assailants were, but he wasn't going to leave Analicia behind at this point.

"We've taken down every Brotherhood member in the area," a man said. "Surrounding villages have also been wiped clean." It looked like he had finished sucking the blood dry of the carriage driver.

"Good," a woman said. "We'll head to our planned meeting point and move from there." She was trying to hurry a man along into the carriage.

As Borely got closer, he could see better the figures gathered at the carriage. They were vampires. And not only that—the woman was Hidif, the banished aristocrat who helped spearhead the destruction and takeover of Istal.

What was she doing here? And why would they turn against the Brotherhood now? Whatever the case, Borely couldn't just let them leave with the carriage, and get away with killing the driver like that.

"Stop it!" Borely yelled. They had surely heard his approaching footsteps already, but he wanted to make it clear he was coming to stop them.

Hidif turned to face him, and the man beside her also stopped before getting in the carriage. Borely noticed he was an eigni man, dressed in a gray robe and brown cloak. There was a pack tied to his back, and it looked like there were several large scrolls tied to it.

The other two vampires moved themselves in front of the carriage. One dropped the carriage driver on the ground, leaving his claws stretched out and bloodstained.

"Ah, this is one of Areo's friends, if I'm not mistaken," Hidif said. "Your group has diminished since last I saw you... Where's your unsightly master? I still owe him the pleasure of slicing him into pieces."

Borely stopped a few meters in front of the nearest vampires. He worked to catch his breath rather than patronize Hidif with a response, and checked to see Analicia running up to join him. She stopped just behind him to his right and began catching her breath as well.

"And it's Analicia," Hidif said, her smile broadening to a grin. "Now's the time for you to join me, my dear. You owe me that much at least, what after saving your life and giving you the one you have now."

"I'm sorry, Hidif," Analicia said. "I have to help Borely now... We need to rescue Areo."

Hidif laughed. "You silly girl. I'm already in the process of doing just that. And I'm afraid I won't allow Borely to try getting in my way."

"You're after Areo?" Borely yelled. "Somehow I doubt you're hoping to free her out of the kindness of your nonexistent heart. Especially after it was her Rite match that led to your exile."

"Areo's no longer a person who can actually think for herself," Hidif said. "She's just a tool, and she will be best used by someone who fully understands a vampire's capabilities. She belongs in Istal, not in the hands of the Brotherhood. And once she's under my control, my world of vampires will never be able to be overthrown."

"Afraid of someone doing to you what you did yourself," Borely said. "And you're not even confident enough in your own power to protect what you've stolen. Instead you betray the people you worked with in order to greedily steal even more power."

"It's the vampire way," Hidif said. "If you can't understand that, my subordinates will be quick to give you a painful lesson in our ways."

"I've learned the ways of the vampires well these past few years," Borely said. "And of the two vampire masters I know, you're the blind one."

"I'd like to see you even attempt to lay a scratch on me," Hidif said.

Borely clenched the Hader in his hand. "As Nivakil's apprentice, and as Jenba and Areo's fellow pupils, I'll gladly be the one to bring you down."

Hidif turned to Analicia. "Are you going to let him fight me, Analicia? I am the one who saved your life. You know where you'd still be if it weren't for me."

"I do," Analicia said. "But for now, I'm sticking close to Borely."

Hidif narrowed her eyes and glanced to the other two vampires. "Very well. Go and kill Borely. She turned to Borely and added, "And then we will see which of our vampire ways is correct."

The two vampires working for Hidif were each dressed in black slacks and suit coats, and each had a pouch at the hip for Nexi stones. The red-haired man with a goatee ran forward, extending his claws further and further. Meanwhile the older-looking man with slicked-back white hair took out two Nexi stones—a green one and a light blue one.

"Stand back!" Borely yelled to Analicia. He held forward his Hader and activated its powers.

First he summoned a long sword with a red Nexi in its hilt. The moment the red-haired man swiped his claws toward him, Borely swung his suddenly-summoned blade across the elongating claws. With the red Nexi activated, Borely sent flames rushing down the length of the man's claws, and on to the rest of his body. The man screamed first from the broken claws, and then from the fire enveloping his entire body.

At the same time, the other vampire sent vines rushing toward Borely from the side. Just as the vines were about to surround him, sections of the vines froze and sprouted thin, jagged icicles straight for Borely. He was forcing ice Nexi energy down the vines and turning that energy into icicles from a far distance.

As Borely turned to face the icicles head-on, he caused his sword to disappear and forced a large rectangular shield to appear in its place. The icicles crashed into the shield, and Borely jumped back with their push to escape the ends of any free vines the vampire was controlling.

Borely turned and saw Hidif using a dark blue Nexi to douse the flames from the other vampire. The man's body was grotesquely charred, but Hidif was already slipping out a vial of blood to give him. He'd be back up and fighting in just a minute.

This was Borely's chance to take the older-looking vampire down. While the man was still surprised by the ability to summon weapons, Borely replaced his shield with a bow and arrow, already drawn and ready to fire. Gripping the Hader and the string of the bow, Borely aimed and fired at the vine-controlling vampire. Though Borely hadn't much experience with the bow, it wasn't a far shot. The arrow sunk into the man's chest, knocking him back to the ground. The enemy was still alive—the arrow hadn't pierced his heart.

As the man was gripping the arrow to pull it out from his chest, Borely replaced his bow and arrow with a tan Nexi. Before the man courld get on his feet, Borely used the Nexi stone to force a narrow stalagmite to jet out of the ground, piecing through the man's back and out his heart. The enemy's body turned limp, finally dead from Borely's series of attacks.

He regretted having to use the Hader so much already. The other vampire was fully healed, despite the charred remains of his clothes barely hanging over his body. Borely felt a little weak, but he knew he'd be able to take this man down. The only question was what to do once Hidif decided to enter the fight.

For now Borely concentrated on the remaining vampire. Though his wounds were healed, most of his hair had been burnt away, and the expression on his face was contorted with rage and fury. He wasn't going to be able to use his claws anymore, so Borely planned for whatever Nexi stone the man would use.

The stones were scattered on the ground, Borely realized—the fires had burned away the pouch. Just as the man hurried to grab the nearest of the Nexi stones, Borely used his tan Nexi to fling out another spike of hardened earth. The man leaped back just in time to keep from getting skewered, and the stalagmite happened to knock one of the Nexi stones toward him. He grabbed the orange Nexi and ran toward Borely. With the orange Nexi charging his entire body, the man sprinted faster than was otherwise possible.

Borely made his tan Nexi disappear and gripped the Hader in his right fist. His metal fistpiece glowed with its own orange Nexi, and he raised his free left hand toward the enemy. Just as the vampire was upon him, Borely elongated his nails into claws, stretching out for the enemy's neck. The man leaped to the side, straight to Borely's jet of water streaming from his headband. Aided with the power of the orange Nexi, the man slinked beneath the water stream and readied his Nexi-powered punch for Borely's chest. Borely powered his fist and slammed it into the man's head, crushing it. His skull shattered, and Borely used the next moment to lob it off entirely with his already-outstretched claws. The man's remains flopped to the ground at Borely's feet, and Borely let out a sigh of relief.

He heard movement and looked up to find ten claws flinging directly toward him. He leaped to the side, but the claws stretched out far too fast for him to avoid entirely. Even from this great distance away—at least five meters—Hidif was attacking him with her claws. At the last moment Borely kept from getting beheaded or staked through the heart, but there were claws pierced through his right arm and hand, his left leg, his left shoulder, and his torso. Knowing Hidif would use these claws to tear him apart from within, Borely fought back the pain and flung himself backward, ripping his body out of the claws pinned through him.

He stumbled backward screaming, but Borely focused on his Hader, struggling to quickly access its energy. A claw flung into the Hader, knocking it out of his grasp. The claw tore open the palm of his hand in the process, and blood poured out along with the blood leaking from all the holes strewn across his body. Borely nearly fell to his knees from the overwhelming pain, but he had to watch for Hidif's claws. Several elongated further and swung for his neck—faster than he'd ever seen a vampire manage, and never at such a great distance. Borely barely managed to duck beneath the claws, but there were already several more coming for his crouched body from his left.

Borely activated the Nexi in his metal headband and blasted the claws back with a jet of water. Using the moment to get back to his feet, Borely turned and deflected back the claws from Hidif's other hand. There was no way to keep back all ten of Hidif's claws though—Borely had to run backward to get out of Hidif's range.

Hidif did not stay standing in place, however. She easily ran forward, keeping up with Borely's wincing pace. Without his Hader, there was no way to defend against all these claws, and he couldn't keep running backward for long. Hidif swung her claws at him, and Borely leaped back as hard as he could. The claws still managed to claw across his chest and stomach, and Borely felt himself going dizzy as blood stained the ground in front of him.

He stumbled backward, realizing this was it. There was no way for him to avoid the next swing of Hidif's claws.

Something stabbed him in the back.

They were claws. Tearing into his back. Borely turned and found Analicia, driving her claws back and forth into his back. Borely fell to his knees, then flat on his face. His entire body overflowed with pain, and Analicia moved closer to continue swiping into Borely's back. She was screaming something, but Borely couldn't make any of it out. He found himself unable to move entirely. Had Analicia cut into his spinal cord? He lay limp on the ground, hot blood pooling across his back. And still Analicia was slicing him up.

Why? Why now? Why did she choose this moment to betray him? Borely found it difficult to think, to put coherent thoughts together. The situation seemed to make no sense, regardless. Analicia could have joined Hidif from the start and helped her fight him. But no... Instead she chose to pretend to be on his side. She chose to wait for the opportune moment to turn against him. To stab him in the back.

Hidif retracted her freakishly long claws into regular-sized nails and took a few steps toward Analicia, now standing a few paces in front of Borely's line of view.

"I did it!" Analicia exclaimed. "Just as he was about to run away, I made my move and finished him! I wish I could've seen the look on his face!"

Hidif stared over at Borely for a few seconds. She looked disgusted, and Borely could only imagine how his remains looked in this state. He surely had to look dead at this point. He couldn't move at all. He couldn't even breathe, he realized. Was he actually dead? No... he wasn't quite dead. He wasn't breathing, and he had suffered fatal wounds, not to mention extreme blood loss... But he was a vampire, and still just barely counted amongst the living. He wouldn't last long, though.

Hidif turned to smile at Analicia and tilted her head a bit. "I must say I'm surprised you denied my invitation to join me."

"I had to keep him fooled a little longer," Analicia said. "He trusted me, and I thought I'd be able to get him if he kept thinking I was on his side."

"That's why you specifically said you'd stick by him 'for now,' then," Hidif said. "I had thought this was a hint, but I couldn't be certain. Regardless, I would have finished him off myself easily enough."

"I was just worried he'd try to escape," Analicia said. "He has a powerful Nexi stone you could use, and I didn't want him to run off with it."

So that was it, then. Had Analicia ever really been on Borely's side? When he thought back, it was possible that every time she had expressed any kind of interest in staying with him, it could have been a lie. Once Jenba was dead, she didn't have any close friends left to turn to. But there was Hidif. She was never there for her, but at least she had been the one to save Analicia's life. Granted, Hidif likely did not actually care about Analicia at all—but in Analicia's eyes, did Borely care about her at all, either?

And all this time, Borely had been hoping he had crossed some kind of bridge with the small girl. Had helped her at least a little in overcoming all these trials they had faced together. Perhaps this was simply Analicia's vampire way...

"Yes... he was somehow summoning weapons out of thin air," Hidif said. "How did that work?"

Analicia pointed to the Hader, lying on the ground a couple meters past Hidif. "It's that stone there. You'll be able to use all the weapons you want with it."

Hidif turned around and looked at the stone. "Ah, is th—"

Analicia's claws slammed through the Hidif's back, and straight through her heart.

The child pulled her claws back out as Hidif spun around, elongating her own claws. Hidif's face was livid with rage. As she crumpled to the ground, she raised her hands forward to extend her claws through Analicia's face. With one quick swoop, Analicia sliced off Hidif's hands entirely. Hidif lay back on the floor, screaming, gagging.

In seconds she was dead. Without a functioning heart, there was no way for any vampire to live—even a master like her.

Immediately Analicia turned back to Borely and began rummaging through his pockets. She found a vial of blood and forced him to drink its contents. As Borely struggled to gulp it down, she got out another vial of blood and pushed that into his mouth as well. She searched each of the fallen vampires nearby for any more vials of blood, and found several more for Borely to swallow down. He still disliked the feel of blood in his mouth, but his vampiric nature loved the taste, and he was undoubtedly thankful for all the pain of his injuries easing away. Once Borely downed a third vial of blood, he felt his back fully repaired, and his other injuries properly healed. He ached terribly and felt weak from Hader use, but he was alive and felt fully able to continue the journey to Niez again.

He sat up and looked up at Analicia, whose face was specked with sweat. She looked even paler than usual, and as worried as Borely had ever seen her.

"I... wow, that was interesting," Borely said. "Thanks, I think."

"I'm sorry I had to lie," Analicia said. "But you were about to be killed, and I thought I could trick her if I made it look like I killed you... I had to take out your lungs and spinal cord to keep you from moving... And I had to count on killing her quickly and finding blood for you before you died for good... It was really dangerous. I was... I was so scared..."

Tears were gushing down her face. "I... I killed her. She saved my life, and I killed her... She... She was such a terrible person. But she was the only one who helped me. My parents were so awful. And she was the one who was there for me, when I had nobody else. And she was evil. And she was never there for me again. And all she wanted was to use me. And I cried and cried for months. And now I've killed her... And I'm evil too. And..."

Borely stood up and placed a hand on top of Analicia's head. "Stop there. You're anything but evil, Analicia. You risked your life to save me. And made an extremely difficult decision. Something no kid should ever have to go through. I owe you my life... again."

This child had somehow managed to play the role of a double agent, killing off a vampire master in the process. And thanks to her, they were going to be able to continue their journey to save Areo... together.

Analicia pushed her face into Borely's stomach and hugged him tight. She cried, and Borely let her. He knelt down and hugged her back, just letting her weep out all the pain and sorrow bottled up in her tiny heart.

•

Borely could hear someone sitting in the carriage, trying to get the horses to move. He recalled there was an eigni person with the group of vampires, and realized the man was trying to escape. Of course, the eigni may have simply been hoping to get away from all the violence that had just ensued, but Borely wasn't going to put any foul motives past the stranger. The eigni may have been in league with Hidif and her followers.

Borely patted Analicia's head and stood up straight. "I have to check on this man up ahead. You can come with me if you wish."

Still crying, Analicia nodded. She took Borely's hand and he helped walk her toward the carriage. After picking up the Hader from the ground, Borely walked up to the right of the stagecoach, away from the corpse of the human carriage driver. The eigni man was cursing, shaking the reins up and down in an exasperated frenzy.

"That's not how you do it," Borely said. "And I wouldn't be surprised if the horses were upset, since their master has just been killed."

The eigni sighed and slumped back on the bench hanging above the horses. He glanced down to Borely with a mix of frustration and resignation in his face. "You seriously killed them all? What... are you going to kill me now, too?"

"If you intend to fight me, I will fight back," Borely said. "Otherwise we could probably get by with a conversation. I doubt I'll take up your whole day."

The eigni leaned forward a bit and clasped his hands together. "What do you want to know?"

"We'll start with introductions. I'm Borely, a vampire from Istal, which recently suffered a large-scale massacre at the hands of the Brotherhood and these vampires you were with. I'm hoping to find a friend who's been captured by the Brotherhood. What's your name?"

The eigni turned away and frowned deeply. "I'm Trilir, a scientist. I specialize in Nexi energies."

When he didn't expound any further, Borely prodded. "You worked for Hidif, and her group of elite vampires?"

"No," Trilir said, shutting his eyes. "That woman kidnapped me. I was working for the Brotherhood beforehand."

"The Brotherhood," Borely repeated. "What were you doing working for the Brotherhood?"

"A variety of experiments," Trilir said. "Many of them have involved the energies of the Elpis stone."

"You've been working with Augurc Shire?" Borely asked, his voice rising.

"Yes, he's the one with the Elpis," Trilir said. "I'd rather not work with him, but it's the chance of a lifetime. Unfortunately it's put my life at risk, what with these vampires trying to force me to work for them instead."

"What experiments were you conducting for Augurc?" Borely asked.

Trilir sighed and gazed back down at Borely. "It would take a long time to explain them all."

"Just tell me what the main objective was for the primary experiments."

"Powerful servants," Trilir said. "The latest is a giant monster capable of destroying an entire city. Before that, a young elf who can not be killed. And before that was the experiment my vampire captors were interested in obtaining. A vampire woman with the power to kill any and all targets given her."

"Areo!" Borely exclaimed. "Where is she?"

Trilir looked worried. "I can't say where, precisely. She's with Augurc Shire, I'd imagine, and likely heading to Niez. Augurc mentioned plans to destroy Niez with his experiments."

"She's here!" Borely said. "Here in this area?"

"Yes... I..."

Trilir didn't get any more out, as Borely leaped up to the stagecoach and pulled the eigni off the bench. Borely jumped down with him and pinned him to the ground.

"Before I head off, let me get one thing straight," Borely said, his eyes ablaze with fury. "You were the one who turned Areo into the mindless killing machine she is today."

"I... I don't know who Areo is," Trilir whispered.

"The vampire woman who can kill any and all targets given her!" Borely yelled. "That was how you put it!"

"S-subject VI," Trilir said. "She was just a test subject. I didn't know anything about her. I didn't think..."

He stopped, fear filling his face.

"You didn't think what?" Borely asked. When Trilir tried looking away, Borely shook him hard. "Keep talking!"

"I didn't think anyone would care," Trilir said. "She was a *vampire*... And apparently one of Augurc's strongest enemies. I just operated as I was instructed."

"You turned her into a murderer against her will!" Borely said. "Who in their right mind does an experiment like that? You gave her all this power so she'd be forced to kill targets for one of the most twisted leaders in history! You are no better than Augurc himself."

"I needed to l-learn about the Elpis," Trilir said. "Augurc was the only one who could use it... I have to perform experiments in order to advance society..."

"Areo was a good woman," Borely said, gripping Trilir's shoulders tighter. "She was selfless, and always quick to make the right choice. You took away everything good about her, and made her suffer in ways no person should ever have to go through. You gave her a fate worse than death!"

"It's... It's possible to save her," Trilir said. "It will take a great deal of energy though..."

"I have this," Borely said, lifting a hand off Trilir in order to hold up his Hader. "This is a Nexi stone refined to combat the Elpis."

Trilir's eyes widened. "Is that... a Hader?"

"Yes. Will that be enough energy?"

Trilir took a few slow, careful breaths. "I can't be certain. I'd have to run tests..."

"I'll assume it's enough," Borely said. If nothing else, Rilv and her people were coming with their Haders as well. Borely would be able to either ask them to assist him or force their Haders from them if he had to. He couldn't back down now, not when he was this close to finding Areo. "What else will I need to do?"

"Subject VI's mind is linked with scenes of murder and bloody violence," Trilir said. "It will take a great scene of that sort to get her attention. At that point you will have to get her to stop following Augurc's orders, either by persuasion or by force. To free her mind entirely, she will need to access the energy of the Hader to counteract the energy of the Elpis embedded within her. If that will be enough. Killing Augurc himself would sever her Elpis-enhanced link to him, but her mind would still be tainted by the desires to murder in his name. But even if you clear her mind of those Elpis-embedded desires, her mind may still be damaged..."

"Even if I do all these impossible things, her mind still might be damaged?" Borely yelled.

"I've never tried undoing the enhancements given to my experiments," Trilir said. "It's entirely possible her body won't even be able to handle the energy of a Hader, given that it barely survived the power of the Elpis..."

"This isn't good enough!" Borely said. "You don't just have a machine or something to reverse the effects of your experimentation?"

"No," Trilir said. "All my research on the Elpis is new and unpredictable. It is an energy extremely difficult to tame, and even more difficult to utilize in any fashion. Not without the royal blood Augurc has."

"So you destroyed everything Areo was," Borely said, "and you can't even propose a safe way to make her normal again."

"I'm sorry," Trilir said. "But there's..."

"I should kill you," Borely said. "I should kill you right now. You're the monster who turned Areo into a Brotherhood servant. How could I ever, ever forgive such an act?"

He gritted his teeth and used his Hader to summon a dagger in his hand. It would be easy to plunge it into the side of Trilir's head. The professor was weak, completely unable to fight back against Borely from this position.

"D-don't," Trilir gasped, tears forming in his eyes. "Please... Please don't..."

"You dare to beg for your life?" Borely asked. "What about Areo? Did she cry when you performed your experiments on her? How much pain did you put her through, Trilir? How much suffering did she have to endure, just so you could glean some more about the Elpis?"

"N-no... Please, don't..."

"How many hours of torment did you put her through? How many tears did she cry as you subjected her to the Elpis energy?"

"No, I can't die... I don't want to die..."

Borely gripped the dagger tighter, pushing the Hader hard against his palm. "How many people have died because of your experiments? How many innocent lives have you forced Areo to kill? How much blood is on your hands, all in the name of your precious science? You are the worst of murderers, Trilir! You deserve no forgiveness! Not in this life—not in any life!"

"Please! No! Don't kill me! Please! No! Help me! No! No! No!" Trilir gagged on his tears, pitifully screaming and gasping out his cries and pleas. There was no reason to give this pathetic man any degree of mercy.

And yet... Borely couldn't bring himself to finish him off. The man's crying rang in his ears, a truly pathetic face grovelling on the dirt beneath him.

Why was he faltering? Perhaps there was still reason to leave Trilir alive. The man didn't know for certain how to save Areo, but he at least had to have useful knowledge pertaining to the Elpis. But Borely didn't care about the Elpis. He just wanted to save Areo. And kill Augurc, he realized—the one truly responsible for this horrendous situation. Could Trilir help him with any of these things?

Borely couldn't stand the thought of working with Trilir. He couldn't even stand looking at the pathetic excuse of a living, sentient being.

Borely shoved him against the ground and stood up. "Stay in this town. If you leave this town, I will hunt you down and kill you. Keep yourself hidden from the Brotherhood."

If the professor stayed in this town, Borely would be able to find him again if necessary. He doubted he'd need to find Trilir again after this, though. It was time to find Areo and put this Hader to use.

Trilir lay sprawled on the floor, gasping for breath, tears still streaming. He wasn't responding to Borely's demands, but it seemed clear the eigni understood his situation perfectly well.

"I will return," Borely said as he climbed up the carriage to the driver's bench.

"Are we really just going to leave him?" Analicia asked, following Borely up.

"Yes," Borely said. "He knows now to never experiment on people, or to assist murderous organizations. He understands now that it'll be extremely bad for his health if he were to use his knowledge of Nexi energies to harm any other living being in the entire world." He said this loud enough to ensure Trilir could hear every word.

The eigni shuddered on the floor, too afraid to sit up and look at Borely. Placing Trilir in a jail would be the best course of action, and Borely considered coming back to do just that once all this was over. But time was crucial, and the vampires had wasted enough of Borely's time as it was.

"Let's go then," Borely told Analicia. "It's time to find Areo."

•

With each passing day, Augurc had found himself growing increasingly agitated. He kept these feelings bottled up, letting them dissipate over time within him. He wasn't going to let himself become anything like his brother. The moment Augurc would be driven by blind passions, he would turn into Delkol. He would lose everything.

The darkness of the forest hid any irritation that may have slipped onto his face. He walked at a rigid pace with Subject VI and a few members of his Brotherhood. Everyone was silent. There was nothing Augurc had to discuss with these people. He only needed to focus.

Soon, many more people would get to witness the terror that was the Brotherhood. They would learn to fear Augurc, and they would learn to fear Augurc's experiments. Subjects VI and EV had proven themselves capable of fulfilling Augurc's demands, and would surely get the chance to shine here as well. And if Augurc felt he was ready, he'd be able to summon the might of Subject MI... Chances were he would save MI for the next stage of his plans, however.

Over the years, Augurc had suffered a great deal following the death of his brother. He did not mourn Delkol's death—in fact, Augurc had seen it coming, so it didn't even surprise him greatly. And in the grand scheme of things, it was best for Delkol to die when he had. The Brotherhood was formed, and Augurc had the means to conduct great experiments on a wide variety of subjects. But Delkol's death brought turmoil to the Brotherhood. Many were killed in the grand battle in Setar, and afterward there were many who defected, not trusting in Augurc to continue Delkol's mission of reuniting the continent under Shire rule.

It was true—Augurc had little reason to care for such petty aims. But he had to pretend he held his royal blood in high esteem. He had to pretend he wanted nothing more than to bring the Shire Kingdom to a new golden age. But the Shire blood meant nothing, and the Shire Kingdom meant nothing. People in general meant nothing.

People were weak. Humans, elves, eigni, vampires... They were all weak. Eternally lost in meaningless, petty squabbles. Everything people concerned themselves with was pointless. They fight over nothing, and then they die. What is the point of their lives? There is no reason for them to exist. They have minds, yet they don't use them. They lose themselves in their emotions. In hatred they kill, and when their loved ones are killed in return, they mourn in despair. An endless cycle of overwhelming feelings. It wasn't that emotion itself was entirely sinful—but as long as people were incapable of controlling themselves, there was no hope for a stable society. There was no hope for any kind of bright future, as long as people were left to do whatever they wanted.

People desire terrible things. Wasn't Delkol a perfect example of that? So was the Shire ruling body in general, for that matter.

And despite all of Augurc's efforts, the Shire royal families could never truly trust him. Most had continued to support the Brotherhood for a while to secretly encourage the disruptive acts across the Fiefs Kingdom, but it was only a matter of time before Fiefs retaliated against Shire. The majority of the Shire royalty did not wish for another war. Soon enough, they would turn against Augurc and the Brotherhood. Funding was already trickling down, and it wouldn't be long before action would be taken against him.

He was too powerful to contain, though. It was too late for anyone in the world to withstand him. The Fiefs Kingdom had failed to find an heir with enough royal blood to wield their half of the Elpis—it was useless to them. And though the Brotherhood had dwindled in numbers, Augurc's experiments had proven themselves capable of fending off large groups of trained warriors. VI could slaughter an entire troop within minutes, and EV simply couldn't die. And MI... MI had the potential to bring down an entire nation.

The more Augurc thought about it, the more he felt it was time to go to the next stage in his plans. Wreaking havoc in Niez would avail him nothing. It wouldn't further his goals. He had already shown the Fiefs Kingdom that his Brotherhood could not be trifled with. It was time to place that same level of fear in the Shire Kingdom.

It was the perfect time to do so, Augurc realized. Niez was near the border of the Shire Kingdom, the city of Zein just on the other side of the border. Zein would be much less protected than Niez, which was expecting attacks from the Brotherhood. It would be much safer to strike against Zein, and therefore much more effective.

Once the Shire Kingdom understood that it could never turn against the Brotherhood and hope to survive, it would be simpler to receive the funds the Brotherhood needed. The experiments would continue on, and Augurc would be that much closer to reaching his ultimate goal.

For one day, he would come to know how to control the emotion of all people. Rather than a detriment leading to chaos, emotion would be contained within each individual, and utilized in the most efficient manner possible. Augurc would come to craft a people incapable of falling into the meaningless cycle of hate and despair.

There would be no weak people left in the world. There would be a little Elpis energy within every individual. Everyone would help create a stable society, a bright future.

Augurc's thoughts lingered on his hopeful visions as he reached a meeting point just outside of Niez. It was a grove with several large boulders, one of them carved flat on two sides. Perhaps it was once the site for some ancient ritual.

Once Augurc reached the site, he found dozens of bloody bodies strewn about. A violent clash. There had to be at least twenty Brotherhood corpses, and a few other corpses Augurc didn't recognize. Only one living figure remained, standing on top of the flat-edged boulder—a small boy with short black hair. His pointed ears marked him as an elf, and he wore a black and silver uniform similar to Areo's. Subject EV.

"What happened?" Augurc asked the child.

"Vampires killed everyone stationed in the city," the boy said. "I killed all the vampires. Then I brought all the Brotherhood corpses here. City guards have surely seen some of them, though. It took hours to find everyone."

The child had done well—far better than Augurc could have ever hoped for in any single follower. Looking over the boy, Augurc saw the child's uniform was riddled with holes and claw marks. The boy's body looked unharmed, but it was clear the vampires he had gone up against were very powerful. Of course, that much was clear, if just a few vampires managed to take down over twenty Brotherhood fighters.

An attack on Niez would be difficult at this point. The city would be on high alert, and troops were likely already on their way from nearby towns. And if top-tier vampires had taken down Brotherhood members here, it was possible they had done likewise in the surrounding towns as well. A terrible blow, and a serious dent in Augurc's plans. He trusted in the power of the Elpis and his two operational experiments, but even their combined might could find difficulty in taking on an entire city—especially one prepared to face them.

With Subject MI, the city would certainly fall, but there was no telling yet if MI would work effectively. Augurc intended to test it out, but he wanted to test it out on a city he knew wouldn't succeed against him in the event MI failed to summon or operate properly.

"We will go to Zein," Augurc said. "You and Subject VI will take down any and all troops on patrol in the city. Any remaining Brotherhood members in the area will join you and assist. In the meantime, I will summon Subject MI and test its capabilities."

One of the Brotherhood members who accompanied Augurc spoke up. "You wish to turn against the Shire Kingdom? You may control your experiments, but none of us will ever accept such a course of action."

"You mean to question me?" Augurc asked. "If you wish to leave, by all means. Otherwise, you may regret speaking ill of my plans."

"I... I apologize," the man said. "I will assist as the Brotherhood needs me."

"I don't understand," another Brotherhood member said. "Why are we attacking Zein? We serve to better the Shire Kingdom..."

"Precisely," Augurc said. "The Shire ruling class is not unified. The leaders of our nation do not believe in us. It is time to wake them up, and make the people in all the land truly understand what the Brotherhood is capable of."

Nobody spoke up further. Whether they agreed with Augurc's plan or not, it did not matter. If any one of them attempted to harm him, he and his two experiment bodyguards would destroy them.

The Brotherhood was in shambles at this point, but Augurc had his experiments to rely on. The Elpis would not fail him now, like it did his brother.

It was time to usher in a new age of terror—one that would eventually lead to an eternity of strength and stability.

And it would all begin in Zein, the last place anyone would be expecting.

•

At the end of a thin alley, Shirm found herself lying on the ground, clutching her grandfather's lucky Nexi stone. Three vampires lay dead in front of her, killed by her hand.

It had all happened so fast. She had finally cornered one of them and drawn her sword, and suddenly a second vampire came from behind and attacked her. After one clawed at her back, the other leaped forward and nearly plunged his fangs into her neck. At the last moment she activated the power of the good luck stone... And somehow managed to slip away from both vampires, then kill them. Along with a third one, who seemed even stronger than the first two... It was a series of miracles. She was badly hurt from the first attack, but she was alive, and would still be able to keep fighting if necessary.

Shirm slipped off her mask so she could stare more easily into the soothing blue and gold glow of the stone. She could count on her hand the number of times she activated Grandfather's lucky Nexi. When he was alive, he had always warned to her to only use the stone in the gravest of emergencies. He said she would draw attention to herself if she used it too much, and her stone of fortune would ironically bring her a life of misfortune.

Grandfather had told her he had formed a contract with a powerful being within the stone—an ancient elf with unbelievable power, and more Nexi energy than an entire mountain full of Nexi stones. The contract enabled his descendants to use the stone, and Grandfather had chosen Shirm to be the one to have it. More than anything, Shirm wanted the Shire Kingdom to become a great, powerful nation. A land that would excel in every way possible.

She could still remember the first time she saw Delkol Shire. A man who truly had a vision for the future. There was no way she could turn down his call to join the Brotherhood—everything Delkol aspired to achieve for the Shire Kingdom was precisely what Shirm and her family had hoped for. Always hoping to keep up with her older brothers, Shirm trained for hours each and every day in order to become a respected member of the Brotherhood. She didn't hold any special position, but she could be counted on for any mission. And as long as she never brought too much attention to herself, nobody ever suspected her necklace contained an abnormally powerful Nexi stone. It was her last resort for whenever she was about to get killed, or when she absolutely needed to succeed for the sake of the Brotherhood's goals.

She wished she could have been there for her brothers, back in the battle against Setar. Or for Delkol. Not only had her beloved leader fallen, but her brothers also died in the face of the adversary. She could never forgive the Fiefs Kingdom. And she could never let the Shire Kingdom falter further.

Which was why she always felt so uncomfortable working for Augurc. Delkol's brother was powerful, but he lacked Delkol's vision entirely. Yes, Augurc always claimed to have the Shire Kingdom's best interests in mind, but it was clear his ambitions were thoroughly personal. All Augurc cared for deep down were his experiments. The Shire Kingdom could burn to the ground, and Augurc would only be concerned about how to fund his next freakish experiment.

Shirm had never cared for Augurc's methods. Delkol was fearless, daring, heroic—a true man. Augurc was... nothing. At the very least, he wasn't the kind of man who could incite any great zeal or fervor in the hearts of the truly loyal Brotherhood members. In the end, all Augurc could really trust was his own power, and Shirm doubted the Brotherhood could last much longer under such leadership.

What was she ever going to do about it, though? She certainly couldn't oppose Augurc. Though he was no Delkol, he was still the leader of the Brotherhood, and contention would not be tolerated. She would be killed in two seconds flat, and she doubted Grandfather's lucky Nexi would change that. Augurc had the Elpis, and even in a fragmented state, there was nothing more powerful than that.

Shirm pushed herself to her feet and put her mask back on. As she slipped her way down the hidden paths of the small town, she didn't find any more vampires. She did find her Brotherhood companions torn to pieces, however. Was she the only survivor?

Eventually she worked her way to a meeting point just outside town. There was a group of Brotherhood members gathered there, and they all recognized her quickly enough. She was smaller than the average Brotherhood member, considering she was a girl in her late teens.

"Glad to see you survived, Shirm," one man said. "Vampires targeted us in every town surrounding Niez. Many of us were killed in the surprise attacks, but it seems most of them have been killed off in return. They underestimated us in the end, but we've still suffered greatly."

"What are we going to do now?" Shirm asked. "What are Augurc's plans?"

"More survivors are gathering elsewhere," the man said. "There will be three groups total, likely with a dozen or so members in each group. Augurc will be traveling ahead with his top experiments. Our task will be to take care of any citizens trying to escape the city."

"Niez, right?" Shirm asked. Everyone was expecting Niez to be the target. It was a large city, and Augurc had been leading things up to a "grand finale" for some time now.

"No," the man said. He waited a few seconds before continuing. "We are actually targeting Zein. It will be an operation to force full cooperation between the Shire government and the Brotherhood."

Shirm nearly screamed "What?" At the last moment she bit her tongue, however, knowing that such an outburst would be read as disloyalty to the Brotherhood. Or at the very least, it would draw attention to her. She couldn't risk people finding out about her Nexi of fortune now.

"Zein..." Shirm said, hardly believing the word coming from her mouth. The very idea of the Brotherhood attacking a Shire city... One of the biggest cities on the entire continent... It was unthinkable.

And yet, she found herself marching with her Brotherhood companions toward the city, just the same. She couldn't argue about it, and she couldn't run away... She simply had to trust Augurc knew what he was doing.

Was this what she wanted to do? She never imagined the Brotherhood would turn against the very nation it was created to serve. What would Grandfather think of this? Or her brothers? Or Delkol?

Was there some reason behind this madness that she simply couldn't see? Perhaps all she needed to do was trust in Augurc, and everything would work out...

Just obey, Shirm thought. *Obey, and hope for the best.* She wanted to clutch her necklace, but she couldn't appear weak now. She had to keep up with the rest of the Brotherhood. She had to keep marching.

Her thoughts rested on the stone at the end of her necklace, prodding quietly against her heart. Would she find fortune or misfortune in Zein? If misfortune... would she be able to use the Nexi stone to turn the tide?

•

Once Borely spotted the airship descending in a distant part of the city, it was only a matter of time for Borely to lead the horses in the right direction. Fortunately Borely recognized the airship as having the same design as the one he had flown in back with Terico, Areo, and Lanek and the rest. This was definitely an airship constructed by Lanek, though this one looked in much better condition than the one Borely had been in several years ago, before he went to Istal.

It was evening, and the streets of Niez were largely deserted. Word must have got around that the Brotherhood had been gathering in the region, and people were afraid to get caught amidst the fighting between the Brotherhood and the city defense forces. Borely had noticed some Setar troops stationed in the city. The government was serious about taking down the Brotherhood once and for all, but Borely wondered if there was much hope against the likes of Areo and any other Elpis-enhanced experiments. Augurc himself also posed a considerable threat, considering he had found ways to utilize the Elpis that his brother hadn't. Unlike Delkol, Augurc had taken the time to study the limitations of the Elpis fragments, and knew how to use it without falling victim to the intense pain of its unbelievable Nexi energies.

Hopefully the Haders would be enough to defeat him and his experiments. Borely had a Hader at the very least, and he was going to combine his strength with Rilv and her team. Borely had to hope that together they would stand a chance against Augurc and his forces.

As Borely moved the horses along at a brisk pace through the city, Analicia sat beside him, hanging on to the side of the bench to keep from slipping off. Borely didn't want to delay meeting with Rilv and the others any longer than he had to—the sooner they got their plans ready, the sooner Borely would know how to go about finding Areo in this huge city. Niez and its sister city across the border, Zein, were two of the largest cities on the continent. Both were in difficult shape, but the people were resilient, hard-working citizens of their respective nations, and managed a stable trading system despite the tenuous relationship between the Fiefs and Shire Kingdoms. Borely didn't want to see these people suffer—or anyone suffer—and especially at the hands of Areo.

All Borely needed to do was free her mind, and then... Then he could decide what to do from there. He could thank Areo for saving his life, at the very least, and call things even between them. But perhaps there was more he could tell her. Perhaps there was more he needed to say.

He led the carriage to the side of the city the airship had landed at. It was an open field at the edge of the city, away from any of the major structures or areas where people lived. There were some worn-down factories in the area, but Borely didn't see many people around. Most everyone was probably at their homes at this point.

Standing a ways in front of the anchored airship were four figures. Borely was quick to recognize those nearest to him—Rilv and Kitoh. It was strange to see Kitoh this tall. The boy had grown quite a bit over the years, but he still looked about as troubled as Borely last remembered him. He wondered if Rilv's group had suffered any significant ordeals during their own search for the Haders.

Borely stopped the horses and carriage a few meters away, and raised a hand toward Rilv. She looked as professional and strict as Borely remembered her in their brief time together at Setar. She nodded at Borely, who got off the carriage and helped Analicia down after him.

"Thank you for arriving here quickly," Rilv said. "Kitoh is about to pinpoint the location of the Hader, as well as Augurc Shire's location."

"Good, we came just in time then," Borely said. He looked past Rilv and Kitoh and found Lanek approaching, carrying a few scrolls. Lanek looked much more troubled than how Borely remembered him. He had his hair in a ponytail now, and looked like he had aged at least ten years.

"How are you, Lanek?" Borely asked.

"I'll be better once this mission is completed," Lanek said. It was a terse answer, and very unlike the Lanek Borely knew. Borely felt he and Lanek had each lost a part of themselves over these past few years. Perhaps that was a large reason why they were both taking part in this mission. They both needed to restore some peace within themselves, and it was going to take something drastic to do so. Something truly meaningful.

"How about you, Kitoh?" Borely asked.

"I... I'm okay," Kitoh said. He looked more than just nervous... He almost looked ashamed to see Borely. Or could he be afraid to see Borely as he was now... a vampire?

"Don't worry, I won't bite," Borely said.

Kitoh looked up at Borely, flustered. "No, I'm not... I'm not worried about you, Borely. I'm glad to see you again. I'm just... It's just that... This mission has been..."

"It has been trying," Rilv said. "It will be over soon, though. We have three Haders amongst all of us now, and we will soon have a fourth. And potentially a fifth and sixth, if we run into Kechi once more."

"Kechi?" Borely asked.

"A servant of Mareba Shire," Rilv explained. "A member of the Shire ruling class. Not much has been heard of him lately, but it seems he has plans to use the Haders to conquer the Shire and Fiefs Kingdoms for himself. If Kechi obtains more Haders, they may pose a greater threat than Augurc Shire and his Brotherhood."

Kitoh accepted the scrolls from Lanek and rolled one of them out on the ground. He placed small metal rectangles at various points around the map, holding it down flat. They were instruments designed for locating points of strong Nexi energy, Kitoh explained, and the map showed all the roads and important structures of Niez.

Lanek folded his arms, staring down at the map with a frown. "So this was how you pinpointed where the Hader was in Velm?"

"Yes..." Kitoh said, suddenly looking very sad. "I drew a map of the village by hand, as Rilv instructed me. The Elpis fragments didn't give a perfect reading, but it was clear the Hader was in the area of the shrine. This along with the fact the shrine was forbidden to non-elves persuaded Rilv to investigate it."

Lanek sighed. "I'm sorry you were pulled into all this, Kitoh."

"I... I'll be okay," Kitoh said.

Rilv didn't look pleased with the conversation, but then again, she never looked too pleased, Borely recalled. She handed Kitoh the half of the Elpis Terico had gathered all those years ago. It was strange to see the shifting colors of the Elpis once more, and to see Kitoh, Lanek, and Rilv for that matter. Borely looked toward the airship and saw there was a fourth member in Rilv's group. Curious, Borely stared at the figure, trying to discern if he knew this person too.

It was a man in the clothes and armor of the Brotherhood. And the mask... It was a Brotherhood mask, but it had a smile drawn across it.

This was the man who killed Febraz and Suran. Borely was never really directly associated with either of these people, but they were important to his associates from five years ago.

"What is he doing here?" Borely asked, pointing at the masked man.

"Lynx is working for us," Rilv said. "His knowledge of the Brotherhood and its actions have been valuable, and he will continue to assist us in tracking down the last of these Haders."

"Are you serious?" Borely asked. When Rilv simply stared at him blank-faced, Borely took it as a *yes*.

He wondered if such a person could actually be trusted though—Lynx could very well be a double agent for the Brotherhood, after all. And how had

Lanek managed to work with this man? Suran was his sister, wasn't she? If Borely had been in Lanek's place...

"I'm not finding anything," Kitoh said. "The Hader isn't in the city, and neither is Augurc."

"Try the next map," Lanek said. "They may be in one of the surrounding towns."

Kitoh replaced the map of Niez with a less detailed one that included Niez, various towns in the region, and Zein. The eigni moved the small Elpis-guided instruments to this map, and then began carefully holding pins above it. He placed a couple pins just outside of Zein, and a third one a little further outside Zein, coming from another direction. It looked like both the Elpis fragments and the Hader in question were heading to Zein. Kitoh then placed two pins right next to each other on a point a ways outside of Niez. It was outside of civilization, and Rilv said this would be Kechi in his small airship, which had been following them all this time.

"If we hurry, we can get to Zein at about the same time as Augurc, as well as whoever has the Hader we're after," Kitoh said.

"Will this person with a Hader..." Borely tried to formulate his words into a good question. "It just seems unlikely for it to be a coincidence this person is moving toward Zein at the same time as Augurc. This person could be in the Brotherhood."

"Or someone who wishes to oppose Augurc, perhaps," Kitoh said. "It's possible there are others who have the same idea as us."

"Will our Haders be enough to take Augurc down, though?" Borely asked. "We could also be running into trouble with this mystery person who has a Hader, as well as that man in the airship with two Haders."

"I will ensure everything goes according to plan."

Borely and the others all turned, finding the Brotherhood member suddenly standing nearby.

"I operate best under a chaotic situation," Lynx said. "I will make sure we obtain all the Haders we need tonight. I will kill everyone who opposes us, be it Kechi, this mystery enemy, or Augurc Shire."

Lanek glared at Lynx for several long seconds, and Borely wondered if the elf was going to lash out against Lynx right then and there. Perhaps Lanek was the enemy Lynx would need to worry about most, before all this was over. Lynx simply stood in place, and nobody could guess where he was staring behind that mask of his.

There was perhaps no telling who would be fighting who by the end of the day.

•

Ever since the disaster at the elf village Velm, Lanek had found himself barely able to even operate his airship. It was something that always came naturally to him... but now he simply could not get himself to care to do anything properly. It made for a shaky ride, and he had to repeatedly correct the airship's trajectory to keep it going toward Zein.

Fenley was dead. He couldn't get the image of her torture and murder out of his head. It had all happened right in front of him. The fact there were psychopaths capable of such horror... It unnerved him. He could hardly eat or sleep. He could barely even think. That small village had held so much promise, so many possibilities... The chance to escape this dark world and live a peaceful, quiet life. The chance to rekindle something in his heart that had flickered into a thin stream of smoke. The chance to be someone other than a hapless nobody unable to move on after the death of his sister.

Lanek's thoughts of Fenley's death only reminded him more of Suran. Had she died in an inhuman way, just as Fenley had? The very idea made Lanek want to strangle Lynx to death with each passing second. That madman had ruined everything for that peaceful village.

No, Rilv was to blame too. Rilv and her obsession with capturing these Haders. And destroying the Brotherhood. Yes, the Brotherhood had to fall, but did they have to stoop down to their level? Did war simply bring out the worst in everybody? Did Lanek just have to accept that there would be innocent lives lost in this struggle?

He wanted to just break down and destroy everything on the ship. Let it go crashing down in flames. Just end everything. It was painful to keep living when he had ruined so many peoples' lives. What was Lanek now? He wasn't what he was just a few days ago. And he most certainly wasn't what he was back in Edellerston. Back when he had Suran, his parents, his friends, and a peaceful village life. Though life wasn't perfect, it was at least... a semblance of a life. What did Lanek have now? Nothing but a quest that may or may not give him some degree of peace or satisfaction or vengeance or something in his heart. There was no way for him to know if anything would work out. He had a Hader. Rilv had a Hader. Borely had a Hader. And so did someone else.

And Kechi had two. Lanek felt he could trust Borely to use his Hader well, but he had to admit it had been a long time since he was with Borely. The man may have changed after all these years as a vampire. As for Rilv, there was no way Lanek could count on her anymore. She was willing to do anything for her lofty goals, it seemed.

And in the midst of all this madness was Lynx, a masked man who admitted to operating best in a setting of madness. Lanek had to keep his eyes on him. If he couldn't kill Lynx right now, he had to be ready to kill Lynx the moment Lynx turned against them.

He glanced back at Lynx, sitting on the floor at the back of the bridge. What was Lynx plotting right now? Who was he watching right now? Borely and his Hader? Rilv and her Hader? Kitoh and his Elpis fragments? At any given moment, Lynx could try killing them all off and take all this power for Augurc. Or for himself. Who knew what the madman was planning. Perhaps it wasn't Augurc or his experiments or Kechi or Mareba or any of these other enemies they truly needed to worry about...

Perhaps Lanek needed to kill Lynx right now.

He wanted to do it. He had the power to do it. With the Hader, he could make himself immaterial whenever Lynx attacked, then make himself material again and stab the masked man in the neck. Then Lanek could take that mask off and wipe that smirk off Lynx's face once and for all. At least, Lanek always imagined Lynx was smirking beneath that mask. It was hard to imagine otherwise.

"You're not piloting the airship very well," Lynx said.

Lanek gritted his teeth. He didn't want to let Lynx make him angry. Angrier than he already was. "Okay."

"You need to do a better job," Lynx said. "This is what you're supposed to be good at. You need to pilot the airship better."

"You think this is easy?" Lanek yelled. "It's not simple to pilot an airship. Especially when your mind is a little preoccupied with all the deaths at a village that were instigated by a certain masked traitor!"

"Enough," Rilv said.

She said nothing more. As if just the mere word was all that was needed to calm Lanek down. He couldn't stand this royal servant. Did she think there was any way he could just keep working with Lynx like this?

"It's not enough," Lanek said. "This is insane. You and Lynx killed a bunch of villagers."

"They failed to cooperate," Rilv said. "Following entry into the shrine, we fought in self-defense."

"We were stealing their Stone of Truth," Lanek said. "We had no right to force our way into that shrine!"

"Perhaps if you had put forth sufficient effort in obtaining it, we would not have needed to take the Hader by force," Rilv said.

"Yes," Lynx said. "Perhaps if you had worked to fulfill the mission quickly—you know, like we were supposed to—we would have gotten the Hader and left before Kechi showed up and killed half the villagers. And the rest of us would have been saved a whole lot of grief."

"Don't you dare try to blame this all on me!" Lanek said. "Those villagers were good people! Stealing the Hader from them was wrong."

"Give me the Hader, then," Lynx said. "Hand it to me, and I'll take all the blame."

"There's no way I'm giving you the Hader!" Lanek yelled. "You're the scum of the earth! The worst type of person imaginable!"

"Tell me how you really feel," Lynx said, standing up. "You know, you could at least try to picture things from my point of view. Maybe I don't want to be this type of person. Maybe I'm working with you people because I'm trying as hard as I can to be someone better. Maybe it's extraordinarily hard for me to maintain any control of who I am, because I'm a product of severe experimentation! Maybe I should rip that condescending head of yours off your neck and take that Hader away, because you certainly don't seem willing to do what is necessary to achieve our objectives."

"Okay, let's stop there, please," Kitoh whispered.

"Everyone will stop," Rilv said. "Right now."

"You feel like you have absolute authority over all of us," Lanek said, "but you don't know when to quit. You go too far, Rilv. We have no good reason to follow you. You're not worthy of our trust."

A hand fell on Lanek's shoulder. He jolted back but stopped when he saw it was just Borely.

"Let's stop," he said. "Maybe Rilv isn't the kind, wise leader we wish we had. And maybe Lynx isn't someone any of us should trust. But we have to cooperate, at least a little while longer. If we fall apart now, we won't be able to obtain the rest of the Haders. And we won't be able to defeat Augurc or his experiments. That's what you and I wish to do at least, right?"

Lanek took a few quiet, shaky breaths. This was all so much to handle, but he had to handle it... "All right."

He said nothing more, and everyone else fell into an uncomfortable silence. The small vampire girl—Analicia, Lanek had learned—was clutching Borely's leg, nervous and afraid. Kitoh also looked nervous, but he mainly just looked depressed. How much had Kitoh emotionally burdened himself with after the devastation in Velm? Meanwhile Rilv looked utterly focused on the windows looking out to the fields below, and Lynx leisurely sat back down on the floor.

How long was this silence going to last? The minutes passed, but they felt like hours. Nobody wanted to be on this airship a minute longer. The sooner they got to Zein, the sooner they could find whoever it was had the Hader there, and the sooner they'd be ready to take down Kechi and get his two Haders. It was a fragile plan, but Lanek had to count on it working. He had to count on it bringing about the end results he had hoped for from the start. He had to hope it would leave him better off than he had been before the mission started.

With Rilv pointing out upcoming city landmarks from the window, Kitoh set up another map with his Elpis-influenced instruments. "We should be close to where the person with the Hader is. Really close."

Rilv stared out the window intently, and Borely and Analicia joined her.

"There are people on that trail leading into the city," Analicia said.

"Those aren't Brotherhood fighters, though," Borely said.

Lanek couldn't see any people at all. Their vampiric vision was even more uncanny than Lanek expected.

"Wait, there's movement in that grove," Borely said. "Just beyond that hill. It's... It looked like a Brotherhood uniform!"

Suddenly there was running. Lanek turned around and saw Lynx sprinting down the hall to the back of the ship.

screamed, getting out of his seat. Lynx was running away...

"Stop!" rejoin the Brotherhood!

Hurry

ship, you moron," Lynx yelled back. He was already forcing open

"p way in the entry room. The moment it was open, Lynx leaped out.

s that madman thinking?

ly the airship lurched hard to the right. Lanek got back to the

ls and readjusted the ship to keep it from tilting too far. Lynx must used a vine Nexi stone to connect himself to the airship, and bring imself safely down to the ground. Lanek looked out the window to find Lynx swinging forward with vines, quickly falling down to the earth. He was heading straight to the hill Borely had spoken of.

"Traitor," Lanek muttered through clenched teeth. "He's done it now."

"We do not know that," Rilv said.

"What are you talking about?" Lanek yelled. "He ran off the moment he found his comrades. Now the Brotherhood will know everything we're planning!"

"He didn't take anything, at least," Kitoh said. "We all have the Haders and Elpis, right?"

Everyone checked to be certain. Lynx hadn't sneaked off with anything important. But now he was free to wreak whatever havoc he wanted.

"We have to take him down," Lanek said. "Before he can give anything away to the rest of the Brotherhood."

"No," Rilv said. "Continue our course to the Hader."

"It should be close to here, actually," Kitoh said. "Or maybe just inside the city..."

Lanek watched as Lynx disappeared amongst the trees. "Keep an eye on him," he told Borely and Analicia.

"We are," Borely said. "There are a couple Brotherhood fighters moving to meet up with him..."

"Wait, look out!" Analicia yelled.

A giant ball of fire launched straight toward the front of the airship.

Lanek immediately turned the airship hard to the right, and the fireball barely missed the canvas blimp keeping them airborne. The massive ship didn't have Nexi cannons, so Lanek had to make sure the airship wasn't hit. It was simply designed to be fast and dexterous—not to be used in combat.

A flurry of icicles flew for the airship afterward. Lanek worked the controls to send the airship diving forward, letting the jagged shards of ice shoot by just in front of the blimp.

"Hang on!" Lanek yelled. At the sight of another huge fireball, Lanek sent the ship turning hard to the left, and then raised it upward to avoid a giant jet of water that followed. There were at least three Brotherhood fighters trying to bring his ship down. From this height, it was unlikely anyone on this ship would survive if it got hit.

"Get us out of here!" Borely yelled.

"Working on it!" Lanek replied. Pulling on one of the control ropes while pushing forward several levers, Lanek sent the ship forward faster, moving it past the hill Lynx had run to. The grove of trees was now just below them, and the blasts of fire, ice, and water were passing behind the airship.

Lanek didn't let up on any of the controls, working the ship to get out of the area as fast as possible. Kitoh could rework the map later to pinpoint the Hader's location—right now they had to get away from Lynx and his Brotherhood friends. They were clearly talented Nexi users, nearly succeeding at shooting down a blimp so high above them. Such accuracy was uncanny, especially with so much power being put into the Nexi attacks.

Once Lanek brought the airship above the city of Zein, he took the time to run a series of checks on the ship, making sure it hadn't been damaged in any way from the attacks. Everything seemed to be operating just fine, so Lanek turned his attention back to the mission at hand.

"We'll have to kill Lynx if we run into him," he said. "But right now, we have to find the Hader. Can you set up the map again, Kitoh?"

"Yes, it'll take a minute..."

Before Kitoh could begin, however, a gigantic burst of light arose from the center of the city. It was a pillar of blinding white light, releasing giant sparks of electric energy from its sides, connecting the dark, clouded heavens with the city structures below. For hundreds of meters around, the center of the city filled with white, ghostly smoke.

"There's something in there," Borely said.

"It's... huge..." Analicia added.

Something had been summoned right in the middle of the city, Lanek realized.

It was a monster. A monster far larger than Lanek had ever thought possible.

Than anyone had ever thought possible.

•

It was the hugest monster Kechi had ever seen. And it was right in the middle of one of Shire Kingdom's largest cities.

"Where did that come from?" Kechi yelled, keeping his hands firmly at the controls of his one-man airship. The city looked unharmed around the smoke-covered creature, so it had to be summoned somehow... But who in the world would summon such a thing? Who in the world *could* summon such a thing?

Kechi had been just about to push his airship to the limit in order to catch up to the airship his enemies at the elf village had escaped in. But now that airship was turning away, sensibly putting some distance between themselves and the gigantic creature that had just appeared. Kechi thought to follow his enemies and obtain their Haders... but there was no time for that now. Mareba Shire would not want this monster to destroy Zein. Saving this city was Kechi's greatest priority now. He was the only one who stood a chance, with the power of two Haders at his disposal.

Using the Haders as much as he had was putting a toll on his mind, Kechi acknowledged. He recognized he had become increasingly willing to do crazy things. Perhaps he had already gone completely insane.

Perhaps willingly going against this monster was the most insane thing someone could ever do. But he was going to do it. Whether he chose to because of the Haders' influence or not, he couldn't let this beast kill off thousands of proud Shire citizens.

The smoke dissipated, and the monster was revealed a ways directly in front of Kechi's little airship. It was... nothing like Kechi could have imagined. It stood on tens of massive, scaly legs, and reached out over city buildings with tens of half-decayed, burning arms. It was an incredibly wide beast, at least fifty meters so, and its back bent at five or six points. It towered well over a hundred meters over the city, with over a dozen different heads, each filled with hundreds of teeth—each larger than a human being. The heads were flattened and contorted, deformed and rotten, oozing red and yellow goo from its many scattered, different-sized eyes. It was in every sense of the word, a monstrosity.

Within seconds it was flattening all the buildings around it. The entire city was in a panic, people screaming and fleeing in every direction. The monster hobbled over the streets faster than Kechi anticipated—it wasn't a slow, lumbering beast. It pounded homes to dust beneath its huge, decrepit feet, and swung its freakishly long, flaming arms down the streets, killing tens of people with every passing moment. The beast was in a frenzy, destroying anything and everything in its path, and anywhere remotely close to it in all directions. Jets of ooze burst from its eyes, and buildings melted in seconds. Fire from its arms flew to the piles of ooze, and explosions began bursting apart dozens of the city's central structures. Hundreds of people were dying... Bodies lined the streets, and everywhere Kechi could see from his vantage point, people struggled in vain to escape the extraordinary reach of the monster.

Kechi sent his airship toward the monster as fast as possible. He personally felt his connection to any of these people was imaginary at best—he knew none of them, and was only concerned about them because he knew Mareba Shire would be. He couldn't let his master down. He couldn't let this city perish at the hands of some enemy Kechi had not yet discerned. Whoever was behind this would surely die—Kechi would see to that. He wasn't going to let any fools have their way with Lord Mareba Shire's glorious new kingdom.

It was time for Kechi to show that nothing—not even the world's largest, most powerful monster—could stand against the might of Lord Mareba Shire.

Kechi filled the front cannon of his small airship with all the red Nexi stones the ship was equipped with. With the ship flying at its greatest speed, Kechi frantically set a trajectory toward one of the monster's many heads. As he quickly drew closer and closer, Kechi couldn't help but laugh. This was a particularly wide head—one of the central ones, as far as Kechi could tell—and it had two mouths and at least a dozen oozing eyes. It was going to go burst to pieces... and amidst the chaos, Kechi would unleash all his power and tear this beast to shreds!

He laughed, knowing this was madness. He laughed, knowing this was suicide. He laughed, knowing his master would be proud.

The ship was now mere meters from the monster's head, and Kechi had set the large fire Nexi stones to detonate on impact. He turned around and ran to the airship exit, forcing the door open and jumping out. Kechi latched vines to the bottom of the airship via a green Nexi stone, and swung himself straight toward one of the monster's other heads.

The airship crashed into the head Kechi had aimed for, and a massive explosion ensued. The monster head blew apart in a collosal fireball that took out the entire airship and snapped the neck of another of the monster's nearby heads. The fiery blast sent Kechi flying straight at another head—this one flat at the top. He swung to avoid a snakelike tongue slinking out from this face's twisted, vertical mouth. The monster then snapped its long, jagged teeth toward Kechi, who activated his fear Hader with all the might he could. The beast held back at the last second, the fear invading its animal senses just before it could devour Kechi.

Kechi landed on the beast's head and accessed the power of the blood Hader. There was an endless supply of blood on the streets far below, and Kechi found that portions of the goo leaking from the monster's eyes also contained useable blood. Kechi immediately sent dozens of metalized blood scythes and lances plunging into the monster's head. The beast lurched left and right, and Kechi used blood to create handholds atop the beast's head, keeping him from falling off amidst the creature's thrashings. Being swung left and right pounded Kechi's body, pummeling him with deep bruises, but he wasn't going to let the pain get to him.

One of the other heads twisted down toward Kechi—several times larger than he was, and it seemed to be entirely made of mouths. It was quite literally nothing but teeth.

The many roaring mouths lunged toward Kechi, who used blood to push himself out of the way and leap toward another head. One of the beast's longer, more bent and jagged teeth sliced Kechi's left side and leg in the process. While in mid-air, Kechi formed a stream of his own blood into a pole which he slammed into the long, feathered neck of one of the monster's other heads. Kechi held on as this monster head flailed about, and the flat-topped head flung its tongue at Kechi. It slammed against Kechi's chest, and for a moment he felt all the life slip out of him.

Kechi swung off his pole of blood and caused all the blood he could to fly beneath him and form a thin path connecting one head to another. Several arms reached in to grab him as he ran, and Kechi caused spikes of blood to slide out from the sides of his path, impaling each of the claw-covered arms and tentacles jerking out for him.

The head of mouths slammed down directly in front of Kechi. He activated his fear Hader to frighten it at the last moment. At the same time, a head with a massive eye surrounded by teeth lurched to the side of Kechi and released a giant blast of red and yellow ooze. Kechi leaped away and caused all the blood amidst the blast to envelop the head decked with teeth. With all the power he could muster, Kechi caused the thick monster blood to squish the freakishly jagged head. The mouth-filled face imploded from the pressure, and Kechi quickly used more blood to stabilize his path to another monster head. Some of the eye-head's ooze had splattered across Kechi's body, burning holes through his clothes and on through his skin. The pain was excruciating, but he couldn't stop now.

He landed on top of a head that had tens of burning, human-sized fingers wriggling amidst broken teeth and a boiling pocket of ooze. Kechi commanded all the blood he could to form into long swords, all of which he sent flying into the torn-apart flesh around him. Using as much blood as he was capable of controlling, Kechi made the swords of blood at least ten meters long, ensuring the head was thoroughly impaled. A few heads were down, but there were plenty more left... And Kechi wasn't even certain the beast would die if he took down all the heads.

One of the behemoth's arms swung toward Kechi. He ducked beneath it, but immediately afterward a curved bone slid out and hooked around Kechi, pulling him back. Its sharp end dug deep into his torso, and Kechi screamed from the pain. He guided a sword of blood to cut through the bone and free him, but there was already a monster head spewing another blast of ooze at him. Kechi used blood to push himself down at the last moment, and the arm melted upon impact with the burning ooze.

Kechi fell to the ground, using blood from some of the killed citizens to slow down his fall. It was still a hard crash, and Kechi felt the wind knocked out of him. The giant monster was hobbling toward him, its cacophony of randomly-sized legs and deep, endless screeches filling Kechi's mind with a pounding headache.

Fighting this beast truly was insane... But Kechi wasn't going to let it win. He wasn't so weak, that a mindless beat could defeat him. He was Lord Mareba Shire's strongest, most faithful servant. He wasn't going to fail now—not when the Shire Kingdom had yet to reach the pinnacle of its glory!

Kechi pushed himself to his feet, realizing he was moments away from being trampled beneath the closest of the gigantic beast's legs. At the last second, Kechi leaped to the side of the first leg, barely avoiding the same massive claws curving out from the sides of the deformed foot. A massive foot covered in burnt fur was about to smash Kechi next—he sliced straight through it with a huge blade of blood, then ran forward through the next series of crisscrossing legs. A pile of ooze dropped down to Kechi's side, and he leaped the other way to avoid a tentacle with hundreds of vibrating claws writhing out from its sides. Once Kechi felt he was directly beneath the center of the beast, he commanded all the blood in the area to gather together and collide into a massive web of spikes and blades which Kechi caused to fly out in every direction.

"Die! Die! Die!" Kechi screamed, flinging jagged, hardened blood into every one of the beast's limbs he could reach.

Tens of the giant legs were impaled or cut apart, and the roaring beast began tripping over itself, lurching from one side to the next. Kechi was slammed in the back by a cut-off portion of one leg, then beat in the head by a small twisted foot that spiraled off another foot. His senses going in and out, Kechi forced his way through the maze of legs and piles of ooze, careful to avoid all the teeth and pillars of fire within the chaos.

Once past all the pounding legs, Kechi turned around and gathered all the blood from the streets around him, forming a giant spear of blood, nearly as wide as one of the monster's heads. The beast fell to the ground, destroying several more building in the process. But it did not slow down in its destructive course. Its arms suddenly unfolded and reached out for tens of meters—hundreds of meters. People were still screaming, running, dying.

"You dare to keep attacking my master's subjects?" Kechi screamed. "I will destroy you for your insolence!"

Tens of arms reached out for Kechi, and he immediately spun his massive weapon of blood through the air, slicing apart each of the arms. One was too fast for Kechi, however, and his left leg was impaled by an incredibly long claw. Kechi screamed and sliced apart the claw, and continued chopping away at all the other arms reaching for him. One arm decked with oozing eyes slunk toward Kechi from above, and he was nearly engulfed by its torrent of boiling pus. He realized his right arm had caught some of the spray, and his flesh was burning apart, turning somewhat gooey itself. The pain was overwhelming, but he could still keep moving. He could still keep fighting. Perhaps if Kechi didn't have the Haders affecting his mind, he would have given up long ago.

But somehow he was crazy enough to just keep going.

Kechi gripped his fear Hader tighter and accessed all the power he could grasp from it. At the same time, he gathered as much blood as possible above the writhing beast's remaining heads.

"Die, you stupid beast!" Kechi yelled at the top of his lungs. Several of the monster's heads stopped their approach toward Kechi, and the remaining arms began twitching uncontrollably. Kechi caused all his gathered blood to rush down at each of the monster's heads, hacking away at all of them at once. The beast was too afraid to fight back—it tried to flee, but the majority of its legs and arms were injured.

As Kechi sliced away at the creature's heads, he gathered together piles of the monster's blood, pushing large quantities of its ooze toward the base of its bent-up body. Through the pain pounding against every pore of his body, Kechi willed himself to keep layering the beast with more and more of the ooze. He nearly fell to his knees and keeled over, but thoughts of letting down his master kept him from giving in.

"It was nice playing with you," Kechi muttered, slipping out a red Nexi stone from one of his pouches. He threw it forward, letting a thin stream of blood guide it to the monster—right in the center of the top of its body, where all the creature's necks connected to. With what little strength he had left, Kechi caused the fire Nexi to explode.

All the monster's ooze covering its body exploded, blasting off what remained of each of its heads. The massive blast sent Kechi flying back, and for a moment it seemed all the city had erupted in a blinding, crimson light.

Kechi lay amidst a street filled with corpses, and to anyone who could see him, he had to look like a corpse himself. A half-melted bearded man lay atop his shoulder, and a small impaled girl was sprawled over his legs.

What weak people, to let themselves get killed like that. Kechi laughed. Here he was, nearly dead himself.

The monster had twitched for a few minutes after the blast, but Kechi listened carefully, waiting for it to stop moving entirely.

Once the street turned silent, Kechi knew the beast was dead for good. He laughed. Why had that monster been so difficult? Now Kechi couldn't even move. These bodies on top of him... He couldn't push them aside. The stench of decay all around him was nauseating. His body was filled with indescribable pain.

But it was all for Lord Mareba Shire. It was worth it. And as soon as he could, Kechi was going to stand up again. And he was going to find all those people with the Haders. And he was going to kill them too. He was going to torture them and enjoy every second of it. And then he'd have all the Haders his master needed.

It was going to be a glorious night.

•

Kitoh held on tight as Lanek violently turned the airship away from the massive monster that began crawling out of the smoke that birthed it. The sheer number of legs, arms, heads, eyes, and teeth... It was like a hundred giant monsters had been crushed into one incomprehensible, disgusting creature. The beast was clearly summoned, but Kitoh couldn't guess who would be responsible. There was Augurc Shire, of course, but what reason did he have to attack a city in his own kingdom?

At any rate, Lanek was driving the airship away from the behemoth, while Borely and Analicia held to the window to keep on the lookout for any of the people they were searching for. Kitoh clutched the map, Elpis fragments, and instruments he was using to locate the missing Hader user. The person in question was definitely in this corner of the city, but the arrival of this monster complicated matters.

"Enemy ahead," Lanek yelled as he worked to stabilize the airship. "It's passing us."

Kitoh looked out the window and saw a small airship in the distance. It was the one Kechi had used to get to the elf village, and to follow them all the way here to this city.

"Ignore him for now," Rilv said. "Our first priority is finding the one with the sixth Hader."

"What about the monster?" Kitoh asked. "It's destroying the city... It's killing everyone!" The monster had pushed its way down the center of the city, taking out everything in its path. Its arms crushed people fleeing in every direction, and its legs trampled all the houses and shops to rubble.

"We avoid it," Rilv said. "It does not concern us."

"What?" Kitoh whispered. He understood that their mission was important, but to just let this beast kill everyone?

"Look for a place to land well outside the creature's range," Rilv told Lanek. "Keep us out of its view entirely if possible."

"We can't just let everyone in this city get killed," Kitoh said. He was afraid to speak up to Rilv like this, but he couldn't just go along with everything she ordered anymore. He had been pushed around by her and her kind for years now... always doing every single thing he was told to do. It was that way back home in Vursa, and it was that way in Setar as well. And no matter where Kitoh was dragged to, he always found himself being forced to use his skills and knowledge in ways he didn't wish to.

And then the incident at the elf village happened. The massacre of Velm... It was something he'd never be able to forget. No matter what he did, he would never be able to undo all the deaths that transpired there. His hands were stained in blood. It wasn't something he could just pretend never happened.

And he couldn't just sit and watch as tragedy unfolded once again.

Rilv was ignoring him, so Kitoh spoke up louder. "We can't just run away. We have to confront that monster!"

Rilv turned to him and frowned a little deeper than usual. "We do not have the means to fight such a beast. Time is of the essence. As soon as we find this next Hader, we will have to confront either Kechi or Augurc. Whatever happens this night, we must be ready to destroy the Elpis once and for all. Do you have your tools?"

"Yes," Kitoh said. During the flight from Velm to Niez, Kitoh had been analyzing Rilv's and Lanek's Haders, comparing their energy signatures and the way their powers resonated under various circumstances. He combined his findings with all the research his team had conducted on the Elpis, and discerned a plausible method of destroying Nexi stones as powerful as the Haders or even the Elpis. With the residual energy of the Elpis fragments, Kitoh managed to create an instrument that would shatter the Elpis upon impact. Its properties were similar to the instruments Kitoh had created to detect high Nexi energies, but there was no way to be certain the destroying tool worked until he tested it out. Of course, Rilv didn't want Kitoh to test it out on one of their Haders, or on their half of the Elpis. Rilv was counting on Kitoh's skills and intelligence, as she always was.

As everyone always was.

The pressure was unbearable. He wasn't perfect. That much was made painfully certain, after all those people died in Velm. And now people were dying here. Should he jump out of the airship and use his transformative Nexi to become a dragon? Would he be able to take on the monster then? Or would he just get himself killed? He didn't want to separate from the rest of the group. And he needed to be there when it was time to destroy the Elpis.

Lanek found a small field to land in—a patch of dead grass between a number of old buildings. They were a good ways from the giant creature now, which appeared to be heading in another direction through the city. People were running down the streets, crying out, searching for their loved ones... It was a state of sheer panic.

"I saw lines of soldiers moving down one of the streets east of here," Borely said. "They were all getting killed off somehow."

"I didn't see Areo there," Analicia said.

"It has to be her, though," Borely said. "I don't think anyone else is that capable of killing so many trained soldiers like that. Except maybe Augurc. And either way, I intend to go there."

Lanek operated the controls to bring the airship down for a safe landing. "Let's stick together, at least. The entire city is a madhouse, and I doubt any of us are going to be considered welcome here in the Shire Kingdom."

"The monster will assist as a distraction," Rilv said. "If we ignore the Shire troops, they should ignore us. They have much bigger problems to worry about at the moment."

Lanek got up, and Rilv turned to hurry out in front of him. She pulled out her telekinesis Hader, and Lanek and Borely followed suit with their Haders. Kitoh followed after them with Analicia.

At the door, Rilv turned to Kitoh and asked him to set up the map and Nexi-seeking instruments one more time. Kitoh worked quickly to discern Augurc's location, which was in the region where the monster was located. Kechi was also apparently in that area, though neither Kitoh nor Rilv were certain if Kechi was involved with the monster summoning in any way. The person with the sixth Hader was inside the city, but quite a ways from their current location. This person was at the south end of the city.

"Augurc is there?" Borely said, pointing to the map. When Kitoh nodded, Borely turned to Analicia. "Are you coming with me?"

"Yeah," Analicia replied. "Where to?"

"Areo can't be far from where Augurc is," Borely said. "We'll use our vampire senses and find her."

"You can not leave us now," Rilv said. "We need to locate the next Hader."

"You and Lanek and Kitoh can handle it," Borely said. "I'll join back up with you as soon as I've rescued Areo." Borely looked to Lanek, and the elf nodded.

"Good luck," Lanek said. "I was hoping you'd stay with us, but I understand your desire to find Areo. If it were Suran... I'd want to head out there too."

"Thanks," Borely said. He leaped out the door, and Analicia ran out after him.

Kitoh had noticed Rilv clutching her Hader tightly, and even lifting it up a little when Borely ran out. She clearly didn't want the group to split up at this point, but starting a fight now would've slowed everything to a standstill.

"We must hurry," Rilv said. She held a hand out to Kitoh, and he gave her the Elpis fragments, as well as the small metal rectangles for Nexi detecting, and the larger curved block intended to destroy the Elpis with. She had told him beforehand that she would want to hold on to all these things upon arrival.

Rilv hopped down to the ground, and Lanek and Kitoh followed after her. They ran through the field and on down a dirt path through a run-down neighborhood, pushing through crowds of people hurrying away from the monster looming far in the distance. The creature's roars were terrible even from this distance—Kitoh could only imagine how traumatizing it was for all the people anywhere near the beast... Of course, anyone near it was probably in the process of being killed. And here Kitoh was, doing nothing to stop it. Perhaps he simply needed to understand that he couldn't go around saving everyone's lives, but he had a greater connection with Nexi energy than the average person—and therefore had a greater responsibility to use his power to help others in need. Terico wouldn't have wanted Kitoh to just let the people of this city perish... Even if this was a Shire city. These were still people, just like the people of any other city in the world.

It was difficult to keep up with Rilv and Lanek. They weaved through the panicking multitude, and Kitoh had to really push himself to make sure he didn't lose them.

An entire troop of Shire soldiers rushed out from between a couple large buildings ahead, and pushed their way past the crowds of civilians. Rilv, Lanek, and Kitoh suddenly found themselves caught in the midst of the troop and their weapons. None of the soldiers were attacking them specifically, but Kitoh worried they would be read as enemies at any given moment, and suddenly they'd have nearly a hundred armed men to deal with...

People began screaming. Louder. More violently. Soldiers were screaming. Kitoh turned left and right, searching for the cause of the commotion. All he could see were people running in every direction. And now Lanek and Rilv were gone... A soldier flailed backward, knocking into two other soldiers. A few meters in front of Kitoh, a screaming civilian fell over, bleeding everywhere. More soldiers were screaming, crashing into each other. The loud, screeching scrapes of metal against metal reverberated all around Kitoh.

Someone was killing all the soldiers, as well as any civilians in their midst.

Kitoh spotted Lanek, getting pushed aside by a couple soldiers. The Shire swordsmen were rushing toward the enemy, which Kitoh finally found a few meters to his left. A young boy dressed in black and silver. An elf, Kitoh realized. And the boy had long, wide blades grafted to his arms, covering them entirely on both sides.

The boy leaped toward one soldier and spun in the air. His blades sliced the man's head clean off, and immediately upon landing, the boy leaped at another soldier, stabbing him beneath the arm where there was no armor. Soldiers tried throwing knives or reaching for the boy with lances, but the boy simply dodged all the weapons. It was almost as if time was passing by more slowly for the boy, and this legion of soldiers had no hope of keeping up with him. One at a time, the boy killed each and every soldier that drew near him.

And these soldiers weren't poor swordsmen or lancers—they were wielding their weapons well. A number of them came together behind the boy and attacked him at the same time. The boy spun around and slashed away at their weapons, deflecting them. But at the same time, a swordsman slipped past some civilians that kept him hidden to the boy's right. The man swung his sword through the boy's side, and Kitoh thought it was all over.

Instead the boy sliced the man's head off, and proceeded to take down each of the other soldiers that attacked him all at once.

Lanek grabbed Kitoh's hand and tried helping him past the last of the gathering soldiers. The elf boy in black slipped past the soldiers surrounding him and began taking down the soldiers in front of Lanek and Kitoh. A couple civilians were killed in the process, and Kitoh realized this child intended to kill each and every single person in this area. Ahead, Kitoh spotted Rilv running toward them, using her telekinesis Hader to push aside a couple soldiers who rushed in front of her, likely recognizing her Fiefs royal uniform. A couple other soldiers spotted Kitoh and Lanek, and yelled out to them, curious what an eigni and elf were doing here.

Before these soldiers could reach them, however, the child with arm blades tore through a few more people and continued running straight into these soldiers, the mangled bodies of his previous victims still impaled through his blades. The child was much faster and stronger than anyone his age had any right to be. He had to be about five years younger than Kitoh... The age Kitoh was when he was first dragged into a series of terrifying adventures.

This child is an experiment, Kitoh realized. This was one of Augurc's Elpis-powered experiments. The very idea that Augurc would use a young boy as a weapon like this...

No, it wasn't that inconceivable. After all, how different was Kitoh? From the very beginning, he had been regarded as a powerful entity... A tool to be used by those above him. A means for achieving specific, bloody goals.

This boy was like Kitoh, but had been driven to the point of losing his mind entirely...

"Look out!" Lanek yelled. He pushed Kitoh aside and activated his Hader. The experiment boy sliced his arm blades straight through Lanek and stumbled forward. Just in time, Lanek had made himself immaterial, saving his life.

The boy recovered instantly and took down another soldier in his way. He tore apart the man and leaped back straight to Kitoh. Immediately Kitoh slipped out a dark blue Nexi and blasted the experiment boy with an especially wide jet of water. Had it been a normal-sized attack, the boy would have easily dodged, but Kitoh knew he couldn't hold back against this opponent. And at this point, Kitoh knew there was no escaping this child. He had to defeat him...

"We need to get out of here!" Rilv yelled, pushing aside a soldier via telekinesis.

Suddenly the child was behind Rilv, about to stab her in the back.

Kitoh turned and blasted a thin, powerful jet of water at the child, careful to keep from shooting Rilv's head or shoulder. She crouched down and Kitoh expanded the blast, moving it toward the experiment boy as he turned back into the crowds.

The boy ran straight into a soldier's lance, impaling him straight through the chest.

Kitoh sighed. It wasn't the ending he wanted... He truly hoped he could have thought of a way to save the poor boy. But what hope was there, really?

The boy leaped back and tore out the lance from his chest. There was a gaping, bleeding hole in the boy's body, but he immediately began jabbing his arm blades into the soldier that dealt him the blow.

Without screaming, without stopping for a second... The boy was attacking more of the soldiers and civilians in the area. What few of them were left.

Kitoh remembered Augurc's experiments on some of his captured Brotherhood members. Back in the battle for Setar, some members of the Brotherhood were capable of fighting on and on, regardless of their injuries. But this was on a different level entirely. This boy was fighting despite wounds that should have been utterly fatal.

Amidst the boy's frenzy, Kitoh noticed the child's huge injury had healed entirely. There was a hole in his shirt, but nothing more, save for some blood that had spilled out back when there was a hole through his body.

The last of the soldiers were finished off—it was just Kitoh's group and a few injured civilians left. Kitoh slipped out his transformative Nexi stone. Would he be able to kill this boy if he had to? He didn't want to... He didn't want to stoop to that level. This boy didn't want to be killing these people. If only Kitoh knew how to save him...

Lanek used a green Nexi to send vines toward the boy. As the boy sliced apart all the vines, Rilv used telekinesis to drive a sword through the back of the boy's head, the blade sticking out the right side of the front of his face. Kitoh gasped, and the boy stumbled down to his knees.

"Good, now let us hurry," Rilv said. "We do not..."

She stopped as the boy stood back up and wrenched the sword out of his head, his arm blades scraping hard against the metal of the sword. Without even a moment's hesitation, he was rushing toward Rilv. She jumped back and used her Hader to push the boy back. He flung backward several meters, but landed on his feet. Lanek released a burst of ice Nexi energy to try capturing the boy by his feet, but the child was too quick, leaping hard to the side immediately upon landing.

There was no way to kill this boy, Kitoh realized. It was simply impossible. The Elpis was used in some way to make it so the boy would survive any painful injuries, and regenerate in the event of a fatal blow.

Rilv used her Hader to send several weapons flying at the boy from multiple directions. The boy was prepared for telekinesis now, and managed to avoid all the attacks. Lanek took out a fire Nexi and released a wave of fire at the boy, which the child leaped straight through. The boy's blade nearly lobbed Lanek's head off, but he managed to wield his immaterial Hader just as the blade cut into his neck. As the boy passed him, Lanek stumbled forward, clutching his bleeding neck.

Before the boy could turn and stab Lanek in the back, Kitoh shot off another blast of water to keep the boy back. Kitoh knew none of his attacks would actually kill the boy, or even harm him... So what was he going to do?

As the boy dodged Kitoh's water blasts, Rilv used a purple Nexi stone to create explosions of violent energy all around the enemy. The boy was pummeled back and forth, and any normal human being would have surely been killed in the process. Instead, the boy fell to the ground and immediately ran straight for Rilv.

At the last moment, Rilv caused a sword to fly in her grasp, and she plunged the blade straight through the boy's neck, severing his head entirely. The boy's body crashed into Rilv, who barely managed to avoid the ends of his blades. The sides of his weapons cut into her as they fell to the ground, and Kitoh ran over to check if she was all right. Gasping, Rilv shoved the boy's headless body aside and clutched at a deep cut in the side of her stomach, and another in her right arm.

"I will be fine," Rilv said. "I only need bandages. Check on Lanek."

"I'll live too," Lanek said quietly, still clutching his neck. "Just get me some bandages."

Kitoh had some on him in a pouch, but he felt certain this battle wasn't over yet. If the boy could survive getting impaled through the heart...

Kitoh looked to the boy's corpse. Something was growing from its severed neck... A thick, bloody mass... A portion of it turned to bone, then eyes formed, and teeth and flesh... Then all the same elements of the boy's face that existed on the boy's severed head, which was still lying on the ground. In a matter of seconds, the boy regenerated his entire head.

Fully alive and well again, the boy ran straight for Kitoh.

There simply was no way to kill him. And with Rilv and Lanek both injured...

Kitoh leaped back to Lanek and grabbed his Hader from him.

Without warning, Kitoh found himself in a different setting entirely. The street was gone, as were all the corpses, and the buildings, and the screams of the distant monster... In their place was a graveyard.

Lanek had told Kitoh about the graveyard world within the Hader... as well as the goddess who inhabited it. Reali, he had called her. One of the divine beings the elves worshiped in that village. Kitoh had not had the time to dwell too much on what any of this entailed, but now he had to decide how he was going to use the power of the Hader to stop the experiment boy. This reality existed outside of time, so Kitoh at least had the chance to think of a plan.

"Another visitor so soon," a voice said.

Kitoh looked and found an elf in a black and white dress—a woman in her twenties. She approached him slowly, cautiously.

"Hi," Kitoh said. "My friends were in trouble, so I grabbed the Hader... I was just planning to use it to defend myself against the enemy, but I ended up here. I guess anyone who wishes to use the Hader is sent here... And I take it you are Reali? My friend told me about you."

"Yes," the woman said. "Your friend said he would use my power for good purposes. Has he done so?"

"He hasn't had much chance to yet," Kitoh said. "I haven't been able to do much good yet either. Our mission has been very... difficult."

"You wish to use my power to defend yourself against an enemy?" Reali asked.

"I don't know," Kitoh said. "I mean... yes, I want to defend myself... But I don't really want to hurt this boy. He's an elf like you, but his mind's been altered by a strong Nexi power—the Elpis. He's just being used. He can't help himself..."

"He reminds you of yourself," Reali said.

Kitoh bit his lip and looked to the ground. "Yes... but I can at least choose what I wish to do. If I really try and stand up for myself... I can achieve something good with my own power."

"Your power alone is not enough to save that boy," Reali said. "Your connection to Nexi energy is great, though. Enough that you can become one with my power."

"What do you mean?" Kitoh asked.

"My power is the power to transcend realities," Reali said.

Kitoh thought over it for a minute. "So... with your power, I could slip in and out of existence... Would I be able to take others with me?"

"If you are strong enough," Reali said. "I am willing to lend my power, and let you try. Are you willing to transcend your own reality?"

Kitoh clamped his hands tight into fists. "You mean... am I willing to die..."

"That is one way of looking at it," Reali said. "The Nexi essence spans across many realities, connecting all the powers and truths a single being can come to hold and understand. Your mind is much clearer, must stronger than any other I have ever seen. If you wish to save that child, I believe you will find a way to do so."

"If not in this reality, then perhaps in another," Kitoh said.

"You may find the answers to all the questions you seek in another realm," Reali said.

Kitoh took a deep breath, and chuckled a little. It was a nervous laugh. He wasn't sure if this was the right course of action to take. Was this his path? He was born with a greater connection to Nexi energy than anyone his people had known for centuries. And yet he had never chosen anything for himself. He was always regulated to fulfilling duties for those in power, wherever that might be. Would that trend continue forever? Perhaps Lanek and Borely and the others would be able to change the world for the better. But what would Kitoh do then? Would he ever get to choose?

This was his chance to take a step forward—in a direction he chose to travel. There was nobody telling him to seek truth in another reality.

And this was his chance to save a life. And if he could save this elf boy's life, perhaps he could learn how to save the lives of everyone else experimented on by Augurc and the Brotherhood.

"I'll do it," Kitoh said. "Reali, please lend me your power. Once I transcend my reality... please resume your contract with Lanek."

"I will be curious to see how far you will go," Reali said.

She disappeared, and so did the graveyard. Kitoh found himself back in Zein, and the elf boy was leaping straight toward him, arm blade raised forward.

Kitoh stepped to the side of the arm blade and thrust his hand forward, pushing the Hader against the elf boy's chest. Immediately upon impact, Kitoh activated the power of the Hader.

His mind cleared, and his body felt light... then lifeless.

He vanished, and the elf boy vanished with him.

Kitoh found himself enveloped in white light, then darkness, then nothingness.

And then... another world. He stood in a bright, grassy field, and the elf boy lay on the ground, unconscious.

The elf boy wasn't prepared to transcend his reality—Kitoh had forced it upon him. The boy was still alive though, and Kitoh knew he could find a way to free the elf's mind. This was a reality with a much greater connection with Nexi energy... The possibilities were endless, Kitoh felt.

He smiled. He was free. For all intents and purposes, he had died...

And yet he never felt more alive.

•

•Part XI•
MADNESS OVERWHELMING

As Lynx had hoped, Lanek managed to pilot the airship well enough to avoid all the Brotherhood's attacks. Lynx had grown a little worried when Lanek had started getting sloppy with his piloting skills, but the elf fortunately pulled through in the end.

There were nine Brotherhood members gathered here, not including Lynx himself. He felt certain one of these people had the Hader that Kitoh had detected. A Brotherhood member would be strong enough to form a contract and utilize the power of a Hader. Lynx just had to keep pretending he was truly on their side.

One of the Brotherhood fighters cursed as Lanek's airship got out of range of their Nexi stones.

"Don't worry, they will land somewhere in the city," Lynx said. "We can ambush them then."

"Lynx, what is the enemy planning?" a large man asked. Lynx recognized him as a higher-up in the Brotherhood—a bald man who wielded a giant axe and went by the codename Iron.

"The enemy has obtained abnormally powerful Nexi stones they intend to use against us," Lynx said. "They believe these stones have the power to withstand the might of Augurc and the Elpis."

"Impossible," Iron said. "But regardless, we must bring them down."

"The stones do pose a threat," Lynx said. "One is capable of granting the user telekinesis, and another allows the user to become ghostlike, able to pass through solid objects. Augurc has asked me to retrieve these Nexi stones so he can study them for future experiments. He wishes to collect all Nexi stones that hold significant power, regardless of their ability." Lynx looked from one Brotherhood member to the next, to see if any of them reacted in a particular way to his words. Unfortunately everyone wore a mask, so it was difficult to read what any of them were thinking. At the very least, none of them spoke up to reveal they had a Hader.

"Understood," Iron said. "We will seek them out and retrieve their Nexi stones."

"Wait a second," one of the other Brotherhood fighters spoke up. A tall, lanky man with green hair. "If you really are Lynx, you would have been able to kill everyone in that airship and take their Nexi stones yourself."

Lynx understood he had a reputation amongst the Brotherhood as one of Augurc's top agents. Over the years he had been given many of the organization's most dangerous missions.

"I tried to take them by surprise," Lynx said, "but as I mentioned, their Nexi stones are extremely advanced. Against multiple enemies, it was simply too much to handle. I timed my attack so that if I had to, I would be able to escape and call in the assistance of other Brotherhood members. Unfortunately you all failed to shoot the airship down."

Emphasizing the power of the Haders and shifting some blame to these Brotherhood fighters seemed to accomplish what Lynx had hoped. Nobody refuted him any further.

"I recognize him as Lynx," Iron said. "If he says he was overwhelmed, then it only means we must take these enemies seriously."

"What are your current orders?" Lynx asked Iron.

"Simply to assist in the invasion on Zein," Iron said. "Augurc is instigating a central attack with his three working experiments—primarily that monster he's summoned... We were asked to take down as many people as possible escaping the city."

Augurc just wanted the Brotherhood out of the way, Lynx realized. This was a massive operation designed to push his experiments to their limit, and perhaps a test of the Brotherhood's loyalty.

"Everyone has agreed to this?" Lynx asked.

"Of course not," one of the Brotherhood members said. A smaller man with a deep voice, perhaps in his late thirties. "It makes no sense for us to attack a Shire city."

Iron turned around and unclipped his axe from his back, pointing the end of it directly in front of the mask of the man who spoke up. "If you wish to run away like all those other cowards, you best do so now. Augurc's orders are law. You may not understand the purpose of each and every mission you are given, but as a member of the Brotherhood, you must fulfill your duties absolutely as you are commanded."

"Yes..." the man said. "Of course."

Perhaps he was the one with the Hader. It made sense for someone questioning Augurc at this time to not admit to having it.

Iron turned back to Lynx. "Of course, we will make it a priority to assist you in retrieving these Nexi stones. How many of us do you require to assist you?"

Lynx looked from one Brotherhood member to the next. He couldn't just have them all come with him.

"Do any of you know or have any kind of experience with abnormally powerful Nexi stones?" Lynx asked. "Or have any knowledge of someone else in the Brotherhood who does?"

Nobody spoke up. Lynx looked to each masked member, trying to read any kind of subtle body language. One person glanced to the side a bit... Was that a sign he knew of a Hader, but didn't want to admit it?

"If anyone knows anything, it's going to be you," a man with a bow and arrow said. "What's the point of asking this? We're wasting time."

Lynx wondered if this man should be regarded as suspicious as well. This man might be eager to get to the city so he could escape with the Hader amidst the chaos.

"We can split up into three groups," Lynx said. If it came to a fight, he felt he could take on up to three members at a time. "Three of you can come with me." He pointed to the three he felt were most likely to have the Hader, based on what extraordinarily little information he had to go off of.

The other two groups formed, with Iron leading one of them, and a small Brotherhood member with long brown hair leading the other. Lynx realized this member was a woman, which was a bit rare in the Brotherhood. There was no evidence, but she could have reason to keep a Hader secret, if she had been using it in order to get into the Brotherhood.

"We will follow the airship to where it lands," Lynx said. "Where will each of your groups go?"

"We will remain south of the monster," Iron said. "If we clear the area, we will head east."

"We will stick west of the monster," the woman said—a rather young woman, judging by her voice.

"Okay, let's go then," Lynx said. He didn't wish the other groups luck. There was a fair chance Lynx was going to be killing many of these people shortly.

He hated to give in to killing people, even if they were his enemies. It was difficult to maintain any semblance of his true self once he started killing... It had been so deeply embedded in his mind and heart that it was right to kill for Augurc, that it was right to end people's pitiful existences...

Somehow, Lynx had to free his mind. Year after year, he had struggled to even think for himself, let alone overcome the overwhelming influences on his emotions. It had taken a very long time for him to reach this point... to be capable of working against Augurc at all... He couldn't fail now. He had to obtain the Haders. Somehow he had to believe they would be powerful enough to save him. If he couldn't find a way to use the Hader to free his mind, then perhaps Kitoh could figure something out. Or even the professor Trilir, if Lynx had to hold up his facade as a Brotherhood member. What mattered was that he obtain a Hader... He had betrayed many people to reach this point—he couldn't stop now.

Lynx led the three Brotherhood members he chose into the city. There were people running as far away as they could from the monster, though some found vantage points from which to gaze in shock at the gigantic beast. As soon as some of the monster's freakishly long arms moved in their direction, they were quick to break out of their stupor and flee.

Lynx could only guess what the rest of the Brotherhood was feeling deep down. These were people they had intended to protect all their lives— people they were willing to fight for and die for. Augurc's ability to summon such an incredible monster surely left many members of the Brotherhood in a state of amazement—perhaps even worship. But for some, the monster surely represented not a wonderful power, but a terror that should have never existed in the first place. Would Augurc's actions this day weed out the unbelieving and make the Brotherhood even more zealous, even more blind and ambitious? Or would the Brotherhood finally crumble and fall, just like these city buildings?

Lynx brought his team through a crowd of soldiers, which was likewise pushing its way through a crowd of citizens. It was time to take on his teammates, one at a time... The best way to find out who had the Hader was to push him to use it.

Lynx weaved between people and sneaked behind one of his teammates. The man turned around just as he realized what was happening. Lynx slashed him across the neck with his knife.

It was unlikely this man had the Hader...

Before the other two members of the team could notice, Lynx sneaked between more people, some of them screaming upon seeing the dead Brotherhood fighter amongst them—but many of the people were screaming already anyways. Lynx spotted one of his teammates and stabbed him in the back. The man spun around and swung his sword at Lynx, who dodged, then drew his own sword to defend against the following swings. It was impressive how well the man could fight while stabbed in the back, but Lynx noted he wasn't reaching for any Nexi stones.

It took a minute to finish him off, by which point the other member of the team had spotted Lynx's betrayal. The man powered his lance with a white Nexi stone, and released a bolt of lightning. Lynx grabbed the man he fought off and used him as a shield. The corpse was shot by the lightning, and Lynx sprinted with his sword drawn forward. The man took out a green Nexi and sent vines for Lynx from multiple directions. Knowing the man would shoot another bolt of lightning at wherever the vines forced Lynx to go, Lynx threw his sword forward. It landed straight in the man's neck.

With all three down, Lynx worked quick to check all their pockets and pouches, just to make sure they didn't have the Hader. As Lynx expected, they only had a few normal Nexi stones. He hurried to where he imagined the Brotherhood group that moved to the western side of the city would be. Some of the Shire soldiers tried attacking him, witnessing Lynx's murder of the three Brotherhood members, but Lynx was too quick for them.

He ran up and down several streets, searching for any sign of Brotherhood members. He had noted where the group had run toward, but he couldn't find any places where people were getting killed off. The Brotherhood team had to be somewhere near the edge of the city, down one of the primary paths... They were probably able to kill all the civilians they wanted, and the Shire troops would be too busy fighting off Augurc's experiments to interfere. A thoroughly reprehensible operation, and yet deep down Lynx could feel some measure of glee in it all.

Wasn't life filled with suffering? The only way to enjoy life was to be the one making others suffer. It was the only to take your mind away from your own suffering...

He had already stained his blade. He could keep going. Just go along with the orders to kill as many people as possible.

No. He couldn't let himself sink to that level. Not again. He had killed enough. Enough for a hundred lifetimes. He wanted the pain to end. If it was possible for it to end.

He had to believe it could end. It was the only way for him to keep living. And he had to keep living. He had to turn his life around. Amend all his wrongs, at least to some small degree.

At last, he spotted a Brotherhood member. A figure sitting at the top of a zig-zagging staircase, leading to the fourth story of an old, weathered brick building. It was the young woman, and she was crouched down, her masked face in her hands. Where were her two companions? Lynx searched amongst the people below, and nobody appeared to be getting killed by anyone.

Lynx hurried to the stairway and ran up it. The woman stood up and turned to run.

"Wait!" Lynx yelled.

She ran across a wood board that acted as a thin bridge between two buildings. She was climbing to the roof of that building as Lynx reached the top of the stairway of the first building.

He looked to her hands and saw it. In one of her fists was a Hader, glowing blue and gold.

"Hold on!" Lynx called out. He ran onto the long wood plank, which inexplicably broke apart as he reached its center. It was thick and sturdy—why did it suddenly break now?

He fell quickly, but managed to use a green Nexi stone to latch onto a stairway railing. He wasn't fast enough to stop the fall entirely, but he landed without breaking his legs, at least. Unfortunately, the Brotherhood woman was getting further away now.

Lynx used the green Nexi to bring himself up the stairway and onto the metal slanted roof. The woman used a vine Nexi of her own to get down the other side of the roof. She ran on down a small side street, which had few people in it. Lynx followed after her, trying to decide why she was running away. Did she know he was taking down the other Brotherhood members? It wasn't very brave of her to run away, though there was sense in avoiding a fight with a much stronger opponent.

But she had a Hader. Did she not believe in her ability to use it effectively in combat? As far as Lynx could tell, she hadn't used it at all yet.

Just as Lynx was about to nab her with some of his vines, a group of people rushed out from behind a building, getting in the way. Lynx ripped the vines off his Nexi stone and continued running down the street. She was even further ahead now, and turning down another small street. Lynx pushed himself to run even faster. He wasn't given this name for nothing... He would catch up with her soon enough.

He reached the side street and bolted down after the woman. Without any warning, a stack of crates fell down on Lynx, knocking him to the ground. It was just a poorly stacked pile of boxes... but the fact they fell at that very moment was disconcerting. Was this woman setting up traps? There wasn't any time for that.

Lynx sprinted after her. "Stop a second, will you?" She only ran faster.

What was she running from? A Brotherhood member. She had done something to betray the Brotherhood. Lynx understood what had happened to the other two members of her team, now. She had killed them.

"You killed them because they were killing Shire civilians, is that right?" Lynx yelled out. "I did the same to my teammates."

The woman slowed down a bit, looking back nervously. She looked like she was considering her options a moment...

She finally slowed down to a walk, taking deep, pained breaths. Lynx caught up to her and worked to catch his breath as well.

"It's okay..." Lynx said. "I understand what you did."

"I... I've betrayed the Brotherhood," the woman said. "I can never be forgiven..."

"The Brotherhood has fallen," Lynx said. He felt he had a good idea for how this woman viewed the Brotherhood, so he had to make it sound like he shared that viewpoint. "Under Delkol, the Brotherhood had a clear vision of a grand future for the Shire Kingdom. But Augurc has squandered that vision."

"Yes," the woman said. "Delkol would never have wanted this. And neither would have my brothers."

"Your teammates were killing helpless civilians, and you lost it?" Lynx said.

The woman nodded. "I... I tried persuading them that we didn't need to kill these people. But they wouldn't listen. They just fell back to Augurc's orders. They told me to start killing people, or they would kill me... So I used the Hader and killed them. I still nearly died in the process... And when I saw you coming, I thought it was over for me... I had to run. I had to get away from this madness."

A voice in Lynx's head told him to just kill this woman and take her Hader. This was his chance to obtain a Hader. All he had to do was kill her, and it was his. He would finally be able to free his mind.

But at the same time, he felt that if he killed her... Perhaps he wouldn't be able to free his mind. Wouldn't that be giving in to Augurc's experimentation? There was no reason to kill this woman. She was willing to cooperate with him. He just needed to rejoin Rilv and the others, and bring this woman with him. They could all work together, and with four Haders all together, it was quite possible they could achieve all their goals that day.

They could kill Augurc. They could finish off his experiments. And they could restore Lynx's mind once and for all. He would finally be himself again, without any of Augurc's Nexi experimentation clouding his mind.

"We need to stop this madness," Lynx said. "We can't just run away. We have to stop Augurc."

"There's... there's no way we can fight Augurc and win," the woman said.

"I beg to differ," Lynx said. "What is your name? Not your code name, but your real name."

"It's Shirm," the woman said. "And what is your name?"

"I am not who I was when I had a real name," Lynx said. "I am Lynx right now... but I won't be for long. Before the night is through, I hope to find the strength to be who I once was. To be myself... A human being."

•

The monster was destroying buildings left and right, and people struggled to get away from the behemoth. The lumbering creature was faster than Borely expected, and scores of helpless people were squished beneath the beast's many giant feet, or torn apart by its many incredibly long arms.

Borely ran down a street leading toward the beast, looking out for any sign of Areo—or Augurc. Borely didn't want to face Augurc right now, but there was a good chance Areo was nearby him.

Pushing through the lines of rushing people was difficult. Borely had to be careful to not hurt anyone, and in turn cause a panic if people subsequently discovered he was a vampire. But perhaps this wasn't anything Borely needed to concern himself with. Who would worry about vampires when there was this massive beast wreaking havoc across the city?

"Let me know if you see her," Borely said to Analicia. He had to keep checking to make sure she was nearby. She was small and blended in with the shifting groups of people passing around her.

"Kind of hard to see anything down here," Analicia said.

Borely led the way to a more open street, careful to watch which way the monster was going. He had to assume Augurc was sticking somewhere near the monster. Would he have sent Areo in a different direction? It probably didn't make sense for Augurc to have both Areo and the monster with him. Areo wouldn't be able to kill many people with the monster right there. She was probably sent to another part of the city.

"Let's find a vantage point," Borely said. "We can get on a tall building—somewhere away from that monster—and search for Areo from there."

There weren't any tall buildings left here in the center of the city. Borely looked north and saw a few grand structures there, and the monster was traveling in another direction.

"We'll head that way," Borely said. "If we run into a really dangerous enemy though, you'll have to promise to get as far away as you can right away. Are you okay with that?"

"Of course," Analicia said.

The fact she agreed so quickly made it way too obvious it was a lie.

"I'm serious," Borely said. "There's no point to all this if you get yourself killed."

"You worry about yourself," Analicia said. "I've handled myself fine this whole time. You just make sure you defeat whatever powerful enemy it is we run into."

Borely couldn't help but smile a little. Though Analicia was a runt, he had to admit it was nice to have her around. He hoped they'd be able to find Areo safely.

But even if they did, how exactly was he going to free her mind? He still wasn't certain how he was going to go about it.

Just find her for now, he told himself. He just had to believe he would know what to do when the time came for him to save her.

•

As Lynx rushed to the center of the city, he watched in amazement as the monster tumbled to the earth. It continued to thrash its many arms in all directions, destroying more buildings in its vicinity—but it wasn't on its feet anymore. Why did it fall? Were the Shire soldiers actually managing to fend off the beast? Lynx understood Augurc's other working experiments had been sent out to take down all the soldiers in the city, though. The city probably wasn't prepared for an all-out attack like this, and the fact the whole city was thrown into a panic had to make the entire situation thoroughly impossible for the city guards.

So who was fighting the monster? And was Augurc nearby? Lynx was hoping to find Rilv and the others. Were they already confronting Augurc? Or were they still making their way through the city? If they got found by one of Augurc's experiments...

Lynx had to count on them pulling through. And he had to make sure he was there when Rilv made her move. He couldn't let her destroy all the Haders or Elpis fragments. He had to make sure his mind was cured first.

He searched down each street they passed, checking on Shirm from time to time to make sure she was keeping up. She still clutched her Hader, its necklace chain tied around her arm. She was on the lookout as well, instructed to yell to Lynx if she spotted anyone suspicious. Rilv and the others could be fighting the Brotherhood, or Augurc, or an experiment, or Kechi, Shire soldiers, or even the summoned monster, for all Lynx knew. Once Lynx brought Shirm and her Hader to them, they'd be able to decide what to do next.

Running up and down the streets away from the fallen monster, Lynx found nothing but rubble, burning buildings, and all sorts of people he didn't recognize. There were corpses, children crying, people stuck beneath pieces of wrecked buildings, mangled bodies screaming for help, and injured people hobbling down the broken paths, leaving trails of bloody footprints behind them.

Lynx kept running and searching. He stopped upon sighting the monster ahead, thrashing its arms against the rubble-covered streets. A giant projectile of some kind was being utilized against the roaring, screeching beast, but Lynx couldn't make out what kind of attack it was. Tens of the creature's arms were sliced apart, and Lynx could only guess what damage the monster's heads were being dealt. Someone extremely powerful was fighting the monster... Lynx thought of Kechi, and his ability to control and harden blood for massive, sweeping attacks. Was Kechi battling the monster himself?

Lynx turned at the sound of a man screaming.

He stepped back in surprise at the sight of Augurc leaping from a building, a dozen vines tearing out of his arms and bringing him down to the ground quickly but safely. Augurc didn't see Lynx and Shirm apparently, as he hurried over to the monster.

The beast exploded.

Lynx stumbled backward, and Shirm turned and shielded her eyes from the massive blast. For several painful seconds, the giant explosion rang in Lynx's ears. He struggled to peer through the fading light, finding rubble and bodies everywhere. There already was plenty of rubble and bodies everywhere, but now there was also blood and monster guts spread all up and down the street with them.

Still screaming, Augurc rushed down the broken, crimson path, using his vines to propel himself forward. He reached the site of the monster's corpse—mostly a pile of dark mush and a pyre of mangled, charred limbs.

"You can not stop now!" Augurc screamed, raising an arm in the air. The multicolored glow of the Elpis fragments shined bright from his clenched fist. "Arise and continue your rampage through this weak and feeble city!"

A pillar of light burst to the sky, enveloping Augurc and what was left of the giant monster he had summoned.

Was he going to heal the monster with the Elpis? It had been utterly destroyed...

Augurc stood still, Elpis energy flowing from his shaking body to the remains of the fallen beast. He was bringing it back to life. Was Augurc actually going to survive such a massive transfer of Nexi energy, though?

It didn't matter, Lynx realized. This was his chance to kill Augurc. There was nothing Augurc could do right now.

"Let's go!" Lynx called to Shirm. He bolted down the street, unsheathing his sword and preparing to stab Augurc straight through the back. Augurc couldn't see it coming... All his attention was on the monster and the Elpis energy.

"Wait!" Shirm yelled.

Lynx kept running. If killing Augurc could free his mind, he would do it... And he would do it now! And if that wasn't enough, he'd use the Haders... And the Elpis... He'd take everything he had to in order to heal himself. To restore his true self. To bring himself back to life.

Lynx leaped toward Augurc and thrust his sword straight into the madman's back.

The flow of Elpis energy deflected Lynx's sword, then knocked him backward, sending him flying hard into the ground. Shirm hurried over to him and tried helping him up, but Lynx's whole body had filled with an excruciating agony.

Was this the pain of the Elpis?

Augurc turned around, his eyes a glowing blank white. "What is this, Lynx?"

The organs of the monster were connecting back to one another, it's scattered flesh and blood flowing behind Augurc in twisting arcs and ribbons.

"You come back here only to betray me?" Augurc asked, his voice echoing, cold and emotionless. "I turned you into something useful. The very concept of betraying me should have never been a remote possibility in your mind. And yet here you are... trying to stab me in the back!"

More of the monster was flowing into the gigantic mass it had been before the explosion. Tens of legs and arms pieced themselves back together. In seconds, the bulk of its body was whole once more.

"Nobody can oppose me," Augurc said. "It is far too late for anyone to stop my glorious work."

Lynx struggled to stand up. Shirm had stepped back a ways, unnerved by the intimidating sight of an Elpis-powered Augurc. There was no way for Lynx to attack him while he was enveloped in the energy of the Elpis.

And there was no way for him to fight an opponent with so much more power than him.

Lynx stood up and held up a knife. "Oh, there's still some time left, Augurc. If I could fight against your experimentation on my mind all these years, I can fight you too."

·

Still clutching his neck, Lanek watched as Kitoh disappeared right before his very eyes. He was barely keeping up with what was happening. Kitoh had grabbed the Hader from him... and at the same time, the elf boy in black was charging for them. And then Kitoh and the experiment child both disappeared.

There was nothing but corpses all around Lanek. Dozens and dozens—perhaps hundreds—of corpses. Soldiers and civilians, all of them powerless to stand against the experiment child for long. But now the boy was gone. Kitoh had somehow finished him off, and had sacrificed himself in the process.

The Hader lay on the ground a couple meters in front of Lanek. He wasn't sure why Kitoh had grabbed it from him, other than to use it against the experiment boy, of course. But it didn't look like Kitoh used it to turn immaterial. He had somehow disappeared entirely, and had taken the enemy with him.

Lanek took a light cloak from a nearby corpse and began tearing strips from it to use as bandages. He had to tend to his wounds, as well as Rilv's. They still needed to find that next Hader, as well as Augurc and Kechi and whoever else they needed to defeat. He had noticed the giant monster was roaring louder now, as if in pain. Was someone fighting it? And actually standing a chance against it? The whole city was just one great collision of madness.

Once Lanek stopped the flow of blood from his and Rilv's wounds, he helped Rilv get up on her feet again, and explained what had transpired with Kitoh and the experiment boy. Though both Lanek and Rilv were badly hurt, they decided they were still able to keep fighting. They just needed to find their next target—whoever it was that had the next Hader.

"I suspect the strength of the Haders is helping us," Rilv said. "The Nexi energy within them has an effect on our bodies... helps us keep going, despite the pain."

"I thought the Haders weren't supposed to affect the user," Lanek said. "I thought that was a major difference between them and the Elpis fragments."

"No," Rilv said. "I have not mentioned this, but I believe the Haders do influence the user in subtle ways. It is not as direct or dramatic as the Elpis. Bit by bit though, the Haders shift the user's mind. I have felt my own mind affected, the more I have used my Hader. It may have... enhanced some of my thoughts, some of my emotions. Affected my judgement. Influenced my decisions."

Lanek hadn't felt anything significant since obtaining his Hader. He hadn't used it much yet, though. Was Rilv saying that since she had her Hader for a while and had used it a fair amount, she wasn't quite in the right state of mind?

It made sense, actually. She was zealous, but Lanek wouldn't have pinned her as one willing to work with the likes of Lynx, or willing to harm innocent civilians—especially those within her own nation's borders. Or would she? It was kind of hard to tell...

Kechi was certainly a madman, and he used his Haders quite a bit. The fact he had two of them may have turned his irrationality into sheer insanity over time. Or was he just a madman in the first place? It was, perhaps, impossible to tell.

"We can't keep using these Haders then," Lanek said.

"We must," Rilv said. "Just a little longer. As soon as the Elpis is destroyed, and as soon as our greatest enemies have been defeated, we will deal with the Haders. If Kitoh's device can destroy the Elpis, it can destroy the Haders as well."

"You're willing to destroy all these weapons?" Lanek asked. "Even though they'd give the Fiefs Kingdom a great advantage?"

"They are too much of a risk," Rilv said. "It has been made clear that there is nowhere these stones can be kept, where they can be truly safe. We even had an Elpis fragment concealed in Setar Castle itself, and still our greatest enemy was able to obtain it. For the safety of Fiefs Kingdom, I must see to it that these Nexi stones are destroyed."

Lanek and Rilv continued their way through the city, noting the movement of the monster's arms. The creature's limbs flung outward all the way to buildings near Lanek and Rilv's location, and they had to run in several instances to keep from getting injured by flying rubble.

They found themselves getting closer to the monster, despite their efforts to keep a somewhat safe distance between them and the beast. But just when they thought they were going to be directly attacked by a couple of its outstretched arms, the limbs were severed and fell to the ground in front of them with a bloody, earth-shaking thump. The beast screamed louder and louder... and then a violent explosion erupted, just a few blocks away.

Lanek and Rilv covered their ears until the explosion's roar faded away. The monster was silent, and Lanek couldn't see it trudging around anymore. Was it actually killed? A man began screaming in utter fury.

"Augurc," Rilv said. "This sounds like our opportunity to deal with him."

It did sound like the monster had fallen, but was this the best moment to confront Augurc? There was still at least one other experiment subject out there, though Borely and his companion were supposedly dealing with her. But Augurc still had his Elpis fragments, and was clearly in a state of rage at the moment—something Lanek found unsettling, considering the man was supposedly known for going about business practically devoid of any emotion.

Lanek and Rilv worked their way down the street, slowed down by the great mounds of rubble that filled the entire area. It was dangerous just climbing over and between the jagged piles of stone, metal, and glass, but they managed to work their way through quickly.

They soon caught sight of the monster in the distance—or rather what was left of it. Amidst the many corpses layered down the street were great globs of organs and goo, its horrid stench some kind of mixture of sewage and rotten food. The entire scene was the very image of a twisted tragedy.

A figure ran to the base of what was left of the monster. He raised a hand up, and a great pillar of light enveloped both him and the creature. From this distance it was hard to tell what precisely was going on, but there were a couple other people rushing to the scene as well. And then... pieces of the monster began floating back together.

"Augurc is restoring the beast with the power of the Elpis," Rilv said, pushing herself more quickly down the street.

They had to stop him now, but as Lanek watched the scene ahead, he saw a man rush at Augurc with a sword. It looked like a masked Brotherhood member, and for a moment, Lanek thought it might have been Lynx. But that didn't make any sense...

And whatever the case, the attack failed. The man flew back upon contact with Augurc, the Elpis energy acting as an impenetrable barrier. There was no way to attack Augurc until he had finished restoring the monster.

Yet Rilv kept running, straight for Augurc. She worked her way around the reconstructing monster while Lanek climbed over an unstable stack of rubble that fell in front of him.

"Wait!" he called out to her. But she didn't stop—she just kept running.

This wasn't like Rilv to go charging in without a plan. Did she have a plan? Or was the Hader affecting her mind, turning her more irrational? Either way, it was too dangerous to go charging straight toward Augurc like this. Lanek didn't want the monster to be brought back to life, but he didn't see any way for them to attack while Augurc was protected by the Elpis energy.

Rilv pulled out the curved block Kitoh had designed for destroying the Elpis. Upon reaching the pillar of light, she swung the device directly into the bright, swirling energy.

The light vanished. The device negated the Elpis energy, allowing Rilv to break through Augurc's barrier. The monster let out a gurgling moan, only a few of its heads partly reconstructed. Gasping for breath, Augurc stumbled back from the impact of Rilv's device against the energy he was enveloped in. Immediately Rilv used her Hader to send Augurc flying back several meters, forcing him to crash into a fallen stone wall.

The Elpis fragments fell from his grasp. Rilv caused them to fly straight to her.

"No!" Augurc screamed, pushing himself back to his feet.

Rilv slammed the end of the curved block against the two connected Elpis pieces. Upon impact, the Elpis half exploded in a burst of multicolored dust, left to scatter and vanish in the passing wind.

Several vines burst out of every green Nexi grafted into Augurc's arms, all rushing for Rilv. Lanek drew his rapier in one hand and his Hader and a fire Nexi in the other. Rushing toward Augurc from his right, Lanek released a burst of fire at the vines. Augurc turned and shot off a blast of frozen air from the light blue Nexi in the palm of his hand.

At the same time, Rilv used telekinesis to push against all the vines whipping toward her. With Augurc distracted by Lanek, Rilv managed to redirect each of the vines to fly around her. Given an opening for a few seconds, Rilv took out her half of the Elpis.

"Stop!" Augurc shouted, realizing what was happening. "I will kill you!"

Rilv smiled.

She floated the Elpis fragments in front of her and smashed them with her Nexi-destroying instrument. Just like the first Elpis pieces, these two blew apart into dust, also left to fade away into nothingness.

The Elpis stone was destroyed. In less than a minute, all four pieces of the Elpis were completely, utterly destroyed.

But there wasn't a moment to dwell on it. Screaming, Augurc regained control of his vines and caused them all to turn back toward Rilv from behind. At the same time, Augurc sprinted forward, using his ice Nexi to create a massive spear of ice from his arm. Lanek chased after him, but he couldn't keep up with an energized Augurc—especially not when Lanek had just been running through the city for so long. He released a ball of fire from his red Nexi, but it barely missed Augurc.

Rilv forced dozens of Augurc's vines to pass to either side of her. One ripped through her hair, tearing off a large chunk of it. She stumbled back, and a vine wrapped around her left arm—the one holding her Hader. In an instant it tore her arm off. Rilv fell to her back, screaming.

Augurc reached her and shoved his lance of ice straight for her chest. Rilv grabbed the Hader from her disembodied arm and held it up directly at Augurc. With telekinesis she sent Augurc violently flying back into the air, tens of meters high. The sheer force of the blast was enough to even push Lanek back a ways, though he was several meters away.

Augurc's vines whipped at Rilv as Augurc flew away. A portion of her right leg tore off, followed by a chunk of her stomach and the entirety of her left hip. Lanek recovered from Rilv's telekinetic push and ran toward her, but a number of Augurc's vines flew in his path, forcing him to hack away at them with his rapier.

Clenching her teeth from the pain, Rilv managed to tear her Hader from the grasp of a passing vine and place it on the ground. Before another vine could grasp the Hader, Rilv slammed her curved block against the stone. Just like the Elpis fragments, the Hader burst apart into miniscule fragments too small for the eye to see once their glow faded away.

"Bring peace to... our kingdom," Rilv got out. A vine slipped around her neck and tore her head off.

Lanek screamed Rilv's name, but it was too late for him to reach her. She had run into the battlefield expecting to die. From the very beginning, her greatest concern was always the safety of the kingdom at large. And to the very end, she was willing to give up her life for that cause. In her last minutes of life, she had managed to destroy the Elpis and one of the Haders...

It was time to finish the job. Lanek turned to Augurc, who was directing his vines to the ground beneath himself. With the support of his vines, Augurc brought himself safely to the ground, standing halfway between Lanek and the two masked figures in the distance. Apparently the second Brotherhood member had grabbed Lynx and brought him a safe distance from the monster, which was struggling to stand upright. The beast gave off a series of tormented, gurgling roars, but it wasn't able to control its arms well enough to attack Lanek or anyone else.

Lanek focused on Augurc. Once the leader of the Brotherhood was taken down, perhaps this nightmare could finally come to an end. Perhaps Lanek could find some semblance of peace in his life. The two people who brought about Suran's death now stood directly in front of Lanek. Lynx, the man directly responsible for her death. And Augurc, the man ultimately responsible for her death.

"It's time for you to pay for your crimes, Augurc," Lanek said.

Augurc's vines returned into their respective Nexi stones. He stood still, silent.

"My experiments," Augurc said, his voice loud but not screaming. "They're supposed to be perfect. Flawless. Unstoppable."

"We've already defeated one of them," Lanek said. "And your creature here has failed you too. Not even the Elpis power that created them was unstoppable. It's time for you to fall as well."

"I can not fall," Augurc said. "I am the only one who can save this world. I won't let you stop me. Not now."

"Save the world?" Lanek said. "You're even more insane than your brother."

"No!" Augurc screamed. Dozens of vines erupted from every one of his green Nexi stones, and a lance of ice at least five meters long formed on his right arm.

"Arise, Subject MI!" Augurc yelled to the monster, which was still flailing about a ways behind Lanek. "Destroy everyone and everything in this city! Show everyone that even in this state, you are a being far superior to any lifeform on this planet! Obedient and omnipotent!"

The monster lurched upward, and giant globs of yellow and red goo began pouring from all the holes and tears in the beast's tattered body.

Lanek ran from the monster, positioning himself closer to Augurc. Suddenly, Augurc flung himself straight to Lanek, propelled by tens of vines. Lanek activated his Hader just as Augurc slammed his gigantic lance of ice through Lanek's body.

Still running, Lanek placed a few meters between himself and Augurc as the madman turned himself around, utter shock etched in his face. Lanek didn't want to give away the power of his Hader without finishing Augurc off in the process, but he only had an instant to react from Augurc's frantic attack.

Footsteps approached Lanek from behind. He turned and found Lynx, struggling to walk forward. He picked up his sword from the ground and made his way toward Lanek.

Lanek thought Lynx was coming for him, but the masked man wasn't facing Lanek. Lynx was facing Augurc.

"I'm sick of these games, Lynx," Lanek said. "You can't keep pretending you're on our side—especially not right after you betrayed us."

"Everything I've done has been either for the sake of obtaining power, or for the sake of bringing Augurc down," Lynx said. "If you're too blind by your hatred to see this, I'll be glad to knock some sense into you once this is over."

"Failed experiments must be eliminated," Augurc said. "All who oppose me must perish."

Apparently Lynx was in fact intending to fight Augurc. Lanek wasn't about to fully trust Lynx, though. If there was a chance for Lynx to kill Lanek, there was no doubt he'd take it. But for now, it was best they cooperate in order to defeat Augurc and this monster.

"How will you fight if you can barely even stand?" Lanek asked.

Lynx pointed back to the Brotherhood member standing a ways behind him. Lanek glanced back and saw the masked figure was a woman. And in her hand was a Hader.

Lynx readied his sword. "I've got Lady Luck on my side."

Stuck amidst the corpses, Kechi watched as Augurc Shire himself rushed into the scene. But instead of going after him, Augurc went toward the base of the destroyed monster. Kechi's vision faded in and out a bit, but he saw a pillar of light envelop Augurc and the monster... and the monster beginning to piece back together? Kechi was in no mood to deal with that beast a second time. This at least confirmed that Augurc was the one who summoned the beast, though.

He's turned against the Shire Kingdom, Kechi thought. *Probably wants to show everyone he's the boss. But he's not the boss. Lord Mareba Shire is the boss, and will be the one to rule this kingdom... and bring it the glory it deserves. Augurc must die now. He has to die. I will kill him. I will knife him. Chop off his fingers and toes. Then his ears. Pull out his teeth. Cut out his tongue. Tear up his arms and legs. Pull out a bone here and there. Dig into his eyes. Rip out each one of those Nexi stones in his body. Make the filthy traitor suffer!*

It sounded like a wonderful plan.

"Where are you right now, Kechi?"

It was Lord Mareba's voice. Was it just in Kechi's head? Or was he actually there? The idea of Kechi's master actually being in this city was frightening.

"I need you to come to Zein immediately," Master said.

It was Kechi's teal Nexi stone. He wearily took it out of his pocket and held it near his mouth.

"Yes, Master," Kechi said. "I am in Zein."

"Good," Master said. "What is your situation?"

"There are at least three Haders in this city, other than the two already in my possession," Kechi said. "I will obtain all the Haders you need, Master."

"I only need four in all," Master said. "Once you have them, bring them to me. I am in my mansion just outside of Zein."

Kechi knew Lord Mareba had a mansion in each of the major Shire cities, but he didn't think Master would be here in Zein.

This was terrifying.

"It is dangerous here," Kechi said. "Augurc Shire and his Brotherhood have attacked the city. And there is a giant monster..."

"I am aware," Master said. "The monster had fallen, but it appears to be coming back to life."

So Master could see the beast all the way from the mansion. It was amazing how Master could be so calm in a situation like this... While the rest of the city was entrenched in chaos, Master spoke as if everything was perfectly under control.

"I fought it off," Kechi said. "I can destroy it again if you wish."

"I do," Master said. "My heart grieves for every innocent Shire life that has suffered this day. See to it that this monster is eliminated for good. I won't settle for this travesty to last a second longer."

"I will not fail you, Master," Kechi said. "I will kill the monster... then bring you four Haders."

"As expected," Master said. And with that, the glow of the teal Nexi faded a bit. Master was done speaking.

It was time to kill that monster again.

Kechi pushed aside the corpses around him and stood up. He nearly screamed from all the pain in his body. Normally he wouldn't have been able to get up at all, but the two Haders he wielded seemed to give him the strength to go on. He had to keep fighting. Failure wasn't an option. He couldn't let Lord Mareba down now. He couldn't let more people in this city get killed by that monster. He couldn't stop and rest until he had brought Master those four Haders he required.

Kechi saw the monster partly reconstructed, flailing about as if in extreme pain. The pillar of light was gone, and Kechi could make out a few figures in the distance. From all the vines emerging from one figure, Kechi could tell Augurc was there. The other three, Kechi couldn't make out, but it seemed they were dealing with Augurc.

It was good that someone else was keeping Augurc occupied—Kechi doubted he'd be able to kill this monster and Augurc at the same time, at least not when he was this injured. Perhaps these other people could keep Augurc busy long enough for Kechi to destroy the monster, and then Kechi could go over and finish Augurc off himself.

But for now, Kechi focused on the beast. It only had half as many legs and arms as it had before, and many of these limbs were in terrible disrepair. Much of the creature's flesh hadn't been pieced back together, so it was mostly a grotesque mass of muscles, bones, and bleeding organs. There were a few heads formed at the top of the beast, but they weren't fully healed either. Random teeth and eyes thrown about oddly-shaped heads, leaking goo from their gaping holes.

"What an eyesore," Kechi muttered. He walked toward the beast, careful to watch for its outstretched arms moving about. There wasn't much left for it to destroy here, but it didn't seem to be anxious to move to another part of the city. Apparently the beast was being directed to stay near its summoner, helping Augurc fight off the three people gathered up ahead.

Kechi used his blood Hader to gather all the blood in the area to one central spot. He wasn't going to let this monster have its way any longer. Lord Mareba Shire demanded it. And Lord Mareba Shire would not be mocked.

Blood flowed upward from hundreds of corpses. Monster blood flowed from piles of goo, as well as from the beast's own gaping wounds.

More... more... more... more!

Stepping aside of a monster arm half-covered with broken claws, Kechi exerted all his strength on gathering more and more blood.

With each passing second, Kechi felt increasingly nauseous. His body wanted to just fall over and die, but he wouldn't allow it. Master needed him to kill this beast. Master needed the Haders. Once these two tasks were done... Then Kechi could die.

He laughed. And laughed. And laughed. He couldn't stop laughing.

So much blood. Enough blood to fill a house. Many houses. Kechi kept forcing more blood to come together. The monster was too busy helping its master to even notice.

I'm going to pulverize this stupid beast!

He formed the massive blob of floating goo into a gigantic spike. It had to be at least ten stories tall, perhaps three stories wide at its base.

The second Kechi hardened the blood into a metallic substance, he sent it flying directly into the base of the monster. Straight through its heads. On through its body. Utterly impaled.

The beast screeched for only an instant. The monster blew apart in a massive display of flying blood and gore. Arms and legs slammed into piles of rubble tens of meters away. There was nothing left of the beast's heads. The torso was thoroughly destroyed.

Kechi felt his mind snap, and all his insides seemed to explode for a moment. Moving such an immense quantity of blood so quickly was far beyond what could ever be considered safe Nexi use.

But he did it! He fell to his knees and puked blood.

It felt like a stream rushing out of his mouth. So much blood, all at once. He forced his mouth shut and gulped down whatever blood was left in throat. His body shook, overwhelmed with the Nexi use.

It was going to be difficult to kill whoever had the Haders he needed. But Kechi knew he wouldn't fail. Master required two more Haders. He was going to get them. It didn't matter how far he had to push himself.

Kechi coughed up some more blood. Once he regained composure, he realized he was coughing and puking amidst bouts of laughter. He had been laughing this entire time.

He forced himself to stop. It was time to get back to his mission.

It was time to get serious.

•

Everywhere Borely went, he heard screaming. Adults and children, men and women. Screams of fear and terror. Screams of pain and agony. The cries of the dying. The suffering of the living.

And somewhere in this city, Areo was playing a role in this turmoil. There were Brotherhood members killing off groups of civilians, but Borely couldn't find her among them. She was likely working alone.

It seemed that if the Brotherhood was being used to take down civilians, then Augurc's experiments were being used to handle the more difficult task of bringing down the city's defenses. And there was no doubt that Areo would be able to make light work of an entire troop of trained Shire soldiers. If she was used to wipe out groups of vampires in Istal, she could be used for even more devastation in Zein.

Borely had to find her and stop her. Save her from this madness. Free her from Augurc's twisted influence.

He had searched from the top of a few buildings, but hadn't caught sight of her. Was she just making her way through the city too quickly for him? Her speed was certainly enhanced by the Elpis, as was her strength and dexterity. There was little that could slow her down at this point. But how was Borely going to keep up with her if he couldn't even find her?

"You haven't found anything yet?" he asked Analicia, who was following him down another street.

"No," she said. She kept looking back at the giant monster, and Borely couldn't help but keep checking on it as well. It seemed there were people fighting it, but Borely couldn't imagine they'd be able to fend it off for long. The beast was so massive, and had the means to attack its enemies from many different directions at once. The landscape exploded around it, and buildings fell beneath its many feet. The fact Augurc could craft such a being was unsettling—about as unsettling as the fact he was able to turn Areo into the killing machine she was now.

Borely climbed his way up a brick building, this one five stories tall. He looked out to some of the streets nearby, searching for any signs of Areo. At the end of one side road he could make out a few Shire soldiers... They were all being killed.

For a half-second, he saw her. It was Areo, dressed in a black and silver uniform. She clawed through each of the soldiers in seconds, then proceeded to slip between a couple buildings, rushing out of Borely's view.

"She's over there," Borely said, pointing so Analicia could see. "She's run off in that direction."

Immediately Analicia climbed down the building, and Borely leaped down in front of her, sprinting down the street upon landing.

He pushed himself as fast as he could. This was finally his time to save Areo. He had a Hader. He had the power to save her. And thanks to that eigni professor, he knew what it was he needed to do. Rattle Areo's mind with the sight of a bloody, murderous scene. Then get her to stop following Augurc's commands—namely, stop killing all the people in this city. Then force her to access a surge of energy from the Hader. And then... hope her mind hadn't been utterly destroyed.

"Areo!" Borely yelled. It was unlikely calling her name would stop her from continuing her onslaught against the Shire forces, but perhaps he could at least get her attention. And perhaps... she could remember him a little, like she did back in Istal. Just before she was about to kill him, she stopped, as if remembering who he was. It hadn't snapped her out of her blind obedience to Augurc, but it was something. Perhaps if she got like that again, that would be Borely's chance to transfer the Hader's energy to her.

He called her name a few more times as he searched down the road he had seen her slip away to. There were more dead Shire soldiers there. He paused a moment to suck the blood of one of the killed soldiers, giving him the strength to keep sprinting down the streets after Areo. Borely could tell this soldier was just killed—Areo had to be close by.

He hurried up another building and caught sight of her just down the next street over. Borely and Analicia rushed down another side road and leaped out just a few meters in front of Areo.

Areo stopped instantly and looked over the two of them while they tried catching their breath. She was trying to decide if Augurc would want her to kill them.

"It's us, Areo," Borely said. "Borely and Analicia. You don't have to keep fighting anymore. We can leave this city, and leave behind Augurc and the Brotherhood."

He doubted just speaking to her would stop her, but if it could somehow get her mind to process some of these concepts, perhaps it would help her fight against the influence of the Elpis.

But Areo simply stared at Borely—or perhaps through him. Her eyes registered no recognition. No emotion at all.

"We just want to help you," Borely continued. "I know you don't want to keep killing people like this."

Areo's fingernails extended into claws, nearly a meter in length.

"Get back, Analicia," Borely said.

In an instant, Areo was upon Borely, swinging her claws for his neck. He activated his Hader and summoned a large, thick shield. As Areo sliced straight through the shield, Borely pushed upward against her claws, then fell back to the ground. Her claws passed directly over him, but the chunks of the shield fell onto him. He pushed them aside and stood up, extending his own claws in the process.

Areo turned and swiped her claws at Borely again. He leaped back to avoid them, but suddenly Areo was directly in front of him, swiping again. Borely summoned two Nexi stones—ice and water—and formed a wide wave of ice between him and Areo. Her claws were encased in the ice, but she was quick to tear through and rush toward Borely again.

Borely thought he'd get more than half a moment to put some space between him and Areo, but she was just too fast. She was trained to end fights in seconds—this was already a much longer fight than she was used to. The fact Borely could summon random weapons at the last instant made him more unpredictable than anyone else she ever had to deal with...

But even then, she was just too fast.

Borely switched his ice and water Nexi stones with a large orange one. He charged up his claws with extra strength and defended against Areo's next attack. She faked for one side, then was suddenly clawing at him from the other side. Borely turned and swiped his claws against Areo's.

Her claws didn't tear through Borely's, but the force of her attack sent Borely flying to the right a meter or so. He stumbled and nearly fell over, when suddenly Areo was in front of him again, jabbing her claws toward Borely's chest. He leaped back, and immediately her claws extended further. He made a frantic swipe and deflected a few of her claws, but the rest plunged through Borely's body.

He clenched his teeth and focused enough to use his Hader to summon a crossbow. Just as Areo was about to tear her claws through Borely's body, he fired an arrow, barely able to aim amidst the suddenness of the moment.

The heavy arrow shot straight below Areo's collarbone. She flew backward, bringing all her claws out of Borely's chest and abdomen. He fell to his knees while Areo fell to her back. He screamed and shakily pulled out a vial of blood, but Areo simply lay still.

"Are you okay, Borely?" Analicia yelled, standing a ways down the road.

"Stay back," Borely groaned. He got to his feet, keeping his eye on Areo. He didn't want to shoot her like that... but it was a last resort move to keep himself from getting killed.

Areo ripped out the arrow and drank a vial of blood of her own. She leaped to her feet, then took two steps to reach Borely. Just as she was about to plunge her claws through his heart, Borely used the Hader to summon a white Nexi and a yellow one. He activated both, creating a flash of blinding light, and shielding himself with yellow Nexi energy.

Areo winced, her eyes blinded by the light. Just as Borely had noticed, she wasn't fighting the way Nivakil had taught them—she was relying on her eyes too much. Jolted by the light, Areo lost her aim and concentration, her claws spreading apart and missing their target. As Borely turned to the side, the claws scraped against his body, but the yellow Nexi was enough to keep them from tearing into his flesh.

Areo flew forward, and Borely replaced the two Nexi stones with a green one. He needed to capture her and get her to witness a bloody, destructive scene... Would he need to kill a bunch of people in front of her? Would a few Brotherhood members suffice? Or would it need to be random devastation, like the kind Areo brought about? Borely couldn't bring himself to kill random people though, even if it was to save Areo... She wouldn't want that.

Areo turned around as Borely sent several vines snapping toward her legs. She clawed through all of them instantly, and reached Borely in a matter of moments. Even anticipating her speed, she was too fast for Borely to capture.

Borely sent more vines flying from his Nexi stone, but this time aimed for the ground. The vines pushed against the earth and sent Borely up in the air. Areo's claws sliced through the vines, just barely missing Borely himself. He landed behind Areo and clawed at her from behind—but the moment he landed, she was leaping forward. Borely's claws missed her completely, and Areo was already turning around again, just outside of Borely's range.

She didn't look flustered in the slightest. She wasn't upset. She was merely continuing the fight, and would continue it for as long as was necessary. There was no chance of capturing Areo—she would always find a way to claw through whatever it was that bound her, even if it was sheer Nexi energy. And Areo wasn't going to give Borely a chance to create a bloody, violent scene in front of her. And he doubted getting killed by her would count.

Areo rushed toward Borely, who used his Hader to summon a tan Nexi. As he ran backward, he created several large, thick stalagmites between him and Areo. It only slowed her down a little, and Borely quickly found this was only tiring himself out quickly.

"Analicia, go kill a bunch of people in front of Areo while we fight," Borely said.

"What?" Analicia screamed.

No, that wouldn't work. If anything, that would direct Areo's attention to Analicia. Borely didn't want to get the child killed in all this.

He had to get Areo to witness the monster's rampage. Borely realized this was a reason why Areo was directed to fight elsewhere in the city. She needed to be killing people all on her own. Seeing extreme acts of murder and terror brought about by others would distract her, and affect her mind in ways Augurc didn't wish for. Her focus would shift away from the mission at hand.

The monster was surely killing many people. Borely didn't want it to, but if he could use the situation to his and Areo's benefit, they'd be sooner able to assist everyone else in saving this city.

He focused back on Areo, who continued to slice her way through all the stone formations Borely crafted with the tan Nexi stone. It was bad to keep using Nexi energy like this. He had to get his plan rolling before Areo overwhelmed him. She wasn't using Nexi stones at all, and it was only a matter of time before Borely exhausted himself.

He turned and ran down a side street, yelling for Analicia to run down another road and watch his back from a safe distance.

Areo was quickly gaining on Borely. Immediately upon reaching the end of one side street, Borely summoned a vine Nexi and used it to latch onto the top of a tall building. He caused the vines to pull him upward, bringing him to the roof while Areo hurried up the wall via her claws, which she shortened a bit to make climbing more manageable.

She climbed really quick. Before Borely could even begin running to the other side of the building, Areo was extending her claws for Borely's head. He fell backward and began rolling down the gradual incline of the roof. He retracted his claws a bit and latched on to the roof before falling off, then swung himself away from Areo as she swiped her claws for his head once again.

Borely sprinted down the length of the roof and leaped onto the next building, heading toward the center of the city where the monster stood. The beast was roaring, and it almost sounded like it was in pain... Were people managing to fend off the creature?

Borely worked his way from building to building, using a vine Nexi to send himself flying across streets. Though Areo was freakishly fast, and she was able to make some rather incredible jumps, she couldn't make it all the way across a street or up and down tall buildings. Green Nexi wasn't his specialty, but he was competent enough to keep from getting killed off in ten seconds flat.

He was getting more and more tired, but the monster was becoming easier to see, especially when Borely made his way up some of the taller buildings still standing in the area. At last he reached a five-story building, just a couple streets away from where the monster stood, shoving its arms through several buildings that stood dangerously close by.

Areo leaped onto the building Borely stood on, and for a moment Borely hesitated. Should he leap down from this building and let the chase continue on, or hope Areo will see a gruesome scene from this building? How long would he have to fend against her before she glimpsed something that truly shook her up? Would she ever glimpse anything at all, if she was entirely focused on fighting Borely?

Borely extended his claws, and as Areo rushed toward him he shot off a jet of water from his headband's Nexi stone. Areo dodged, and Borely swiped his claws toward where she landed. He knew her speed, and aimed right where he anticipated she'd be running from.

Amazingly, she slowed down the very instant Borely swung his claws for her. She avoided his attack and jabbed her claws at Borely's neck.

The building shook, and Borely and Areo each fell backward. Borely glanced back and watched as a colossal crimson spike slammed down into the giant monster. Waves of blood and monster guts flew up and down the street, some of it splattering all the way onto the building Borely and Areo stood on.

Areo remained where she sat, staring straight at the incredulous scene. Never in Borely's life could he have imagined such a horrifically spectacular display of unsightly death.

Areo's mind was affected by the one thing that could affect it in its current state—the terrifying sight of a gruesome, violent murder. Now Borely needed to get her to give up on the mission Augurc gave her. And the one way he was going to get her to stop killing people, he decided, was to defeat her.

Now was the time for Borely to use all the power he had.

•

•Part XII•
THE SHATTERED FRAGMENTS OF REVENGE

As the monster flung its arms toward him, Lanek leaped to the side, knowing his rapier wouldn't be able to cut through the thick, heavy limbs. While stepping back from the giant claw at the end of another arm, Lanek took out an orange Nexi and slid it down the length of his blade. With his rapier strengthened with Nexi energy, Lanek proceeded to slice straight through the next arm that reached out for him. Meanwhile Lynx was ambushed by several arms at once, and was bashed in the torso by a thick, knotted-up tentacle. He managed to charge his own sword with orange Nexi power, and struggled to fight off the other arms rushing toward him.

Lanek didn't see how Lynx had luck on his side. But for now, Lanek had to focus on how to defeat Augurc in a situation as trying as this. The man was taking some time to recover from the injuries Rilv had given him, allowing the giant monster to fight off Lanek and Lynx.

The arms Lanek hacked away at seemed to be growing longer. The giant beast had no problem with continuing to attack Lanek with its injured arms, no matter how much Lanek cut off. The arms just kept extending toward him, their sliced ends releasing more than just blood. Thick red and yellow goo flowed out freely from every arm, and as Lanek fought back more arms, he realized other arms were releasing goo around him. He was being surrounded by the horrid-smelling material, and he wasn't certain about any of its properties.

"Get out of there!" Lynx yelled.

Lanek's first thought was this was a trick—but would Lynx want him to die at this very moment? Right now they were both needed to fight off Augurc.

Lanek activated his Hader and turned himself immaterial. In this spirit-like form, he managed to run straight through the attacking arms and the walls of goo that surrounded him. As soon as he passed through, the goo burst in a large explosion. Several arms were knocked back and blasted apart, and the ground which Lanek had stood on was turned into a smoking crater. He would have been utterly pulverized had he ignored Lynx's cry.

There wasn't time to dwell on this. As soon as the explosion passed, Lanek returned to physical form, knowing he couldn't keep using the Hader for long without growing exhausted.

Lanek rushed out from amongst the writhing arms, and immediately made eye contact with Augurc. Tens of vines launched out for Lanek, who slipped out a fire Nexi and blasted a wall of flames at the approaching plants.

Suddenly a massive spear of ice plowed straight through the fire. Lanek activated his Hader at the last moment, and both the ice weapon and Augurc himself passed directly through Lanek.

Augurc continued past Lanek and charged straight for Lynx, who was busy dodging more of the monster's arms. The beast was trying to pound a fist on Lynx with one arm, while slipping a mouth-covered tentacle toward him from behind. Lynx spun in place, his sword outstretched, and somehow managed to step directly to the side of the fist, proceed to slice through the fist, continue his attack through the tentacle of mouths, and finish off by jabbing the end of his sword directly into the end of Augurc's ice lance. The weapon of ice shattered upon impact, and the thrust sent Lynx flying back— just in time for another of the monster's arms to miss slamming into him. It was all far too unlikely for it to have all been done on purpose. It was practically a series of miracles in the span of just a few seconds. Was this what Lynx meant by having luck on his side? Was the Brotherhood woman's Hader somehow manipulating Lynx's fortune, of all things?

Augurc reformed a giant ice lance and just continued sprinting onward, leaving Lynx behind to avoid more of the monster's attacks. Lanek found another arm reaching out for him as well, and he ran to avoid it, as well as the arms that followed directly in front of him. He sliced his way through the bent-up arm that swung for him afterward, and searched for Augurc amidst the chaos of limbs and goo. The monster began lurching toward them—was it going to try trampling them, even with Augurc there?

Lanek spotted him in the distance, running straight for the Brotherhood woman. She fled, and her Hader began glowing brighter. Vines rushed out for her, but she managed to dodge each one of them as she ran away. She didn't even need to look back—she simply knew where to run to avoid all the vines.

"Don't run!" Lynx yelled. He was counting on her to use her Hader to help them.

Lynx rushed after Augurc and took out a brown Nexi stone. He blasted a burst of swamp-like material, far too fast to avoid. Augurc turned around and aimed his giant ice spear for the swamp blast, forcing it to spray off to either side of him.

The spear of ice launched off of Augurc's arm, blasting straight through the swamp material. Lynx pulled out a fire Nexi and threw it at the giant ice formation. The Nexi stone exploded, and the spear shattered into large chunks of ice directly in front of Lynx. Unfortunately, several of the jagged blocks of ice slammed into Lynx, knocking him hard into the ground.

Augurc looked back for the Brotherhood woman, but she had used Lynx's diversion to escape. Apparently even with the fortune Hader, she found the situation against both Augurc and the monster too much to deal with.

Lanek fought through a couple more arms, and noticed that Lynx wasn't getting back up. Was he dead? It was too hard to tell. It was the worst moment for him to get beaten down, though. Augurc turned to Lanek and formed another giant spear of ice over his forearm.

Continuous laughing filled the air. It sounded familiar. Lanek turned, finding the sound coming from the other side of the monster. He looked up and found a colossal spike of blood floating in the air, high above the beast. So it was Kechi who fought off the monster...

The blood hardened, forming the largest weapon that had likely ever existed. Amidst Kechi's maniacal laughter, the ridiculously huge spike plummeted into the beast. With the creature this close to Lanek, he realized he was going to get pummeled by its bursting remains.

Lanek used his Hader to render himself immaterial, allowing the giant piles of monster flesh and goo to pass through him. The collision between the blood spear and monster shook the ground beneath Lanek's feet, and the incredible noise of the impalement made him scream in pain.

The earth-shattering crash sent waves of blood and mangled organs flying up and down streets in every direction. The instant it all passed though, Lanek turned material again and ran toward Augurc. As Lanek expected, Augurc had used his spear as a shield, plunging it into the walls of gore flying toward him. Fending off such a powerful blast was forcing Augurc to take a few seconds to recover.

Lanek charged his rapier with another swipe of an orange Nexi stone. It was time to plunge through all of Augurc's defenses and bring him down, once and for all.

•

Shirm felt terrible for abandoning Lynx, but she couldn't allow herself to fight her master. Even if Augurc wasn't half the man Delkol was, she was still a member of the Brotherhood. She couldn't turn against Augurc like this.

Perhaps Augurc would kill Lynx and that elf, and the Brotherhood would finish off the rest of the city, and things could resume from there... Things could return to normal somehow.

She clutched her good luck Nexi tighter and continued to run through the ruinous city. She had evaded Augurc's arm vines—a miracle in itself, considering just how quickly and precisely the man could control them. But she couldn't let herself be found by Augurc again—not any time soon. Perhaps once all this was over, she could explain that she was forced to help Lynx, and the moment she realized Augurc was in danger, she fled, not wanting him to come to harm. Would he believe her?

No... that was ridiculous. There was no way Augurc would let her live. She needed to give up on the Brotherhood. She had to leave this city—perhaps leave the Shire Kingdom entirely.

Or was there anywhere in the world that was safe for Shirm now? As long as Augurc lived, she would be in danger.

Why did she listen to Lynx? Yes, Augurc's actions here were terrible, and it was unsettling how so many in the Brotherhood were willing to join in on the acts... But it wasn't for her to decide if the destruction of Zein was right or wrong. Perhaps this city was a necessary sacrifice. Perhaps Shirm just needed to do what was expected of her... Obey, and perform her assigned duties with exactness.

She slowed down to catch her breath. Her lucky Nexi stone had weakened her significantly—she had never used it so many times in one day before. She wasn't supposed to use it so much. Now there were people who knew about its existence. Lynx, the elf, and Augurc, at the very least. Would word of her powerful Nexi stone spread further? She had put herself in grave danger. This was exactly what she was warned to try to avoid. The lucky Nexi needed to be kept a secret to everyone but her.

She sat down in a niche hidden behind some rubble, tucked in a section of wall that was still standing. The sight of so much devastation, so much death... It made her dizzy. And then there was the fact she failed to do anything to actually stop it.

What was she supposed to do now? She couldn't run, hide, or fight. Or could she? Could she use her lucky Nexi once more? Was there a way she could use it to truly change her fortune?

Someone was approaching her. She could hear footsteps. Shifting wreckage. Rubble slipping and settling.

A man stood a couple meters in front of her. In each hand he held a stone, each filled with a glow of two swirling colors. Just like her lucky Nexi stone.

"Hand over that Nexi," the man said in a hoarse, sickly voice.

The man had several bad wounds, and just one good eye—but Shirm's attention was drawn to a gash on his arm. Blood was leaking out of it... and starting to float into the air. A thin ribbon of blood, weaving toward Shirm. The end of the thin stream shifted, then gave off a metallic sheen, just like the sharpened blade of a dagger.

Shirm leaped to her feet and shoved against the broken-down wall she hid in front of. The loose bricks collapsed, and the piles of wood and stone she hid behind fell over as well. The man leaped away from the crashing rubble, and Shirm ran for it, activating her lucky Nexi once more. She had to get away. The lucky Nexi had to protect her... just a little longer. Just long enough for her to escape.

Something slammed against her hand holding the lucky Nexi. She screamed, and dropped the stone in the process. Her hand felt broken, and she realized it was a rock that was flung at her.

She turned and found the man had made several streams of blood in the air, the ends of them picking up stones and bricks from amongst the city's rubble. He was somehow controlling the blood, using it to shoot off these projectiles at her.

All at once, the man sent stones and bricks flying at her. She was too exhausted to dodge them all—she avoided the largest of the stones, but got hit in the shoulder by a brick, then got a leg scraped by another. And the man was already picking up more of the primitive weapons.

There was no fighting him in this state, and the lucky Nexi had failed to protect her. And the man wasn't going to stop until he got that Nexi stone...

She turned and ran as hard as she could. If she stayed, she would die.

She clenched her teeth, fighting back the pain as a stone slammed into her back, followed by a brick that hit her elbow. Leaving behind her lucky Nexi, the last thing she had that connected her to her family... She couldn't believe she could give it up. Even with her life at stake, she had never wanted to leave it. Especially not now. Especially when she had lost everything she had worked for all these years.

She kept running, on and on down the streets. The stranger had stopped attacking her, perhaps satisfied with obtaining the good luck Nexi. Her precious heirloom. The one thing she had left.

What had she come to this city for? What had she been working for her entire life?

She collapsed on the ground, unable to even crawl. Barely even able to breathe. Her entire body was in pain, her injuries accentuated by her extensive Nexi use... And yet she wasn't dying. She was still alive. But what for? What was there left for her to do? Was there anything left for her to even attempt at this point? And if she did try, was there any hope for her to succeed?

She couldn't change anything even when she had the stone of good fortune. How could she change anything now?

•

There wasn't much time left. Kechi could tell he was dying, and that every time he pushed himself to use a Nexi stone a little more, he was pushing a dagger deeper into his own heart.

That was okay. He only needed one more Hader. The elf fighting Augurc had one. He just needed to let them finish duking it out, and then he could take the Hader. And then he could present four total Haders to Lord Mareba Shire. And then...

It depended on whether he survived or not. If Kechi lived, he would remain by Master's side forever, completing all the tasks given to him for the sake of a land unified under the glory of the Shire Kingdom. But if Kechi died, then that was that. He would die having fulfilled Master's wish.

Once Master had the Haders, it didn't matter what happened to Kechi. Technically, there would be nothing Master would not be able to do on his own, so Kechi wouldn't really be needed anymore.

And that was fine. Master had given Kechi a life when he had none. If by giving back his life Kechi could repay Master back even the slightest bit, it would be worth it.

It was difficult to keep walking. Though Kechi was willing to keep walking even if all his flesh was torn off, it was difficult to force his body to do that which was past its capability. The three Haders were helping. Their power was so great, they were allowing Kechi to keep going. But his mind felt clouded. As if it weren't exactly there in his head. Only a reflection of his soul remained intact. He didn't mind, but it was getting difficult to figure out where to go, or where everything was... Everywhere Kechi looked, there was nothing but rubble, blood, and corpses. It was beautiful. It was horrifying. It was Kechi's life.

He heard a commotion nearby, and looked up to two figures fighting atop a battered yet stable building. A man and a woman, both of them fighting with long needles. Or were those claws? They were vampires, Kechi realized. He had always wanted to kill a vampire.

But what surprised Kechi even more was the glow coming from the Nexi stone the man held. It wasn't just a Nexi stone—it was a Hader. Who was this vampire, and why did he have a Hader? What were the chances that yet another person in this city would also have a Hader?

Kechi wanted to kill the elf that had taken his eye from him, and he wanted to kill Augurc as well. But Kechi needed to make sure he got a fourth Hader, no matter what. That had to be the first priority. That was why he didn't push himself to kill the Brotherhood woman he stole a Hader from. If he had been able to use his fear Hader against her, it would have been a quick and easy kill. The vampire man with the Hader would also not be easy to kill. Perhaps Kechi could use his blood Hader in a way to make it easier for the woman to kill the man, and then Kechi could just use his fear Hader on the woman and kill her off.

It was too painful to laugh, so Kechi simply focused on walking to the building, and finding a way to get to the roof.

He had some vampires to kill, and a final Hader to obtain.

•

Borely fired off a jet of water from his metal headband, forcing Areo to his left. He immediately turned and swiped his claws at her, but she ducked beneath the attack and dived forward, her claws elongating further. Borely leaped above her claws and landed to Areo's left. She was already turning once Borely landed. Before she could slice through him, Borely used his Hader to create a fire Nexi, which he tossed in front of him as he leaped backward. Just before the fire Nexi detonated, Areo stopped her attack and ran.

While Areo avoided the explosion entirely, Borely was knocked back, and nearly rolled right off the building. He latched on with his claws, and forced himself back to his feet. Areo sprinted around the hole in the roof and was upon Borely in seconds. Borely used the moment to summon a lance, which he threw to Areo's right while he fired his headband Nexi's water stream to Areo's left. Areo kept running straight for Borely, who rushed forward and caused his claws to lengthen as far as he could manage. At just the right moment, Areo was unable to leap to the right or the left, and Borely's claws had grown a half-meter longer than Areo's.

Areo suddenly stopped and leaped backward, just out of range of Borely's claws. The jet of water passed by to her left and the lance passed by her to her right. Borely kept charging, but Areo was too quick. She rushed to her right, spun in place, and swiped her claws toward Borely's side. She tore deep gashes into his arm and side, but Borely kept running to keep from getting sliced up further.

He turned around and found Areo already running to him. Borely swiped his right claws toward her, and his left claws toward where he predicted she'd leap aside to. Areo's paused for the slightest second, and Borely saw his claws about to tear straight through her chest.

Then Areo was suddenly crouched to the side of Borely's right claws. Then slicing through those claws with her own claws. Then all the way past Borely's left claws. Borely stumbled forward, screaming, realizing all his claws had been sliced off. Areo's burst of speed had rendered every one of his claws useless, and she was already turning back to slice through his neck.

Still screaming, Borely turned and caused what little was left of his claws to slide back into bloody fingernails. At the same time, Borely focused all the energy he possibly could into the orange Hader of his right metal fist, which he was already winding up for a punch. Areo's claws swung at Borely's neck, and at the last moment Borely used all his strength to punch into the sides of the claws.

Rather than snapping them off as he'd hoped, he merely pushed the claws aside, spinning Areo a bit. Her attack missed Borely, and he used the moment of her forced spin to leap toward her, his fist still charged with extra strength.

Areo dropped to the ground, rolled to the side, and swung her claws up for Borely. She sliced off each of Borely's metal fists, sending the pieces flying from his grip along with the orange Nexi stones in each.

Borely ran past her, screaming in surprise. His hands were badly cut up, but not sliced off entirely, fortunately. He turned to Areo and fired a jet of water at her, but she rolled to the side and was on her feet the next instant. Borely leaped back just as Areo was swiping her claws at his face.

He nearly collapsed as blood began flowing down his face. He hadn't even felt Areo's claws dig into his skin—it was as if the force of her swing had happened directly in front of his face, and that alone was enough to leave gashes from his forehead to the right side of his jaw. The claws had missed his right eye, but his metal headband was sliced apart. The pieces of Borely's special weapon fell off, along with the dark blue Nexi embedded within it.

The pain of all these attacks was getting to Borely, but he had no time to drink blood. He had to constantly move as fast as he could to keep from getting chopped up into bits.

His weapons were gone and his claws were torn off. He had to defeat Areo with the Hader right away—but he was injured, and Areo showed no signs of slowing down.

Just as Areo was swinging her claws at his chest, Borely used the Hader to summon a purple Nexi stone, which he immediately used to create a burst of loose energy. Areo caused her claws to shorten back into fingernails to keep them from getting blown off, and she spun her body to the side of the blast, which had shoved Borely back violently. He realized he had shot off a chunk of his side off in the process, and Areo was already lunging toward Borely, her claws lengthening again and her fangs exposed.

With no time to come up with an attack or defense, and too exhausted to use the purple Nexi again so soon, Borely simply took the stone and bashed it into Areo's forehead. Her claws pierced through Borely's chest and stomach, but Borely's punch knocked her back, pushing her claws right back out. She tumbled back across the roof, her forehead leaking blood all across her face.

She shakily got back on her feet while Borely took out a vial of blood. Immediately Areo rushed for Borely, and swiped her claws straight through the vial, slicing it clean in half. Borely leaped back to avoid the next swipe of Areo's claws, and ran for it, working his way down the length of the roof.

He caught a glimpse of Areo's face at that moment of her rushed attacks. She was livid.

Borely smiled. He was getting to her. That wasn't just a blank expression of anger. That was the look Areo got specifically when she was furious.

He wasn't going to last much longer at this rate, though. He had to defeat her to end the mission Augurc gave her, and then use the Hader to cancel out the Elpis energy embedded within her.

Borely turned around to face Areo once more, knowing he wouldn't be able to put much more space between them. He readied his Hader, and Areo swung her claws. Just as Areo's claws reached Borely, he summoned a white Nexi stone and released a bolt of lightning. At the same moment, a crimson material appeared between Areo's claws and Borely's white Nexi. Borely thought it was blood, but it hardened, and the blast of lightning was spread out in multiple directions. Instead of blowing Areo's claws clean off, her claws were merely pushed back. But due to the positioning of the blood-like substance, Borely was shot in the stomach by a portion of the lightning attack. He flew backward, launched straight off the roof of the building.

He was falling, and he could barely form a thought in his head, let alone find the energy to try and save himself. The pain was overwhelming, and his chances of saving Areo seemed to shatter in front of him. Borely crashed hard against the ground, the pain in his body only increasing. He couldn't move. He couldn't even tell if he had broken his back or neck. He lay there, unmoving.

A man walked over to Borely and bent down to pull the Hader out of Borely's grasp.

"All four at last," the man whispered. He had one good eye, and quickly looked over Borely a moment, as if trying to tell if Borely was still alive. The man pulled a knife from a holster and held it over Borely's heart. "Just to be sure."

Before the man could finish Borely off, Areo leaped down from the building, landing just behind the stranger.

"Get away from Borely!" she screamed as she swung her claws for the man's neck.

The man caused one of his Haders to glow brighter, and Areo stopped her attack. She simply stared wide-eyed at the man. It was as if she had suddenly regretted trying to kill this man.

Apparently not wanting to continue the fight, the man turned and ran for it, falling into a coughing fit as he escaped.

Borely could hardly make sense of the situation, but there was no time left to worry. Areo was right there. Was she going to finish him off right now?

She looked down at Borely for a couple seconds.

"Areo..." was all Borely could get out.

"Target down," Areo said, her voice monotone and detached.

She turned away and ran. Apparently to seek out new targets.

Borely couldn't move. And even if he could, what would he be able to do now? He lost his weapons. His claws. And now his Hader. There was nothing he could do now.

Areo was lost to him.

•

Lanek sprinted toward Augurc, who launched off a series of vines straight for him. Lanek swung his rapier through the vines and kept running. More vines arced toward him from the left and right. Lanek spun in place and swung through the attacks. More vines rushed at him head on. He activated his Hader and leaped through them, stepped to the side, deactivated the Hader power, and continued running. Augurc redirected tens of his vines to rush at Lanek from all directions.

Instead of using his Hader again, Lanek simply charged forward, pushing himself faster, hacking away at the freakishly fast vines with every bit of his strength.

Was this for revenge? Was this for Suran? Or was this simply what he needed to do? Was it simply the right thing to do? He wasn't even certain, but he knew Augurc couldn't be allowed to continue this nightmare any further.

Lanek sliced through every vine, turning in place to face each one of them, and continuing to run every moment he had an opening. Augurc forced even more vines to burst out from his arm Nexi stones, and Lanek had to anticipate where all of them would be at every given moment.

It was draining to keep using the orange Nexi, but it was the only way to keep the vines from overwhelming him, and he needed to save the Hader for just before the finishing blow.

Lanek approached Augurc, who continued launching vines at him. As soon as Lanek was in Augurc's range, the man slammed his giant ice spear into Lanek's body—just as Lanek turned immaterial.

Lanek rushed for Augurc, running straight down the length of his huge weapon. Augurc's expression turned from slightly flustered to genuinely worried. He had no Elpis to turn to. And with Lanek in a spirit form, how was Augurc going to fight him? As soon as Augurc was within range of Lanek's rapier, Lanek was going to leap out of the ice spear, return to physical form, and slam his blade into Augurc's heart. If Augurc managed one final attack at that moment, Lanek could leap back and turn immaterial one last time, just long enough for Augurc to die, once and for all.

Lanek continued running through the long, thick weapon of ice, and kept careful watch over each of the vines arcing in the air around him. They were going to lash out at him the moment Lanek would jump out of the ice lance—he had to be ready to avoid them all as soon as he was material again.

Just before Lanek was preparing to leap out of the ice lance, Augurc brought all his vines back to him, and began surrounding himself in the vines. In seconds, a thick cocoon of vines was formed around Augurc. But was that really enough to keep Lanek's orange Nexi-charged sword from piercing through?

As Lanek leaped out and returned to physical form, he discovered the cocoon had shifted into more of a sphere, with Augurc hanging in the direct center of it. Vines slipped out the bottom of the sphere, forming long legs that raised the ball high in the air. Augurc's massive ice weapon still stuck out the side, and through a thin hole in front of him, Augurc was able to see Lanek standing several meters down below. The sphere of vines shifted easily under Augurc's control, and the man quickly twisted it in order to swing the giant ice lance down at Lanek.

Lanek leaped to the side, and the earth shattered into pieces around him as the weapon of ice came crashing down beside him. A number of vines shot out from the sphere of vines, trying to grab Lanek as he was airborne. Lanek managed to hack away at them, but by the time he landed, Augurc was already attacking with the ice lance again.

Lanek dropped to the ground, lying flat directly beneath the swing of the giant weapon.

The fact Augurc could manage such an incredibly complex application of simple Nexi stones was a testament to the madman's genius, as well as his incredible Nexi-wielding capacity. Lanek was exhausted, but it seemed Augurc was capable of continuing this fight for some time.

Augurc turned to swing his lance again, and this time there were dozens of vines arcing toward Lanek from the other direction. Lanek was going to have to use his Hader again, but he was certain that would push him to the brink of Nexi poisoning. The vines approached faster, and Lanek began swinging his rapier at them, while still watching for the approaching ice lance.

Just before it reached him, a blast of swamp material hit the side of the ice spear, keeping it from swinging into Lanek.

Lanek glanced back and saw Lynx, still lying on the ground, but able to at least hold up a Nexi stone and wield it. Once again, Lynx had saved Lanek's life.

Not because Lynx cared for Lanek, of course. He just needed Lanek to bring Augurc down, right? But then, why did Lynx want Augurc killed in the first place? Lanek couldn't understand whose side Lynx was truly on, if he was on anyone's.

"Run!" Lynx screamed.

Lanek sliced through the next few vines and ran for it. Just moments later, an explosion went off behind Lanek. Apparently Lynx had placed a fire Nexi inside the swamp stream he fired at Augurc's weapon. The ice spear shattered into pieces, and Lanek had to turn and dodge the largest of the ice chunks to avoid the same grievous injuries Lynx had suffered. Lanek was battered by a few brick-sized chunks of ice, which only left him badly bruised. As soon as the detonation passed though, Lanek was rushing toward Augurc's sphere of vines, which was tilting far backward from Lynx's explosion.

Fire was rushing up many of the vines, and Augurc was focused on disconnecting these vines from the vine ball he hid in. It gave Lanek the few seconds he needed to sprint to the thick vine legs holding the sphere up, and charge his rapier with orange Nexi energy one more time. Upon reaching the first leg, Lanek plunged his rapier straight through the vines, then tore through to sever the thick mesh of plants entirely. As soon as one leg was cut, Lanek rushed to the other and sliced through that as well.

The ball of vines fell to the earth. There was no time for Lanek to get out of the way. He was going to get flattened.

No. This is my chance.

He activated the Hader and ran beneath the center of the vine sphere. For one second, Lanek leaped through the air in an immaterial form. As soon as he was inside the vine sphere with Augurc, Lanek returned to physical form and plunged his rapier into Augurc's chest. The man had no time to react, or even realize what was happening—not amidst all the chaos of that moment.

Augurc screamed and swung a punch for Lanek's head. Lanek ducked in time, then pulled his rapier back out so he could fend off the vines rushing for him from Augurc's arm Nexi stones.

He wasn't sure if Augurc was stabbed through the heart, but Lanek felt the man was at least out of the fight. Lanek used his orange Nexi-charged rapier to force an opening through the ball of vines, and ran before Augurc's new vines could strangle him or tear him into pieces.

Lanek ran back a ways and watched as the vine sphere fell apart, dissolving into a lifeless pile.

Augurc ran out of the pile, clutching the bleeding wound in his chest. Vines were wrapping around the injury, holding him together. As he ran, he looked back to Lanek and yelled, "As soon as Lynx is dead, I will come back for you! I will not be stopped by you, or by anyone in this inferior world!"

Lanek was about to run after Augurc, but the thought of Lynx dying made him hesitate. Was Lynx really dying for good? For some reason the thought was... unsettling.

He looked back to Lynx, and the sight didn't fill him with glee. If anything, the sight was pathetic. A bleeding body, covered with gashes, and impaled with ice in several places. The man lay on the ground, motionless, ready to die.

It was precisely what Lanek had wanted to see ever since he had been dragged into this Hader-searching mission. And yet... he didn't feel relieved. He felt guilty. Though this man had killed Suran, he did save Lanek's life multiple times now. What did any of this mean? Why did Lynx have a change of heart? It would have been simpler if Lynx was nothing but a traitor. Lanek would've felt no remorse.

He hurried over to Lynx and discovered the man's mask was broken apart. Only about half his face was covered. The idea that Lynx had a face was strange in itself... Lynx was supposed to be faceless. Nothing but a twisted, wicked being. Someone who wasn't actually someone.

And as soon as Lanek lifted off the rest of the mask, he realized Lynx was not just someone.

Lynx was Turan.

This was a fellow villager from Edellerston. A classmate in school. A friend of Terico and Suran. Someone Lanek had seen often. Someone Lanek *knew*.

A flood of memories rushed through Lanek's mind. He had never been particularly close to Turan, but this was someone Lanek was truly familiar with. It was as if Lanek had suddenly traveled back in time, to a time when he lived a peaceful life. He had his parents, his sister, his friends...

No kingdoms to save. No people to kill. No monsters to become.

"Why?" Lanek asked. "Why are you here, Turan? Why are you Lynx?"

Turan's eyes had trouble focusing on Lanek's. "Sorry... I couldn't help it."

"Why are you Lynx?" Lanek screamed.

When Turan couldn't respond, Lanek worked quickly to tend to Turan's wounds as best he could. He managed to remove the chunks of ice impaled in Turan's limbs and torso, then stopped the bleeding with strips of clothes Lanek could find. It seemed likely Turan was going to die though, even if Lanek had access to better first aid equipment.

"Why... Why are you Lynx?" Lanek asked again, once he felt Turan was able to talk again.

"I... was captured," Turan said. "Turned into Lynx... Nexi experiments... Lost my mind... I need my mind back... That's all I want..."

"Why couldn't you tell us this?" Lanek asked.

"Couldn't..." Turan said. "Lost my mind..."

Apparently there had been a terrible struggle going on in Turan's mind all these years. He had been trying to fight his identity as Lynx, an identity crafted by the likes of Augurc Shire. Lynx and the other Brotherhood experiments were a precursor to the Elpis-powered experiments to come, it seemed.

"Also..." Turan continued, "I didn't... I didn't want you to know... I'm so sorry..." Tears trickled out the sides of his eyes. "I'm so sorry about Suran..."

"I... I don't know what to say," Lanek said. The thought of Suran's death wasn't something Lanek could simplify. It wasn't something he could just forgive, even if the perpetrator didn't intend it. Nothing he or Turan could do would ever bring Suran back. She was lost to him.

And this whole mission... None of it had made Lanek feel closer to her.

And now that Suran's killer was dying, Lanek felt nothing but grief. Tears filled his own eyes, and he was too exhausted to hold them back. In his heart, Lanek almost felt as if he were witnessing Suran's death all over again.

"You can kill me... if you wish," Turan said. "I long wanted to kill myself... but I never could. And then I learned of the Haders... A part of me... A part of me always held on to hope. Hope that... somehow... something could work out. I wanted to be me again... I wanted to right all my wrongs... somehow."

Lanek shut his eyes and gritted his teeth. Suran wouldn't want her friend to die. Even if Turan did kill her, she wouldn't want him to die. Perhaps if Lanek had been even a little bit like Suran, he would have been able to do what was right from the very beginning. Perhaps he would have been able to move on after her death, and not suffer like this so much...

He realized what he needed to do.

"Take this," Lanek said. He placed his Hader in Turan's grasp. "If you have the desire to use this, you will enter a realm outside of time. A goddess named Reali lives there, and she will help you. If your motives truly are just... She will give you the power to turn that which exists... into a nonexistent state. I believe you will be able to take your madness and make it disappear forever."

Tears flowed freely down Turan's face. "But... I'm dying..."

"The Hader will help you live," Lanek said. "Just do as I said, and you will make it. I have to go after Augurc now, but as soon as I'm through with him, I will return here."

"Lanek... How will you fight without the Hader?"

"I've fought my whole life without one. I'll manage."

Lanek turned and ran down the path Augurc had taken. There were far too many thoughts passing through Lanek's head, and he had no time to deal with a single one of them.

He had to stop Augurc. He couldn't let that madman get away. He couldn't let another person suffer as Lynx had.

As Turan had.

Kechi made it to the steps of his master's mansion. It was excruciating to keep walking, but the Haders kept him going. He couldn't fail his master. He had to get the Haders to him. He made it to the mansion. He just had to give the Haders to Master. Kechi couldn't stop. He had to fulfill his master's wishes. All he had to do was hand Master the four Haders. He was there. He was opening the door. He couldn't just collapse and die now. He needed to find Master. Give him the Haders. Master needed the four Haders. And then it would be over. He couldn't fail Lord Mareba Shire.

The inside of the mansion was all a blur. Gazing out of his one good eye, Kechi trudged through rooms, down hallways, up stairs... Where was Master? All Kechi wanted was to find Master. All he wanted was to give Master the Haders. Then it would be over. Master would be pleased. That's all Kechi wanted. What purpose would Kechi have, if it weren't for Master? If he didn't fulfill Master's wishes, there wasn't a point to his existence.

There. There was Master's room. Master was sitting in his bed.

A skeleton.

Kechi stared blankly, trying to make sense of what he was seeing. In Master's bed was a skeleton.

But now that Kechi thought about it, Master had died a while ago, hadn't he? Not long after Kechi was given his mission for seeking out the Haders. Some Shire royal had gotten Master killed, not wanting him to bring trouble to the Shire Kingdom. But little did those fools know, Lord Mareba Shire lived on in Kechi. Master was still alive in Kechi's heart. That's all that really mattered.

The skeleton sat propped up in the bed. Completely motionless. Completely silent. Staring off into nothingness.

But Kechi could see Master for who he truly was. The man who would bring the Shire Kingdom to its full glory. Nobody could stop Master's dream from coming true. Kechi had devoted his whole existence to Master. And he could still hear Master's voice, instructing him from time to time. Kechi knew what he was doing.

And now was the time for the ritual. He had four Haders. It was time to give Master all the power he needed to conquer this world and lead it in fear and justice.

Kechi set the four Hader stones on the bed, arced past Master's feet. On the wooden base at the front of the bed, Kechi painted a series of symbols with his own blood. The creators of the Haders had come up with an entire language that could manipulate the abilities of the stones. And when several of the stones were gathered together... they had powers that could rival the full Elpis itself.

In this case, four stones could be used to do all sorts of things.

Kechi lay himself down on the floor in front of Master's bed. His head lay beneath the bloody symbols, and after a couple minutes, he could begin to feel a tense energy building up in his heart. He wanted to scream, but all feeling in his body had turned numb, meaningless.

His soul split in two.

Kechi could feel a portion of it fading away. As it transferred to Master's skeleton, Kechi got on his knees and watched as Master's organs, flesh, and clothes all pieced back together. It only took a couple seconds.

Lord Mareba looked just as Kechi always remembered him. An older man, unable to walk, but commanding an aura that could bring entire nations to their knees.

"What is the situation, Kechi?" Lord Mareba asked.

"I have brought you back, Master," Kechi said.

"I know," Lord Mareba said. "I saw it happen."

"It's my soul that was split," Kechi said. "A central part of you is me now."

"And you are everything I have told you to be," Lord Mareba said. "My aspirations are your aspirations. We are one in mind."

"I will not fail you, Master," Kechi said. "I will do whatever you ask of me. Even die, if I must."

"You are dying already," Master said. "But if you wish, you can assist in this city's cleansing."

"Yes," Kechi said. He walked over to help Master out of his bed and into his wooden wheelchair, but Master set Kechi's hand aside.

Instead, Master caused the four Haders to float over to his hands. "I have no need for the wheelchair." The four stones glowed brighter all at once. With this much energy, Master could bypass any contracts need with the beings inside the stones. He could do whatever he wished.

Master pushed aside his blanket and stood up on the bed. In his white and green uniform, Master looked like the commander of the entire world. A silver and golden glow enveloped his entire body, obscuring the features of his face.

"It is time to test my power," Master said, his voice now sounding much younger, much stronger. "I will vanquish all my enemies in this city, restore every building that fell, and then proceed to the nearest city of the Fiefs Kingdom. I will wipe Niez off the map, and then proceed to the next closest city. Once the Fiefs government surrenders, I will return to the Shire Kingdom, and take my place as ruler of the entire continent. All who resist will perish."

It sounded like a perfect plan. Lord Mareba would not fail, and neither would Kechi.

They could not fail each other now. To fail Master would be to fail himself.

And he could not fail himself. How would Kechi exist, if he hadn't come into being?

•

Without the Hader, the pain in Borely's body built up more and more. He shut his eyes and tried to focus on anything but the pain. He wanted to get up. Find Areo again. Keep trying to save her. This was his chance to do so, but he didn't know how he was going to overpower her. She had been a talented vampire even before the Elpis experimentation. What chance did he ever have against her, even when he had the Hader?

Something nudged him in the shoulder.

"Are you dead?" It was Analicia.

Borely opened his eyes and saw the child standing behind his head. "Not quite."

"Then get up!" Analicia said. She placed a vial of blood at Borely's mouth and forced him to drink. "Areo's getting away."

Borely gulped the blood down and felt his wounds healing, and energy returning to his body. Analicia didn't have any more blood to give him, so Borely didn't feel in perfect condition, and his claws weren't going to heal any time soon. He wasn't going to be able to fight Analicia with his claws, and he didn't have the means to fix his metal gloves or headband. And of course, the Hader was gone too. He got up and took the Nexi stones out of his broken weapons, so he could use those at least.

"I don't see how I'll be able to stop her," Borely said. "I was giving my all, and I simply couldn't keep up with her..." The only thing hopeful about his fight with Areo was the fact she had stopped the stranger from killing Borely off. There were a few possibilities for why she did so, but Borely felt that deep down, Areo had recognized him. Or at the very least, had recognized the scene of him nearly dying, and reacted in a way to keep Borely alive—just as she had before she was captured by Augurc.

"Don't give up," Analicia said. "You've been in worse pinches than this."

"I'm not so sure about that," Borely said. "I can't use my claws, or my weapons, or the Hader."

"Maybe you don't need to use those things," Analicia said. "See if you can save her some other way."

"I've already tried talking to her," Borely said.

"Try some more then," Analicia said.

"She'll just kill me," Borely said. "In her heart, she may recognize me, but she can't stop herself from fighting everyone she deems an enemy of the Brotherhood."

"Find a way to reach her without getting killed," Analicia said.

Borely looked over the Nexi stones he had. A couple orange ones, a light blue one, a green one, and a teal one. He had used the teal Nexi to speak with Rilv from a great distance away. But two Nexi stones were needed in order to communicate, as Rilv had a teal Nexi as well. Areo didn't have one, so she wouldn't be able to hear Borely's words. And the moment Borely shouted anything to her, she would sprint over to him and stab him in the heart.

Perhaps he could use the green Nexi in some way...

"I think I have a plan," Borely said. "Which way did Areo go?"

Analicia pointed. "She went a few blocks that way, and I saw a group of soldiers ambush her the next street over."

Areo would surely kill off all the soldiers, but if they slowed her down a bit, Borely would be able to catch up with her.

"Let's go, then." He ran off down the street, weaving his way through the remains of fallen buildings, while Analicia followed behind him.

After making their way down a few blocks, Analicia directed Borely to run left. Once down another street, Borely found the corpses of dozens of Shire soldiers, many of them sliced clean in half.

He searched the area for Areo, but only found more corpses. The furthest corpse was to Borely's right. He turned that way and hurried down the street, guessing this was the direction Areo must have taken.

He stopped at a crossroads, noticing a figure standing in the distance to his left.

It was Areo. She was directly facing Borely. He turned and gazed at her, and realized she was crying. Tears were streaming down her face.

Was she realizing everything she was doing? Perhaps the moment she chose to save Borely again had a deeper effect on her mind than Borely thought.

She turned and ran. She didn't want to face Borely again.

She knew that if she did, she would kill him.

Borely ran after her, pulling out his green and teal Nexi stones. If he couldn't stop her from fulfilling Augurc's requests by force, perhaps he could tell her the right words she needed to hear, and she would decide to stop on her own. Her mind had been twisted by Augurc, but it still was her mind. Deep within that Elpis-tampered body of hers was a soul that was fighting to return to who she once was. Borely had to believe in this. And he had to believe he could help her overcome those destructive emotions Augurc had enhanced in her.

He created a bit of vine from his green Nexi stone and tied the teal Nexi to the end of it. With the teal Nexi properly secured, Borely caused the vine to extend and reach out toward Areo.

Once the teal Nexi was hovering a few meters above Areo, Borely focused on the stone, directing his energy to it through the green Nexi stone, and on down the length of the long vine. Areo was running faster, placing a good ten meters between her and Borely.

But Borely wasn't going to lose sight of her. He pushed himself harder, running as fast as he could.

"Areo, it's me... Borely," he said between breaths, his voice echoing from the distant teal Nexi. "Analicia and I came to this city to find you. We're not sure if we're going about this the right way, but we really want to help you. Augurc has forced you to kill a lot of people today, but I know you don't want to be a part of this a second longer...

"I know I can't persuade you to stop. You've always had a stubborn personality, and I'm sure Augurc took advantage of that when he twisted your mind with the Elpis. But I'm stubborn too—perhaps even more so than you. I suppose most people wouldn't want to stick around someone who kept trying to kill them... but I can't give up on you. I can't just leave you behind, or let you leave me. Not again."

Areo kept running, but she seemed to be slowing down a bit. Or perhaps Borely was just starting to run faster.

"You saved my life five years ago," Borely said, still channeling his words down the vine and out the teal Nexi stone a ways above Areo, careful to keep the vine out of reach of her claws. "I wouldn't be alive if it weren't for you. I was upset about becoming a vampire, but I know now... What you did was the right thing.

"And it's time I returned the favor. At least, that's what I felt I was doing, when I finally managed to leave Istal and go search for you. But I don't think that's how it should be... I didn't go through all this just so I could feel we were even. I've been trying to find you because I want to, Areo. Our time together five years ago wasn't exactly full of happy experiences, but there was nothing wrong with you."

"Stop it," Areo said. Borely could hear her voice from his green Nexi stone, its vine connected to the teal Nexi. "Stop it. Stop it. Stop it."

"I told you, I'm never going to stop," Borely said. "I wouldn't have come all the way here and gone through so much pain just to give up now. Even if I never did stand a chance against you. I'm still willing to give my all for you, Areo."

"Go away!" Areo yelled, her pace starting to stagger and slow down a bit. "Don't come near me!"

"I'm coming," Borely said. "Whether you like it or not, I'm coming."

He ran faster, struggling to maintain his breath. He couldn't let her get away. He couldn't let himself slow down. He had to reach Areo.

"I don't want to kill you!" Areo screamed.

"I don't want you to suffer anymore!" Borely replied. "Nobody's going to kill anyone. You don't want to kill anymore. And... neither do I. I just want this all to end. I want us to be together again. I'll help you through your pain. I'll help you recover. You can count on me, Areo. I'm here for you."

Borely found himself gaining on Areo quickly. Areo slowed to a stop, and Borely brought the vine back into its Nexi stone. He pocketed the green and teal Nexi stones, and ran right up to Areo.

Just as Borely reached her, Areo turned around and extended her claws, jabbing Borely through the chest. Borely collapsed into Areo, and wrapped his arms around her.

Borely gripped her tight and whispered into her ear. "And I'm not going to let you go."

He turned his head and sunk his teeth into her neck. Areo didn't move—she simply held her position, her claws still impaling Borely's chest. Borely injected his venom into her body, and let his blood flow amongst her own.

You know this blood, Borely thought. It was the blood she drank just before Augurc captured her. For vampires, there was nothing that affected the senses as strongly as blood.

Borely kept his fangs in Areo's neck. He couldn't let her forget him. He couldn't let her give up on her life. Her real life.

Areo slid her claws back into her fingernails. Borely released his teeth from Areo's neck. He slumped forward, but managed to hold on to Areo's shoulders. He felt the life fading from him, but he couldn't let himself let her go.

"Drink my blood," Areo said. She forced Borely's mouth back on her neck.

Borely smiled and accepted her request. He sunk his teeth back in her neck and sucked her blood, healing the deep, fatal injuries in his chest.

Once he felt strong enough to stand on his own once more, he released his teeth from Areo's neck again. Still holding his arms around Areo, he leaned back a bit and looked into her eyes. She was crying again... and her eyes looked genuine. They were Areo's eyes.

Areo was back.

"You look better," Borely said.

"You look terrible," Areo said.

Borely laughed. His clothes were tattered, and he must have looked a few levels beyond exhausted by now. He had pushed himself far beyond what was safe. Regardless of how much blood he drank, he couldn't exert himself forever.

"First thing you tell me is I look terrible," Borely said. "You really are back to normal."

Borely was surprised Areo was in control of her mind again. He hadn't used the Hader to cancel out the Elpis energy implanted inside of her. Had Rilv, Lanek, and Kitoh managed to destroy all the Elpis pieces? Perhaps with the Elpis itself gone, Areo was able to overcome the effects of the experimentation.

Borely kept a hold over Areo. "You're really okay now, though?"

Areo nodded. "I... I think so. But everything... I can't forget. I can't forgive myself for this..."

"None of it was your fault," Borely said. "You couldn't control yourself."

"I still let myself get captured though," Areo said. "And I wasn't strong enough to overcome Augurc's experiment."

"The Elpis is the strongest Nexi power in the entire world," Borely said. "You can't blame yourself for this."

"My... mind... It hurts..." Areo said. Tears flowed from her eyes again. "I can't..."

"It's okay," Borely said. He placed a hand on the back of her head and placed her face against his shoulder. He realized it would take some time for Areo's mind to heal.

"I'll take care of you, Areo. I won't let us get separated again."

•

Everything had failed him. Everything Augurc had ever worked for... Everything, everything, everything—everything was weak. Everything was meaningless. Everything was utterly imperfect.

The Elpis, his experiments, his Brotherhood... He couldn't rely on anything.

He worked his way through the ruinous city, the very embodiment of what had become of his every dream and ambition.

His experiments had failed him. And Augurc could blame nobody but himself. Not his father, not his brother, nor any of the Shire dukes. Not even his enemies. His experiments were supposed to be perfect. They were formed just as he intended them to be.

But they failed. From several vantage points, Augurc searched the city over, and he could find no sign of Subject VI or EV. They must have been defeated, just as MI was—the creature that was supposed to rival the power of a god, and the obedience of a flawless servant.

There was nothing Augurc could rely on. Not even himself.

He sat atop a roof of one of the only tall buildings left in the city, and found nothing but ruin and failure.

It was the cycle of hatred and despair.

Augurc shut his eyes and gripped his fists. Everything he had worked his whole life for... None of it changed a thing. If anything, his life's work only strengthened the cycle. He wanted to eradicate hatred. He wanted to extinguish despair. He wanted to break down the walls of the world's meaningless nations, and replace the meaningless peoples of the land with a superior form of life.

With years of dedicated research and the power of the Elpis, Augurc was to bring the world into an era of thought, complacency, and unity. People would no longer hate. People would no longer despair.

But it was an impossible dream. Augurc's experiments—the most powerful beings the world had ever seen—even they weren't enough to bring a single city into submission. All the world would resist, and Augurc was helpless to change a thing.

And if even the Elpis was not strong enough for him to achieve his goals, there was no use in focusing on them any further.

What was he supposed to do with his life now? It was meaningless. Just as meaningless as every other life in the world. He couldn't break the cycle, no matter what he did. All he could do was make it more painful.

He gripped the vines holding his chest together. It was possible he was going to die, without the power of the Elpis lending him any of its healing glow.

Perhaps it was time for him to die.

"Augurc Shire."

He turned around and saw a man hovering in the air behind him. He looked to be an older man, and an aristocrat—one of the Shire noble, Augurc realized. An aura of gold and silver light glowed about him, and all color had faded from his eyes. It reminded Augurc very much of his brother, charged with the power of the Elpis. The man dropped a large bloody canvas on the flat roof. It was not tied together, so the canvas spilled out its contents all about.

About twenty masked heads rolled out.

"These strange people were murdering Shire citizens for some reason," the nobleman said.

"You have the Elpis?" Augurc asked. He couldn't see how the man had the Elpis, considering how Augurc saw each of the fragments destroyed by the Fiefs servant woman.

"No, the Haders," the nobleman said. "Much more reliable and stable than the Elpis."

"I doubt it." Augurc had no idea what the Haders were, but he couldn't get himself to care. There was always a price to pay for such power.

"You accomplished a great deal of destruction with the Elpis," the nobleman said. "But it pales in comparison to what I can accomplish with the Haders."

"You've destroyed what was left of the Brotherhood," Augurc said. "Kill me and be done with it."

"You've given up?" the nobleman asked. "That simplifies matters. I can only hope the Fiefs Kingdom will be as weak and feeble as you!"

Augurc stood up and stared at the man. "You plan to destroy the Fiefs Kingdom?"

"Just enough of it for the kingdom to surrender to their rightful Shire ruler. And anyone who gets in my way of becoming the ruler of this continent will likewise perish."

It was the cycle all over again. This man was making the same mistakes Delkol made.

The same mistakes Augurc made.

He formed a lance of ice on his arm and caused more vines to emerge from the Nexi stones on his arms. The nobleman floated back a bit, a long, thin grin spread across his weathered face.

"I can't let this destruction go on any longer," Augurc said. "I'll never stop the cycle of hatred and despair... And I can never hope to atone for the destruction I've inflicted on this meaningless world. But I can still do something. And in doing so... One day, perhaps I can find some meaning in it all."

•

Lanek searched the city for Augurc, catching sight of him from time to time, but never quite able to reach him. The man was looking for something. His experiments? The monster had been killed, and Kitoh had dealt with the young elf. And if all was going well for Borely, Areo was being dealt with as well. There were only the Brotherhood members Augurc could turn to now, and Lanek hadn't seen any of them during his chase through the city.

In fact, it seemed the ambush of the city had come to a close. What exactly was going on? Did Augurc give up, and call off the attack? The defeat of his treasured experiments must have been humbling, but Augurc didn't seem the type to ever give up.

Or was he? He wasn't really like his brother Delkol, all things considered. Perhaps Augurc could be reasoned with.

At last, Lanek found Augurc again—he had made his way up another building, which was easy for him thanks to the many vine Nexi stones at his disposal. But this time Augurc was just sitting there. He wasn't searching for anything. It looked as if he just wanted to sit and think. Perhaps his mind was having trouble grasping how his experiments could have failed him. He clearly didn't foresee the Haders being used against him, and certainly not this effectively. And with his Elpis gone, his experiments defeated, and his own body critically injured, he was at the end of his line.

Someone appeared near Augurc, floating in the air. Lanek stopped, taken aback. It looked like an older man—an aristocrat, from the looks of it—and he was bathed in silver and gold light. The scene reminded Lanek very much of Terico and Delkol, when they were powered by fragments of the Elpis.

But the Elpis was destroyed. What was giving this man so much Nexi energy? It couldn't be a Hader... Could it be the combined power of multiple Haders? Yet this wasn't a man Lanek knew to have a Hader. And the only person Lanek knew to have more than one Hader was Kechi.

"Are you left breathless at the sight of my master—the omnipotent Lord Mareba Shire?"

Lanek turned and found Kechi a ways behind him, struggling to trudge down the block. He looked like he had been killed ten times over already. What happened to him, and how was he still standing? He wasn't carrying any Haders. Did he give them to the man floating in the air... Mareba Shire?

"What are you trying to do?" Lanek asked.

"I will always live for my master," Kechi said, his one good eye open wide. "I will never stop serving him. Not even death can disrupt my master's vision."

"And what would that be?" Lanek asked.

"A land as it should be," Kechi said. "A land ruled by Lord Mareba Shire."

"Even if the Fiefs Kingdom is conquered," Lanek said, "the people won't just submit themselves to your power-hungry master."

"They will have no choice but to," Kechi said. "With the power of the Haders, nobody will be able to resist Lord Mareba's rule and glory."

"If your master was so great, he wouldn't have to force people to follow him," Lanek said.

"People are foolish!" Kechi yelled, before falling into a wretched coughing fit. "People don't understand him. They don't care for anything but themselves. They're complacent. They're afraid of change. They don't truly care for the Shire Kingdom. They just want things to stay as they are. They don't think—"

Lanek stabbed him through the heart.

Kechi slumped over the blade of Lanek's rapier. Lanek pulled the sword out and let Kechi's body collapse on the ground. Lanek had expected Kechi to attack Lanek at some point, to get revenge for the loss of his eye at least— but Kechi had become completely absorbed by his devotion to his master. Kechi wasn't able to react in time once Lanek was sprinting toward him, rapier already drawn forward.

Lanek turned to Augurc and the man Kechi called his master.

The fight was already over.

•

Augurc doubted he could fight for long. He was in poor condition to fight, and this nobleman seemed to have a power that rivaled the Elpis itself.

"You will pay for your crimes with your life," the nobleman said. He raised a hand toward Augurc and grinned.

Augurc leaped toward the nobleman and sent a series of vines rushing for him from multiple directions. Just before Augurc could slam his lance of ice into the nobleman's chest, he stopped, frozen in place. His body shook, and sweat trickled down his face. His heart felt like it was beating in his neck— his entire body filled with fear. At the same time, all of Augurc's vines missed the nobleman entirely. It was true that Augurc was in a great deal of pain, but the chances of every single one of his vines missing their target... It was unfathomable.

Why was he suddenly afraid to attack this nobleman? And how did every one of his vines happen to fly around the nobleman like that?

The nobleman laughed. "This is the future, Augurc Shire. All my enemies shall be filled with fear, and fortune will forever be on my side."

A mass of crimson liquid—blood, Augurc realized—appeared above the nobleman's head. The blood split apart into small, thin needles, which quickly hardened and turned metallic. The blood... How it was floating in the air and turning into needles, Augurc couldn't even guess.

At the same time, several swords materialized out of thin air, floating to either side of the nobleman. Augurc had never seen such power within any kind of Nexi energy before.

The ability to instill fear in enemies, have luck on your side, control blood, and summon weapons... In one moment, Augurc felt his entire understanding of Nexi power was entirely altered. What were these Haders, and how did they contain powers that were entirely unrelated to anything found within regular Nexi stones?

Augurc couldn't just let himself die. He didn't understand. There was so much he didn't understand. So much he had misunderstood. There was so much more to learn. So much more to discover. Perhaps there was still a way for Augurc to break the cycle. Perhaps there was something more for him to do in this world, even if it wasn't anything remotely similar to what he had been working for all these years.

"I'm not done," Augurc said.

The nobleman laughed. "I killed your giant monster! I can kill you too. There is nothing I can't kill. And nothing that can—"

He stopped mid-sentence, and his whole body began shaking. He gasped for air, and for a moment Augurc thought the man had been stabbed in the back. Yet there was nothing...

Augurc found the artificial fear left him, and immediately stepped forward and slammed his spear of ice through the nobleman's heart.

"My... soul..." the nobleman coughed.

The mass of blood liquified and rained on the nobleman, and the summoned weapons fell to the roof of the building. The silver and gold glow faded away, and the nobleman fell limp over Augurc's ice spear.

Four Nexi stones fell to the floor beneath the nobleman's body. Augurc pulled his arm out of his lance and dropped it, letting the nobleman's bloody corpse flop to the side.

Each of the Nexi stones glowed with two different colors, swirling and shifting about.

What are they? Augurc thought. *And how should I use them?*

•

Lanek found a ladder and used it to climb to the top of the building Augurc sat upon. From what Lanek could tell, the moment he killed Kechi, it seemed Mareba Shire had suffered in some way in reaction. It looked like it was only a brief moment of weakness, but a moment was all Augurc needed to kill him.

As Lanek climbed up the ladder, he didn't hear Augurc try to run away or even move. Lanek had his rapier ready once he reached the roof, but Augurc didn't make any movement, vines or otherwise. Was Augurc too weak to fight anymore? Or was he dying?

It looked like he was still breathing. He sat hunched over, his eyes focused on some Nexi stones lying a few paces in front of him. They were Haders.

Lanek sprinted toward the Haders, expecting Augurc to grab them and use them.

But Augurc didn't move. Lanek ran up to the Haders and knelt down to pick them up. He took all four of them and walked back a few steps. Augurc still sat motionless, his gaze still focused on the spot where the Haders had been.

Lanek stood in silence, wondering what to do next. Was Augurc going to attack him or not? It made no sense for Augurc to just let Lanek take the Haders, if he understood what they were at all. With the loss of his Elpis fragments, Augurc should have been desperate to obtain these Haders.

"What do you intend to use those Nexi stones for?" Augurc asked, breaking the silence.

"The plan was to destroy them," Lanek said. "We've gotten tired of your lot using these things to wreak havoc in our kingdom."

"How pointless..." Augurc sighed. "And yet, it's just as pointless to try using them, too."

"When you fight the Fiefs Kingdom, you're going to face resistance," Lanek said. "And now you must pay for your crimes, Augurc."

Lanek pointed his rapier at Augurc, and a flood of emotions passed through Lanek's heart. This was the moment for him to avenge Suran's death, once and for all. This was the man who brought so much pain and misery to the kingdom these past five years. It was time for Lanek to find some measure of peace in his life. It was time to make this haunting mission worth something. It was time to bring this all to an end.

Someone climbed up the stairs. Lanek turned and found Borely walking onto the roof, followed by Areo.

Lanek looked back to Augurc, who still hadn't moved. Had he simply accepted death?

He kept his eye on Augurc as he spoke to the vampires. "I see you've succeeded at what you set out to do, Borely."

"I helped Areo stop following Augurc's orders," Borely said. "Unfortunately, it seems Areo's mind has been severely scarred. At first she acted and spoke like her old self, but now she's simply following me, not even aware of who I am. It might take a long time for her mind to fully heal."

"You probably would like the chance to finish off Augurc as well then," Lanek said. "He is the one responsible for your near-death five years ago, and the one who brought Areo down to this lowly state."

"I know," Borely said. He didn't say anything more for a bit, apparently thinking over his words carefully. "But Areo is alive, and I can help her through her pain. And the Elpis has been destroyed, I take it."

"It has," Lanek said. "I also have four Haders, which I intend to destroy once Augurc has been dealt with."

"Will you kill him, then?" Borely asked.

Lanek was still pointing the tip of his rapier down toward Augurc's head. The man still hadn't attempted to stop Lanek. His vines hung limp to his sides, and he didn't try to create any more weapons from his ice Nexi.

"I can not stop you," Augurc said. "I can not blame either of you in your desire for revenge. It is a central part of the human mind. I have brought you despair. It is only natural you retaliate in hatred."

Augurc bowed his head toward Lanek. He was fully accepting his fate. He was ready to die.

Lanek gritted his teeth. Why was this happening? He needed to kill this man, didn't he? Augurc had killed so many people. Brought pain and agony to so many lives. Ruined entire cities. Augurc had to pay. He was a monster. He was a monster who killed *Suran*. He couldn't be forgiven.

"I won't kill you," Borely said.

Lanek loosened his grip on his rapier. His mouth dropped open a bit, and his heart slowed its beat—it felt as if time itself had slowed down.

"Why would you say that?" Lanek asked. "You have every reason to kill this man."

"I know," Borely said. "I want to kill him... very badly. But we've already won. The Brotherhood has been defeated. The experiments have all been dealt with. The city is safe now. And the Elpis and Haders will no longer pose a threat on the Fiefs Kingdom. But the Shire government will be in an uproar over what happened today. The destruction of Zein could be used as a reason for war against the Fiefs Kingdom."

It took a few moments for Lanek to understand what the situation entailed in the political scheme of things.

"So what you're saying... is we need Augurc alive," Lanek said, the words painful to his lips.

"We can't just keep killing each other," Borely said. "Somebody has to choose peace. Otherwise... the cycle of revenge will just go on forever."

Lanek turned away from Augurc and sheathed his sword. Tears trickling down his face, he stared at Borely and took a few deep, quiet breaths.

"You're... right," Lanek said. He shut his eyes, his whole vision turning back to Suran.

Was she pleased with this decision?

Deep down, Lanek knew Suran wouldn't want him to keep walking this bloody path. Suran wouldn't want Lanek to kill people in revenge. She would just want Lanek to move on with his life, and find happiness somewhere... Create meaning in his life. Do good things for those around him. Live a dignified life. One their parents could be proud of.

"We will let the Shire Kingdom deal with Augurc as they see fit then," Lanek said.

"What if they decide to let him live?" Borely asked.

"I will only concern myself with my kingdom," Augurc said, still looking at the ground. "I have influence in my kingdom, regardless of all I have done. I will accept my punishment, and do whatever is left in my power to ensure the fighting ends between our kingdoms."

It was unlikely Augurc would be given any actual say in the government of the Shire Kingdom from this point on. But as a direct descendant in the Shire family line, he could in time come to influence the decisions of the governing court, even from the prison walls of the Shire's royal castle.

If there was even a small chance of peace, Lanek would accept letting Augurc live. Even if Augurc was a monster who had every reason to die, Lanek recognized that Borely's decision was the better path to take. Lanek had seen enough blood over the course of this mission.

"Let's deal with this then," Lanek said. He placed the four Hader stones on the ground and took out the device Kitoh had designed to destroy the Elpis. Lanek had seen Rilv use it on her own Hader, so there was no doubt it would work on these ones as well.

With four strong whacks, Lanek destroyed the four Haders. They each burst into dust, and Lanek felt as if a great weight had been lifted with the loss of each one. The Haders were truly incredible, but it was time for them to pass on. They had served their purpose in bringing down the Elpis. The world was a much less dangerous place now.

Not long afterward, a troop of Shire guards arrived at the scene, led by a Brotherhood woman named Shirm. She had abandoned her mask, and apparently had turned against Augurc during the invasion of the city. She explained that she would see to it that whatever was left of the Brotherhood would be disbanded, and that any of Augurc's ongoing experiments would be brought to a halt.

The guards tied Augurc up and brought him down from the building, leading him to a prison carriage intended to head to the Shire Kingdom's capital city.

"I am probably the only Brotherhood member left in this city," Shirm said to Lanek. "There are probably only a few others spread out across the continent. Augurc had brought most all of them together for this invasion... He led us into a massacre."

"What will you do now, without the Brotherhood?" Lanek asked.

"I will act as mediator between Augurc and the royal council," Shirm said. "I failed to help the Shire Kingdom as I had always hoped to. I apparently went about it entirely the wrong way... from the very start."

"People have strong wills," Lanek said. "I think Augurc has realized this himself."

"We're not as weak as he thought," Shirm agreed.

Borely placed a hand on Lanek's shoulder, his other hand holding one of

Areo's hands. "Well, we are pretty weak. We're just not the types to let that sort of thing stop us."

Lanek couldn't help but smile a little. It seemed this mission was finally over with, and though his body was still in great pain, his heart felt lighter than it had in years.

He didn't have to let his despair or hatred control him.

He could do whatever he wished.

•

After everyone took the time they needed to heal in Zein, it took a week for everything to be cleared up in Setar. With Rilv a casualty of the mission, it was up to Lanek to explain to the Fiefs royal council everything that had happened. The Elpis and Haders were destroyed, the Brotherhood disbanded, and the likes of Augurc, Mareba, and Kechi were all dealt with. Rilv, Kitoh, Nivakil, Jenba, and many civilians of the elf village Velm were all lost amidst the conflict, not to mention the many lives which perished in Istal, Zein, and a number of Fiefs towns and villages.

But at long last, the threat was thoroughly extinguished. As Lanek and Borely hoped, the Shire Kingdom's governing body learned the full story of what happened in Zein from Augurc and Shirm. Augurc took full responsibility for the lives lost there, and any potential conflict between the two kingdoms was thankfully averted. Augurc was imprisoned rather than executed, but from the sound of things it seemed the Shire leadership agreed with Augurc's assessment that more measures should be taken to ensure a stable peace between Shire and Fiefs.

Perhaps there were still those who felt the two kingdoms should be united by force, but given the bloody devastation of the last couple weeks, there didn't appear to be anyone eager to promote any further violence anytime soon.

Lanek piloted his airship to Velm, not certain what anyone there would think of him. He brought Turan, Borely, Areo, and Analicia with him, since none of them had homes to return to at this point. The vampires could have returned to Istal now that the city was back in the hands of the citizens, Lanek supposed. But the three each had the necessary Nexi stone for them to live in the light now, and they wanted to go to this village Lanek kept telling them about.

It seemed they all wanted to find someplace peaceful to live at. All five of them had rejected the Fiefs government's honorary positions offered them in the castle, and they didn't even feel the need to accept the monetary rewards they were given. There was no need for any of that. They just wanted to go somewhere quiet.

Velm was the perfect place for them.

It took some time to explain to the villagers the full situation, and why the tragedy happened the way it did. Many of the elves were reluctant to let Lanek, Turan, or the vampires step foot in the village, but once Lanek handed the village elder the Stone of Truth, the villagers were more willing to forgive. Lanek had told the Fiefs governing body that this Hader was destroyed along with the rest of them. And since only Lanek, Turan, and the three vampires knew it was a Hader, the Stone of Truth was safe once more.

Over the following weeks, Lanek and the others helped the village in rebuilding their shrine. In a way, Lanek felt he was rebuilding his own life, and he imagined his four companions felt the same.

Turan had successfully used the Hader to clear his mind of the madness Augurc had forced upon him via raw Nexi energy. Lanek didn't know if he would always feel a little uneasy being around Turan, as Lanek still couldn't get over Suran's death. It was simply a feeling that would never leave him. But he found himself slowly becoming more accepting of Turan, who was acting more and more like his old self, rather than like Lynx did. Turan would never be as he once was, of course, but he did have his mind again. As far as Lanek was concerned, Turan was a friend, and the two had a connection with one another through their home village, Edellerston, and the times they all spent together with Terico and Suran.

Areo's mind was unfortunately much less stable. She no longer had a desire to kill anyone, and at times she seemed to have forgotten who Augurc was entirely. Lanek had tried using the Hader to try to clear her mind of madness, similar to what Turan did—but it was no use. Her mind was clear and free, but it was still damaged by the Elpis. That simply wasn't going to go away, and it was left up to Borely to help Areo. At times she would be entirely oblivious of what was going on around her, and at other times she would have terrible headaches. But then there were times where her old personality resurfaced, and Borely treasured every moment they spent together during these brief minutes.

Then again, as time passed, Borely seemed to treasure every moment he spent with Areo, regardless of her mental state. Along with Analicia, the three vampires became valued members of the elf community, and animosity between the villagers and the five newcomers slowly dissipated.

It was difficult to win everyone's trust. Beloved friends and family members had died, including a few who were killed by Turan himself. Turan apologized in every way he could, and it was made clear he was not himself at the time, thanks to Augurc's brainwashing. It was painful, but over time, the village came to accept Turan and Lanek. They worked hard, helping with a number of the village farms, and with other chores that kept many of the families busy.

Lanek visited Fenley's grave often. In some ways, she represented everything Lanek had longed for in a friend and companion. And in other ways, her personality triggered memories of all the time he spent with Suran. There was no way to bring either Fenley or Suran back. He had to accept their passing. He would never forget them, but he wouldn't let their deaths bring him to despair, either. He had to keep moving on with his life. Finding new things to do. New ways to help the people around him.

The village was a very simple, quiet place. It was difficult for everyone to move on after so much turmoil had befallen them. Perhaps there were many who would have liked to kill Lanek and Turan in revenge. And perhaps there were some who would have liked to kill Borely, Areo, and Analicia out of fear.

But nobody ever tried to hurt them. Lanek, Turan, Borely, Areo, and Analicia had all proven they would never bring any harm to the villagers. In fact, they each vowed to never let any harm befall the village at all. It was unlikely anyone would ever want to disrupt such an out-of-the-way village, but just in case—Lanek and his companions were ready to defend it. This was their home now.

Eventually the shrine was fully repaired, and it opened again for elves to enter and glean wisdom from the Stone of Truth. For several days there were constantly villagers at the shrine, eager to come to a better understanding of how to press forward with their lives. About a week passed before the shrine began having its normal, quieter flow of participation.

One cool evening, Lanek walked to the shrine entrance, passing Turan and Analicia, who happened to be serving as guards that day.

"Going for a swim?" Turan asked.

"Don't drown," Analicia added.

"I'll stay in the shallow end," Lanek replied.

He walked in and went to the back, where he could change in the gray clothes needed for the ritual Fenley had shown him. Once he was ready, he lay in the water in front of the fixed statue of the goddess Reali. She was looking up to the invisible Stone of Truth once more, and ready to help him feel at ease.

Lanek lay in the water and closed his eyes. He couldn't pretend that everything worked out perfectly. Life simply didn't work that way.

But once he was willing to let go of his hatred and despair, it was possible to find some measure of contentment.

He smiled and let the glow of the Hader give him peace.

•

The End.